To

....

From

....

On this date

....

ONE
GOD
ONE
PLAN
ONE
LIFE

ONE
GOD
ONE
PLAN
ONE
LIFE

A 365 Devotional

BY MAX LUCADO

ADAPTED FOR TEENS BY JAMES LUND

THOMAS NELSON
Since 1798

The devotional text was adapted from several of Max Lucado's previous books. The "One More Thought" sections after the devos were written by James Lund specifically for our teen readers.

Published in Nashville, Tennessee, by Thomas Nelson.

Thomas Nelson titles may be purchased in bulk for educational, business, fund-raising, or sales promotional use. For information, please e-mail SpecialMarkets@ThomasNelson.com.

Cover design by Micah Kandros.

Library of Congress Cataloging-in-Publication Data

Lucado, Max.
  One God, one plan, one life : a 365 devotional / by Max Lucado ; adapted by James Lund.
    pages cm
  ISBN 978-1-4003-2263-3 (hardcover)
1. Devotional calendars. I. Title.
  BV4811.L774 2014
  242'.2—dc23   2013021929

Printed in Thailand
24 DSC 17

With great appreciation, Denalyn and I dedicate this volume to a dear and wonderful family: Keith, Sarah, Josh, Jake, Ryan, Mathis, Hope, and Hannah Kennington.

Acknowledgments

Special thanks to James Lund for his skillfully written adaptations, to Michelle Burke for her careful oversight of this project, and to teen editors Owen Di Giosia and Mari Arana for their helpful insights.

JANUARY

"Do not remember the former things,
Nor consider the things of old.
Behold, I will do a new thing,
Now it shall spring forth;
Shall you not know it?"

[Isaiah 43:18–19]

"Love the Lord your God with all your heart, all your soul, and all your mind."

[Matthew 22:37 NCV]

The Purpose of Life

Dig deep enough in every heart and you'll find it: a longing for meaning, a quest for purpose. As surely as a child breathes, he will someday wonder, *What is the purpose of my life?*

Some search for meaning in a career. "My purpose is to be a dentist." Fine job, but hardly a reason for living. They choose to be human "doings" rather than human "beings." Who they are is what they do; consequently they do a lot. They work many hours because if they don't work, they don't have an identity.

For others, who they are is what they have. They find meaning in a new car or a new laptop or new clothes. These people are great for the economy and rough on the budget because they are always seeking meaning in something they own. Some try sports, movies, drugs, friends, sex, you name it. All mirages in the desert of purpose.

Shouldn't we face the truth instead? Our purpose is to love God. Nothing else will satisfy.

ONE MORE THOUGHT

Your life is so confusing. There's so much to figure out. What to study? What are you good at? Why are you here? There is One who has the answers you seek, who knows your future. One God. One plan. One life. Love him, and everything else will fall into place.

> "I will give you a new heart and put a new spirit within you."
>
> [Ezekiel 36:26 NASB]

The Grace Adventure

Do we *get* grace? We talk as if we understand the term. The library gives us a *grace* period to pay a late fine. The no-good politician falls from *grace*. We use the word for hospitals, baby girls, and premeal prayers. It politely occupies a phrase in a hymn, fits nicely on a church sign. Never causes trouble or demands a response.

But is this all there is to grace? What's it *really* about?

Grace is everything Jesus. Grace lives because he does, works because he works, and matters because he matters. To be saved by grace is to be saved by him, not by an idea, rule, or church membership, but by Jesus himself, who will sweep into heaven anyone who so much as gives him the nod. Not, mind you, in response to a finger snap, religious chant, or secret handshake. Grace won't be stage-managed. It's like Jesus himself: uncontainable, untamable. Like a wild, whitewater kayak ride that is thrilling and scary and joyful. Grace isn't merely an app to be acquired. It's an adventure to be lived.

ONE MORE THOUGHT

Are you living the grace adventure? Have you been changed by it? Strengthened by it? Softened by it? If not, turn to Jesus and let it wash over you. His wild grace is just what you need.

We love Him because He first loved us.
[1 John 4:19]

Does Anybody Love Me?

God loves you with an unfailing love.

England saw a glimpse of such love in 1878. The young son of Princess Alice was infected with a horrible disease known as black diphtheria. Doctors quarantined the boy and told the mother to stay away. But she couldn't. One day she overheard him whisper to the nurse, "Why doesn't my mother kiss me anymore?" The words melted her heart. She ran to her son and smothered him with kisses. Within a few days, she was buried.[1]

What would drive a mother to do such a thing? What would lead God to do something greater? Love. And, oh, what a love this is—"too wonderful to be measured" (Ephesians 3:19 CEV). I urge you to trust it. You may be hungry for such love. Those who should have loved you didn't. Those who could have loved you wouldn't. You were left at the hospital. Left off the party list. Left with a broken heart. Left with your question, "Does anybody love me?"

Please listen to heaven's answer. As you ponder him on the cross, hear God assure you, "I do."

ONE MORE THOUGHT

You have days where you feel unloved. Mom snaps at you. Best friend snubs you. Even your dog seems to give you a mean look. But God? There's never an instant when he doesn't love you wholeheartedly. Count on it. Always. Forever.

4

Let the message about Christ, in all its richness, fill your lives.

[Colossians 3:16 NLT]

God's Word Is Alive

Has any other book ever been described like this: "For the word of God is alive and active. Sharper than any double-edged sword, it penetrates even to dividing soul and spirit, joints and marrow; it judges the thoughts and attitudes of the heart" (Hebrews 4:12 NIV)?

"Alive and active." The words of the Bible have life! God works through these words. The Bible is to God what a surgical glove is to the surgeon. Haven't you felt his touch?

In a late, lonely hour, you read the words "I will never fail you. I will never abandon you" (Hebrews 13:5 NLT). The sentences comfort like a hand on your shoulder. When anxiety tears away at your peace, someone shares this passage: "Do not be anxious about anything, but in every situation, by prayer and petition, with thanksgiving, present your requests to God" (Philippians 4:6 NIV). The words stir a sigh from your soul.

Put them to use. Don't make a decision, whether large or small, without sitting before God with an open Bible, open heart, and open ears.

ONE MORE THOUGHT

Teachers pile on reading assignments like football players after a fumble. Texts for history. Workbooks for math. Novels for English. None will have the impact on your life like a book called the Bible. Don't forget the most important reading assignment of all.

> For it is by believing in your heart that you are made right with God, and it is by confessing with your mouth that you are saved.
>
> [Romans 10:10 NLT]

Say It and Believe It

Do you ever have doubts that you belong to God and are headed to heaven? Do you wonder if you are truly saved? How can you know?

The Bible says, "If you confess with your mouth, 'Jesus is Lord,' and believe in your heart that God raised Him from the dead, you will be saved" (Romans 10:9 HCSB). First, *confess* that Jesus is Lord. Say it out loud or quietly in your heart—either way. Just mean it. Then *believe* that Jesus was resurrected. He's not a man in the grave but God in the flesh with the power over death.

Catch what Romans 10:9 does *not* say—live perfectly, be nice to everyone, don't mess up, don't doubt, always smile . . . and you will be saved. Nope. Just confess and believe. Salvation will follow— along with the peace and inner joy that come from knowing your ultimate destination.

ONE MORE THOUGHT

We try to make it hard. In our minds, we add conditions to going to heaven with God: more good deeds, more As at school, more godly thoughts. But he keeps it simple. Speak of the authority of Jesus. Believe that he was killed and returned to life. Simple. Salvation.

God Never Changes

God will always be the same.

No one else will. Friends call you today and ignore you tomorrow. Teachers love your work one week and hate it the next. Parents shift between understanding and criticizing. Not God. With him "there is no variation or shadow due to change" (James 1:17 ESV).

Catch God in a bad mood? Won't happen. Scared you might use up all his grace? Think he's given up on you? Wrong. Did he not make a promise to you? "God is not a human being, and he will not lie. He is not a human, and he does not change his mind. What he says he will do, he does. What he promises, he makes come true" (Numbers 23:19 NCV). He's never sullen or sour, sulking or stressed. His strength, truth, ways, and love never change. He is "the same yesterday and today and forever" (Hebrews 13:8 ESV).

The resurrection of Jesus will not lose its power. The blood of Christ will not fade in strength. God never changes. You can count on it.

ONE MORE THOUGHT

Change is exciting. Yet when everything around you is changing—your friends, classes, family, school, body, dreams—sometimes it's nice to know someone stable, someone you can depend on. And when that someone happens to be the all-powerful Creator of the universe, overflowing with love for you? *That's* exciting.

All things are worth nothing compared with the greatness of knowing Christ Jesus my Lord.

[Philippians 3:8 NCV]

The Reward

The reward of Christianity is Christ.

Do you journey to the Grand Canyon for the souvenir T-shirt or the snow globe with the snowflakes that fall when you shake it? No. The reward of the Grand Canyon is the Grand Canyon. The wide-eyed realization that you are part of something ancient, splendid, powerful, and greater than you.

The prize of our faith is the person God sent to pay for our sins. Not money in the bank or a computer in the bedroom or a healthy body or a better self-image. Yes, these count for something. But the Ironman of faith is Christ. Fellowship with him. Walking with him. Pondering him. Exploring him. The heart-stopping realization that in him you are part of something ancient, endless, unstoppable, and unfathomable. And that he, who can dig the Grand Canyon with his pinkie, thinks you're worth his death on a Roman cross. Christ is the reward of Christianity.

ONE MORE THOUGHT

You may think that when you become a Christian, the idea of rewards goes out the window. Not true. It's just that your reward comes not in cash or good grades but in a relationship with the Creator. Hard to measure. Hard even to imagine! But what a reward.

Guide me in your truth, and teach me, my God, my Savior.

[Psalm 25:5 NCV]

Honest Evaluation

Raise your hand if any of the following describe you. *You are at peace with everyone.* Every relationship as sweet as fudge. Even your former friends speak highly of you. Love all and loved by all. Is that you? *Or maybe you have no fears.* Failing French—no problem. Heart condition discovered—yawn. Just call you Superman. Does that describe you? *Or maybe you need no forgiveness.* Never made a mistake. As square as a game of checkers. As clean as Grandma's kitchen. Is that you? No?

Let's evaluate this. A few of your relationships are shaky. You have fears and faults. Do you really want to walk through life all on your own? The trail ahead looks tough. Sounds to me as if you could use a shepherd. "Even though I walk through the darkest valley, I will fear no evil, for you are with me" (Psalm 23:4 NIV).

ONE MORE THOUGHT

Let's be honest. No matter how pumped up you get over your latest achievement—the test you aced in English, the points you scored on the basketball court, the volunteer award you received—you still could use some help in this life. A friend. A guide. A shepherd. A Savior.

"For even the Son of Man came not to be served but to serve others."

[Mark 10:45 NLT]

Stinky Feet

On the night before his death, Jesus "wrapped a towel around his waist, and poured water into a basin. Then he began to wash the disciples' feet" (John 13:4–5 NLT).

I don't know about you, but if I knew I was about to die, my first thought wouldn't be to grab soap, water, and someone's ankle. I'm not even a fan of feet. Look you in the face? I will. Shake your hand? Gladly. Put an arm around your shoulders? Happy to do so. But rub feet? Come on. Feet smell bad and look ugly. Which, I believe, is the point of this story.

Jesus touched the stinky, ugly *feet* of his disciples. Knowing he came from God. Knowing he was going to God. Knowing that all authority was his, he exchanged his robe for the servant's wrap, lowered himself to knee level, and began to rub away the grime, grit, and grunge their feet had collected on the journey.

He wants to wash away every dirty part of your life too.

ONE MORE THOUGHT

Do you see how much Jesus cares for you? How much he values you? Enough to bend down to your level. Enough to touch and clean even the ugliest parts of your past. Enough to die for you. That's grace. That's love.

> "The things impossible for people are possible for God."
>
> [Luke 18:27 NCV]

Dare to Dream

God always rejoices when we dare to dream. In fact, we are much like God when we dream. The Master exults in newness. He delights in stretching the old. He wrote the book on making the impossible possible.

Examples? Check the Bible. Eighty-year-old shepherds don't usually play chicken with Pharaohs . . . but don't tell that to Moses. Teenage shepherds don't normally have showdowns with giants . . . but don't tell that to David. Night-shift shepherds don't usually get to hear angels sing and see God in a stable . . . but don't tell that to the Bethlehem bunch.

And for sure don't tell that to God. He's made an eternity out of making the earthbound airborne. And he gets angry when people's wings are clipped. So go ahead and give your dreams to God. Watch him turn them from barely visible ideas into a reality beyond your wildest dreams.

ONE MORE THOUGHT

Don't put limits on yourself. Not every dream will come true, and not every dream is from God. But when your dreams connect with God's plans, you'll find open doors that you never thought you'd see. Dare to dream.

Do Something

Faith is not the belief that God will do what you want. Faith is the belief that God will do what is right. "People may make plans in their minds, but the LORD decides what they will do" (Proverbs 16:9 NCV). God is always near and always available. Just waiting for your touch. So let him know. Demonstrate your devotion:

Write an encouraging letter. Ask forgiveness. Be baptized. Feed a hungry person. Invite a classmate who needs a friend to church. Tell someone about Jesus.

Pray.

Worship.

Go.

Do something that demonstrates faith. For faith with no effort is no faith at all. God will respond. He has never rejected a genuine act of faith. Never.

ONE MORE THOUGHT

Read James 2:14–26. Do your deeds show your faith? Our love for God isn't something that we hide in a backpack. It should move us into action. What can you do this week to demonstrate your faith? God will be pleased and will meet you there.

> But don't just listen to God's word. You must do what it says.
>
> [James 1:22 NLT]

Good Habits

Someone once said to me, "I'm a new Christian. Over the years I've developed some bad habits. How do I get rid of them now?" My answer to him then and advice to you now? Develop good habits. Here are four to start with.

First, pray: "Steadfastly maintain the *habit* of prayer" (Romans 12:12 PHILLIPS). God wants to hear from you daily. Second, study: "The man who looks into the perfect mirror of God's law . . . and makes a *habit* of so doing, is not the man who sees and forgets" (James 1:25 PHILLIPS).

Third, give: "On *every Lord's Day* each of you should put aside something from what you have earned during the week, and use it for this offering" (1 Corinthians 16:2 TLB). You don't give for God's sake, but for yours. And last of all, fellowship: "Let us not give up the *habit* of meeting together" (Hebrews 10:25 GNT). You need support every week from other Christians.

Four habits worth having. Isn't it good to know that some habits are good for you?

ONE MORE THOUGHT

When you give your heart to God, your room in heaven is reserved for all time. No more payment is needed. But if you want to grow in your faith and be more like him, adding a few good—and godly—habits will put you well on your way.

> "If people want to follow me, they must give up the things they want. They must be willing even to give up their lives to follow me."
>
> [Mark 8:34 NCV]

It's Your Choice

On one side stands the crowd. Some are the "cool" people. Some are your friends. They're taunting. Booing. Demanding.

On the other side stands a peasant. He's alone. Has swollen lips. Lumpy eye. Lofty promise.

One pledges acceptance, the other a cross.

One offers flesh and flash, the other offers faith.

The crowd challenges, "Follow us and fit in."

Jesus promises, "Follow me and stand out."

They promise to please. God promises to save.

God looks at you and asks, "Which will be your choice?"

ONE MORE THOUGHT

Your salvation in Christ may be secure, but the choice to keep following Jesus is made a thousand times a day. In the moment, choosing God over the popular people can seem awkward. But in the long run, there's no choice that feels better.

He gave up his place with God and made himself nothing.

[Philippians 2:7 NCV]

Why Did He Do It?

Holiday travel. It isn't easy. Then why do we do it? Why cram the trunks and endure the airports? You know the answer. We love to be with the ones we love.

The four-year-old running up the sidewalk into the arms of Grandpa. The bowl of cereal with Mom before the rest of the house awakens. That moment when, for a moment, everyone is quiet as we hold hands around the table and thank God for family and friends and pumpkin pie. We love to be with the ones we love.

May I remind you? So does God. He loves to be with the ones he loves. How else do you explain what he did? Between him and us there was a distance—a great span. And he couldn't bear it. He couldn't stand it. So he did something about it.

"He gave up his place with God and made himself nothing."

ONE MORE THOUGHT

Are there loved ones in your life you rarely get to see? A friend who's moved away. A grandmother overseas. Wouldn't you do most anything to spend more time with them? That's what God did. He couldn't stand the separation, so he did something about it.

Not to us, O LORD, not to us, but to your name goes all the glory
for your unfailing love and faithfulness.

[Psalm 115:1 NLT]

We Need His Glory

God has one goal: God. "I have my reputation to keep up" (Isaiah 48:11 MSG). Surprised? Isn't such an attitude, dare we ask, self-centered? Why does God broadcast himself?

For the same reason the pilot of the lifeboat does. Think of it this way. You're floundering neck-deep in a dark, cold sea. Ship sinking. Life jacket deflating. Through the inky night comes the voice of a lifeboat pilot. But you cannot see him. What do you want the driver of the lifeboat to do? Be quiet? Say nothing?

By no means! You need volume! Amp it up, buddy! In biblical jargon, you want him to show his glory. You need to hear him say, "I am here. I am strong. I can save you!" Drowning passengers want the pilot to reveal his supremacy.

Don't we want God to do the same? Look around. People thrash about in seas of guilt, anger, despair. Life isn't working. We are going down fast. But God can rescue us. And only one message matters. His! We need to see God's glory.

ONE MORE THOUGHT

Make no mistake. God has no ego problem. He doesn't reveal his glory for his good. We need to witness it for ours. We need his loud voice so we can find him and his strong hand to pull us into a safe boat. Let's thank God that he is the pilot of our lives.

You made me so happy, GOD. I saw your work and I shouted for joy.

[Psalm 92:4 MSG]

Defiant Joy

My friend Rob cried freely as he told the story about his young son's challenging life. Daniel was born with a double cleft palate, dramatically disfiguring his face. He had surgery, but the evidence remains, so people constantly notice the difference and occasionally make remarks.

Daniel, however, is unfazed. He just tells people that God made him this way, so what's the big deal? He was named student of the week at school and was asked to bring something to show his classmates for show-and-tell. Daniel told his mom that he wanted to take the pictures that showed his face prior to the surgery. His mom was concerned. "Won't that make you feel a bit funny?" she asked.

But Daniel insisted. "Oh no, I want everyone to see what God did for me!"

Try Daniel's defiant joy and see what happens. God has handed you a cup of blessings. I suggest you sweeten it with a heaping spoonful of gratitude.

ONE MORE THOUGHT

You could say that being happy is the temporary good feeling that comes from eating ice cream or finishing first in a race. Joy, however, is something deeper. It defies bad days and hard lives. No matter what the circumstances, it lets the love and light of God shine through.

He faced all of the same testings we do, yet he did not sin.

[Hebrews 4:15 NLT]

Perfect

Jesus stands before Pilate, accused of crimes he did not commit. The Roman governor does all he can to release Jesus. Why? "I find no fault in Him at all" (John 18:38). With these words, Pilate unintentionally steps into the sandals of spiritual teacher. He states first what Paul would record later: Jesus "knew no sin" (2 Corinthians 5:21). Of equal ranking with Jesus' water walking, dead raising, and disease healing is this skyscraper-tall truth: he never sinned.

Jesus was God's model of a human being. Ever honest among hypocrites. Relentlessly kind in a world of cruelty. Heaven-focused in spite of countless distractions. It's not just that Jesus passed every test. He posted a perfect score on every test.

Can you imagine such a life? No mistakes? Not a single red mark on your essays? Me either. That's why God found a way to punish the sin and preserve the sinner. Jesus took your punishment, and God gave you credit for Jesus' perfection.

Sounds perfect to me.

ONE MORE THOUGHT

We all want perfect hair, perfect skin, perfect grades, perfect lives. We never get it, do we? And we won't. That's why we need Jesus so desperately. He's the One who covers our cracks and fills in our flaws. Only his work is picture-perfect.

> "In the same way I loved you, you love one another."
>
> [John 13:34 MSG]

God's Family of Friends

God offers you a family of friends and friends who are family—his church. When you transfer your trust into Christ, he not only pardons you; he also places you in his family of friends.

Family far and away beats any other biblical term to describe the church. *Brothers* or *brothers and sisters* appears a whopping 148 times between the book of Acts and the book of Revelation. The church isn't a place to go but a group of people who care for each other in faith.

God heals his family through his family. In the church we use our gifts to love each other, honor one another, keep an eye on troublemakers, and carry each other's burdens. As his children, we belong to the Father. It's what he had in mind from the beginning: "God decided in advance to adopt us into his own family by bringing us to himself through Jesus Christ" (Ephesians 1:5 NLT).

ONE MORE THOUGHT

Membership in God's family is a pleasure and a privilege. By putting our faith in Jesus, we instantly gain millions of brothers and sisters around the world. A perfect family? No. But when we focus on the Father, we experience a perfect love.

> I look at your heavens, which you made with your fingers.
> [Psalm 8:3 NCV]

Don't Lose the Wonder

We understand how storms are created. We map solar systems and transplant hearts. We measure the depths of the oceans and send signals to distant planets. We have studied our universe and are learning how it works.

And, for some, the loss of mystery has led to the loss of majesty. The more we know, the less we believe. Strange, don't you think? Knowledge of how things work shouldn't cancel out wonder. Knowledge should stir wonder. Who has more reason to worship than the astronomer who has seen the stars?

Ironically, the more we know, the less we worship. We are more impressed with our discovery of the light switch than with the One who invented electricity. Rather than worship the Creator, we worship the creation (Romans 1:25).

No wonder there is no wonder. We think we've figured it all out. My advice? Don't lose the wonder.

ONE MORE THOUGHT

We humans can be an arrogant bunch. We always seem to think we know more than we really do. It used to be established fact, for example, that the earth was flat. Maybe we should look beyond all our learning about the world to the Lord who makes it possible.

He will rejoice over you.

[Zephaniah 3:17 NCV]

God Won't Forget You

God is *for* you. Turn to the sidelines; that's God cheering your run. Look past the finish line; that's God applauding your steps. Listen for him in the bleachers, shouting your name. Too tired to continue? He'll carry you. Too discouraged to fight? He's picking you up. God is for you.

God is for *you*. Had he a calendar, your birthday would be circled. If he drove a car, your name would be on his bumper. If there's a tree in heaven, he's carved your name in the bark.

"Can a mother forget her nursing child?" God asks in Isaiah 49:15 (NLT). What a bizarre question. Can you imagine your mother feeding you when you're an infant and then later asking, "What was that baby's name?" No. I've seen mothers care for their young. They stroke the hair, touch the face, sing the name over and over. Can a mother forget? No way. And God says, "Even if she could forget, . . . I will not forget you" (Isaiah 49:15 NCV).

ONE MORE THOUGHT

God has a better memory than a computer. He remembers your name. He remembers the good things you've done and the faith you've held in your heart. He remembers his exciting plan for your future. Forget you? Forget it.

Then God said, "Let Us make man in Our image."

[Genesis 1:26]

Made in His Image

Imagine God's creativity. Of all we don't know about the creation, there is one thing we do know—he did it with a smile. He must've had a blast. Painting the stripes on the zebra, hanging the stars in the sky, putting the gold in the sunset. What inspiration! Stretching the neck of the giraffe, putting the flutter in the mockingbird's wings, planting the giggle in the hyena.

What a time he had. Like a whistling carpenter in his workshop, he loved every bit of it. He poured himself into the work. So intent was his creativity that he took a day off at the end of the week just to rest.

As a finale to a brilliant performance, he made man. With his typical creative flair, he began with a useless mound of dirt and ended up with an invaluable species called a human. A human who had the unique honor to bear the stamp "In His Image."

ONE MORE THOUGHT

The next time you doubt that you're special, consider that you are God's crowning achievement. He created the heavens and earth, oceans and forests, and animals of every type. But he finished his work with people—men and women in his image. And he said it was good.

> Devote yourselves to prayer with an alert mind and a thankful heart.
>
> [Colossians 4:2 NLT]

Let's Pray

Most of us struggle with prayer. We forget to pray, and when we remember, we hurry through prayers with hollow words. Our minds drift; our thoughts scatter faster than friends at the end-of-school bell.

Our battle with prayer is not entirely our fault. Satan seeks to interrupt our prayers. The devil knows what happens when we talk with God. "Our weapons have power from God that can destroy the enemy's strong places" (2 Corinthians 10:4 NCV). Satan does not stutter or stumble when you walk through church doors. Demons aren't flustered when you read this book. But the walls of hell shake when one person with an honest, faithful heart prays, "Oh, God, you are so great."

Satan scampers like a spooked pooch when we move forward in prayer. So let's do. "Humble yourselves before God. Resist the devil, and he will flee from you. Come close to God, and God will come close to you" (James 4:7–8 NLT).

ONE MORE THOUGHT

Are you aware of the power of prayer? One way to see this in your life is to keep a prayer journal. Record your conversations with God and how he answers your requests. You just might be surprised by what you learn and how much closer you grow to him.

Praise the Lord, God our Savior, who helps us every day.

[Psalm 68:19 NCV]

Lay Down Your Failures

Do you carry a backpack to school? Are there days when lugging your textbooks around feels like a workout all its own? As weighty as your backpack may be, perhaps the heaviest load we try to carry is the burden of mistakes and failures. What do you do with your failures?

Even if you've fallen, even if you've failed, even if everyone else has rejected you, Christ will not turn away from you. He comes first and foremost to those who have no hope. He goes to those no one else would go to and says, "I'll give you eternity."

Only you can surrender your concerns to the Father. No one else can take those away and give them to God. Only you can put down your worries and leave them with the One who cares for you. What better way to start the day than by laying your cares at his feet?

ONE MORE THOUGHT

Even the most successful people fail. I guarantee that you'll do it too. So how will you respond when you blow it? Going over it constantly in your mind and telling yourself how dumb you are isn't the answer. Put down that load. Let God carry it. His backpack is far bigger than yours.

> "I have good plans for you, not plans to hurt you."
>
> [Jeremiah 29:11 NCV]

A Plate of Experiences

Last night during family devotions, I called my daughters to the table and set a plate in front of each. In the center of the table I placed a collection of food: some fruit, some raw vegetables, and some Oreo cookies. "Every day," I explained, "God prepares for us a plate of experiences. What kind of plate do you most enjoy?"

The answer was easy. Sara put three cookies on her plate. Some days are like that, aren't they? Some days are "three-cookie days." Many are not. Sometimes our plates have nothing but vegetables—twenty-four hours of celery, carrots, and squash. Apparently God knows we need some strength, and though the portion may be hard to swallow, isn't it for our own good? Most days, however, have a bit of it all.

The next time your "plate" has more broccoli than apple pie, remember who prepared the meal, and eat hearty. This is a chef you can trust.

ONE MORE THOUGHT

What are your favorite foods? Pizza? Ice cream? A sauerkraut sandwich? I'll bet you don't eat your favorite every day. We've all been taught the importance of a balanced diet. Balance is important in our life experiences too. God knows it, and he can help you to be thankful no matter what life

> Put on all the armor that God gives, so you can
> defend yourself against the devil's tricks.
>
> [Ephesians 6:11 CEV]

Lost in the Wilderness

The wilderness can be a dark and lonely place. In the wilderness you think the unthinkable. Jesus did. He was "in the wilderness for forty days, being tempted by the devil" (Luke 4:1–2 NASB). I wonder if wild ideas crossed his mind. Teaming up with Satan? Becoming a dictator instead of a Savior? Torching Earth and starting over on Pluto? We don't know what he thought. We just know this: he was tempted.

"We are tempted by our own desires that drag us off and trap us" (James 1:14 CEV). What was unimaginable prior to the wilderness becomes possible in it. Gossiping. Cheating. Humiliating a friend. Drugs. Drinking. Sex. Pornography. Suicide. When your world is so dark that you can't see the way out, you give thought to the unthinkable.

How to avoid the trap of temptation? Rely on the Word of God. He "will show you how to escape from your temptations" (1 Corinthians 10:13 CEV). Listen hard for his voice, and leave the wilderness behind.

ONE MORE THOUGHT

We all wake up in the wilderness at some point. You may be there now. Feels overwhelming, right? Count on this: God always gives you a way out. Look for it. Listen for it. Grab it as soon as you get the chance. He'll guide you every step.

The Question

Jesus turns to his disciples and asks them the question. *The question.* "But who do you say that I am?"

He doesn't ask, "What do you think about what I've done?" He asks, "Who do you say that I am?" He doesn't ask, "Who do your friends think? Who do your parents think? Who do your peers think?" Instead, the question is intensely personal. "Who do *you* think I am?"

You have been asked some important questions in your life: Will you go to the dance with me? How do you feel about moving to Alaska? What do you want to do after you graduate from high school?

Yes, you've been asked some important questions. But the grandest of them is an anthill compared to the Everest found in the eighth chapter of Mark. *Who do you say that I am?* Your answer will be life-changing. It will decide your future forever.

ONE MORE THOUGHT

We answer questions all day long. What do you want for breakfast? What is the capital of Panama? Do you like him? But none compares to Jesus' question: "Who do you say that I am?" If you're not sure of your answer, read again about his life in the books of Matthew, Mark, Luke, and John. This is one answer you need to get right.

"I am with you always, even to the end of the age."

[Matthew 28:20]

"Here Is God"

When ancient sailors sketched maps of the oceans, they disclosed their fears. On the vast unexplored waters, cartographers wrote such words as "Here be dragons" and "Here be demons."

If you drew a map of your world, would we read such phrases? Over the unknown waters of friendships and romance, "Here be dragons." Near the sea of school and classes, "Here be demons."

If so, take heart from the example of Sir John Franklin. He was a master mariner in the days of King Henry V. Distant waters were a mystery to him, just as they were to other navigators. Unlike his colleagues, however, Sir John was a man of faith. On his maps he had crossed out the phrases "Here be dragons" and "Here be demons." In their place he wrote the phrase "Here is God."[2]

Mark it down. You will never go where God is not. You may be moved to another class, school, or city, but—brand this truth on your heart—you can never go where God is not. "I am with you always," Jesus promised (Matthew 28:20).

Don't be afraid; just believe.

ONE MORE THOUGHT

The next time you venture into unexplored waters, talk to God about it. Playing a solo at the band concert? Trying out for the varsity team? Talking to a classmate about your faith? Wherever you are, he's right beside you.

> "I am the way, and the truth, and the life. The only way to the Father is through me."
>
> [John 14:6 NCV]

One Path

Tolerance. A prized virtue today. The ability to be understanding of people who are different from you shows that you're classy. Jesus, too, was a champion of tolerance:

Tolerant of the disciples when they doubted.
Tolerant of the crowds when they misunderstood.
Tolerant of us when we blow it.

But there is one area where Jesus was intolerant. There was one area where he would not bend or compromise.

As far as he was concerned, when it comes to salvation, there aren't several roads . . . there is only one road. There aren't several paths . . . there is only one path. And that path is Jesus himself.

That is why it is so hard for people to believe in Jesus. It's much easier to consider him one of several options rather than *the* option. But such a philosophy is no option.

ONE MORE THOUGHT

There are times to be tolerant and times when that's a bad idea. Your friend talks too much? You can handle that. Your friend plans to steal the principal's car? No way. When it comes to your faith, it's time to give

God gives each of us chance after chance.

[Job 33:29 CEV]

God Wants You Back

When I was fifteen, I made a plan to get drunk. The details involved me, a friend, and a case of quarts. I drank beer until I couldn't see straight then went home and vomited until I couldn't stand up. My dad came to the bathroom, smelled the beer, threw a towel in my direction, and walked away in disgust.

That was the beginning of some wayward years for one Max Lucado. I lied to my parents. I lied to friends. I focused on me, me, me. And I drank. With gusto.

I was a sophomore in college the last time I got drunk. I'd quit going to church because I didn't think God would want me back. But the influence of a few good friends and a minister helped me see that the whole reason Jesus died on the cross was for people like me.

It was a life-changing discovery. I realized that God is always ready to grant a second chance. So I grabbed it—and have been grateful ever since.

ONE MORE THOUGHT

Do you see? Nothing you do will end God's love for you. Not drinking. Not drugs. Not the terrible thing you did to your dad, sister, or friend. So own up to your mistakes and ask God to forgive you. Start living again. He wants you back.

The true children of God are those who let God's Spirit lead them.

[Romans 8:14 NCV]

Who Is the Holy Spirit?

The Trinity—Father, Son, and Holy Ghost—is not your typical family. In fact, it might not make much sense to you. We talk about the Father and study the Son, but when it comes to the Holy Spirit, many of us are confused at best and frightened at worst. Confused because we've never been taught. Frightened because we've been taught to be afraid.

May I simplify things a bit? The Holy Spirit is the presence of God in our lives, carrying on the work of Jesus. The Holy Spirit helps us in three directions—inwardly (by granting us the fruits of the Spirit, Galatians 5:22–24), upwardly (by praying for us, Romans 8:26), and outwardly (by pouring God's love into our hearts, Romans 5:5).

When you invite God into your life, you invite the Spirit too. "And the Spirit himself joins with our spirits to say we are God's children" (Romans 8:16 NCV). You might call it the best family reunion you've ever been to.

ONE MORE THOUGHT

It's one of the wonderful mysteries of our faith—Jesus is the Son of God, an individual, yet also God himself. The same is true of the Holy Spirit. He works inside us, with God and as God, leading us to the life we were meant to live.

> I keep trying to reach the goal and get the prize for which God called me.
>
> [Philippians 3:14 NCV]

A Higher Standard

Most of my life I've been a closet slob. Then I got married. I enrolled in a support group for slobs. ("My name is Max, I hate to vacuum.") A physical therapist helped me rediscover the muscles used for hanging shirts. My nose was reintroduced to the smell of Pine-Sol.

Then came the moment of truth. My wife, Denalyn, went out of town for a week. Initially I reverted to the old man. I figured I'd be a slob for six days and clean on the seventh. But something strange happened, a curious discomfort. I couldn't relax with dirty dishes in the sink. What had happened to me? Simple. I'd been exposed to a higher standard.

Isn't that what has happened with us? Before we met Jesus we didn't care about the world around us. We were mainly focused on ourselves. Our lives were a mess. But now we're so much more aware of God's people and God's standards. Today we have a new model to follow—the best ever.

ONE MORE THOUGHT

Jesus is our model in life. It can be a little intimidating at times—he is perfect, after all. God doesn't expect perfection from us, but he does call us to try every day to be more like Christ. The nice thing about that is, the closer we get, the better our lives and the greater our joy.

FEBRUARY

And we have known and believed the love that
God has for us. God is love, and he who abides
in love abides in God, and God in him.

[1 John 4:16]

You received God's Spirit when he adopted you as his
own children. Now we call him, "Abba, Father."

[Romans 8:15 NLT]

Trust God's Verdict

To accept God's grace is to accept God's offer to be adopted into his family. Your identity is not in your friends, possessions, talents, tattoos, grades, or accomplishments. Nor are you defined by your family's divorce or debt, or your dumb choices. You are God's child. You get to call him "Papa." You receive the blessings of his special love (1 John 4:9–11) and provision (Luke 11:11–13). You will inherit the riches of Christ and reign with him forever (Romans 8:17).

The adoption is horizontal as well as vertical. You are included in the forever family. A community is created on the basis of a common father. Instant family worldwide!

Rather than try to invent reasons to feel good about yourself, trust God's verdict. If God loves you, you must be worth loving. If he wants to have you in his kingdom, then you must be worth having. God's grace invites you—no, *requires* you—to change your attitude about yourself and take sides with God against your feelings of rejection.

ONE MORE THOUGHT

On a scale of one to ten, how good do you feel about yourself right now? If you're having trouble seeing your value, maybe it's time for a second opinion. God loves you and wants you in his family. Don't you think he knows what's truly valuable?

> I will sing your praises! You are my mighty fortress, and you love me.
>
> [Psalm 59:17 CEV]

A Strong Hand to Hold

With life comes change. With change comes fear, insecurity, sorrow, stress. So what do you do? Hibernate? Take no risks for fear of failing? Give no love for fear of losing?

A better idea is to look up. Set your bearings on the one and only North Star in the universe—God. Although life changes, he never does. Consider his strength. Unending. According to Paul, God's power lasts forever (Romans 1:20). The words "I'm feeling strong today" he has never said. He feels equally strong every day.

Think about it. God never pauses to eat or asks the angels to cover for him while he naps. He never signals a time-out or puts the prayer requests from Russia on hold while he handles South Africa. He "never slumbers or sleeps" (Psalm 121:4 NLT). Need a strong hand to hold? You'll always find one in his. His strength never changes.

ONE MORE THOUGHT

You probably know some strong guys at school. They're the ones who major in weightlifting and make it look easy. Compare their strength to God's, though, and they are as puny as a paper clip. No matter how strong your opponent in life, God's strength is so much greater.

This is the day the LORD has made; We will rejoice and be glad in it.
[Psalm 118:24]

God Made This Day

What of those days of double shadows? Those days when hope is doused by disaster? You wake up remembering you wrecked the family car. Or that your dad just lost his job. Or that your mom was diagnosed with cancer. Who has a good day on these days?

Most don't . . . but couldn't we try? After all, "this is the day the Lord has made; we will rejoice and be glad in it." The first word in the verse leaves us scratching our heads. "*This* is the day the Lord has made"? Perhaps holidays are the days the Lord has made. Wedding days are the days the Lord has made. Easter Sundays . . . snow days . . . vacation days—these are the days the Lord has made. But *this* day?

"This is the day" includes every day. Final exam days, surgery days, detention days. God made this day, ordained this hard hour, designed the details of this wrenching moment. He isn't on holiday. He still holds the conductor's baton, sits in the cockpit, and occupies the universe's only throne. Each day emerges from God's drawing board. Including this one.

ONE MORE THOUGHT

Every day is a gift from God. That may be hard to believe when it seems your life is going up in flames. But just as a forest uses fire to replenish itself and give birth to new life, God uses the burning embers of our days to

Your word is like a lamp for my feet and a light for my path.

[Psalm 119:105 NCV]

God's GPS

The purpose of the Bible is simply to proclaim God's plan to save his children. It tells us that we are lost and need to be saved. And it communicates the message that Jesus is God in human form sent to save his children.

Although the Bible was written over sixteen centuries by at least forty authors, it has one central theme—salvation through faith in Christ. Begun by Moses in the lonely desert of Arabia and finished by John on the lonely isle of Patmos, it is held together by a strong thread: God's passion and God's plan to save his children.

This is important! Understanding the purpose of the Bible is like understanding how to read a GPS. When you know what you're looking at and adjust your direction as needed, you'll journey safely. But if you fail to pay attention to the coordinates, who knows where you'll end up. If you want to know where you're going, use God's GPS for your life. Read your Bible every day.

ONE MORE THOUGHT

We all have times when we're not sure what to do or where to go. If you're in the woods, it's sure helpful to have a map or compass or GPS. But if you're lost in life, the surest way to find your way again is to pull out your Bible. It's the blueprint for getting to where you want to be.

The One who died for us . . . is in the presence of God
at this very moment sticking up for us.

[Romans 8:34 MSG]

Standing Up for You

Picture a woman in bed, her sleep interrupted by voices. "Get up, you harlot." "What kind of woman do you think you are?" Her accusers marched her through narrow streets and thrust her before the holiest judge of all. "Teacher," they said, "this woman was caught in the very act of adultery. The law of Moses says to stone her. What do you say?" (John 8:2–5 NLT).

Jesus stood on behalf of the woman, placed himself between her and the lynch mob, and said, "'All right, but let the one who has never sinned throw the first stone!' Then he stooped down again and wrote in the dust" (vv. 7–8 NLT). Name-callers shut their mouths. Rocks fell to the ground. Accusers slipped away one by one.

Jesus stands up for you too. In the presence of God, in defiance of Satan, he rises to your defense and offers a future free from blame—not just from your past mistakes but also from the ones ahead. Christ forever stands in on your behalf.

ONE MORE THOUGHT

You'll always have critics. Teachers. Parents. Enemies. Friends. Older brothers. But you'll also always have an advocate. The One who loved you enough to die for you is ready to stick up for you. Anytime. Anywhere.

> So let us go on to grown-up teaching. Let us not
> go back over the beginning lessons
> we learned about Christ.
>
> [Hebrews 6:1 NCV]

Move Closer

I like the story of the little boy who fell out of bed. When his mom asked him what happened, he answered, "I don't know. I guess I stayed too close to where I got in."

Easy to do the same with our faith. It's tempting just to stay where we got in and never move.

Pick a time in the not-too-distant past. A year or two ago. Now ask yourself a few questions. Do you talk to God more today than you did then? Has your joy increased? What about Bible reading and understanding? Can you tell you've grown? Is your faith growing deeper and your love for Jesus stronger?

Just like friendships, a relationship with God works best when you make the effort to get closer. Don't make the mistake of the little boy. Don't stay where you got in. It's risky resting on the edge.

ONE MORE THOUGHT

At the swimming pool, some little kids (and big kids) dip only a single toe in the water to see what it's like. Imagine how little swimming they'd get in—and how much fun they'd miss—if that was as far as they went. Faith is like that too. Don't settle for dipping one toe. Dive in!

> You did not save yourselves; it was a gift from God.
>
> [Ephesians 2:8 NCV]

He Chose the Cross

Jesus' obedience began in a small town carpentry shop. His uncommon approach to his common life prepared him for his uncommon call. "When Jesus entered public life he was about thirty years old" (Luke 3:23 MSG). In order for Jesus to change the world, he had to say good-bye to his world.

He had to give Mary a kiss. Have a final meal in the kitchen, a final walk through the streets. Did he ascend one of the hills of Nazareth and think of the day he would ascend the hill near Jerusalem?

He knew what was going to happen. "God chose him as your ransom long before the world began" (1 Peter 1:20 NLT). Every ounce of suffering had been scripted—it just fell to him to play the part.

Not that he had to. Nazareth was a cozy town. Why not build a carpentry business? Keep his identity a secret? To be forced to die is one thing, but to willingly take up your own cross is something else.

ONE MORE THOUGHT

You may think that because Jesus is Lord, it was easy for him to give up his life on Calvary. Not so. Because Jesus chose to be human, he suffered on the cross just as you or I would. What's really amazing is that he knew what was coming and did it anyway. For us.

40

Home

All of us know what it is like to be in a house that is not our own. You've spent the night at a friend's. Perhaps you've visited your older brother's dorm room. Maybe you've slept in your share of hotels or motels. They have beds. They have tables. They may have food, and they may be warm, but they are a far cry from being "your father's house."

We don't always feel welcome here on earth. We wonder if there is a place here for us. People insult and reject us. Tough times leave us feeling like strangers. We just don't seem to fit in.

We shouldn't. This isn't our home. To feel unwelcome is no tragedy. Indeed it is healthy. We are not home here. This language we speak, it's not ours. This body we wear, it isn't us. And the world we live in, this isn't home.

Where's home? Heaven. It has rooms designed specifically for us. It's filled with love. It's the place we belong. It's where our Father is. I can't wait. It's home.

ONE MORE THOUGHT

You really shouldn't expect to feel too comfortable in this world. It's filled with ideas and attitudes that make no sense—and they shouldn't. A house, in fact a kingdom, is waiting for you. A place of purpose, yet peace. A place that's inspiring and loving. A place you can finally call home.

Christ in you, the hope of glory.

[Colossians 1:27]

Christ in You

When grace happens, Christ enters. No other religion or philosophy makes such a claim. No other movement implies the living presence of its founder *in* his followers. Mohammed does not indwell Muslims. Buddha does not inhabit Hindus. Lady Gaga does not reside in even her most fervent fans. Influence? Instruct? Entice? Maybe. But occupy? No.

Yet Christians embrace this puzzling promise. "The mystery in a nutshell is just this: Christ is in you" (Colossians 1:27 MSG). The Christian is a person in whom Christ is happening. He moves in, making himself at home. We sense his rearranging. Confusion turns into clear direction. Bad choices are replaced by better ones. Little by little a new self emerges. "He decided from the outset to shape the lives of those who love him along the same lines as the life of his Son" (Romans 8:29 MSG).

Grace is God as heart surgeon—cracking open your chest, removing your heart, poisoned as it is with pride and pain, and replacing it with his own. His dream isn't just to get you into heaven, but to get heaven into you.

ONE MORE THOUGHT

Ever gulp down a steaming cup of hot chocolate on a cold winter's day? You can feel it spreading a wonderful warmth to every corner of your body. That's the tiniest glimpse of what Jesus does in you. Spreading to every corner of your life. Warm. Wonderful.

Resentment kills a fool, and envy slays the simple.

[Job 5:2 NIV]

Forgive the Felonies

Some of us (most of us?) find it hard to forgive the people who bring pain to our lives. We forgive the one-time offenders, mind you. We dismiss the parking-place takers and date breakers. We can move past the misdemeanors, but the felonies? The repeat offenders? The ones who take our friends, our virginity, our parents?

Can you forgive the scum who hurt you?

Failure to do so could be fatal. "Resentment kills a fool, and envy slays the simple" (Job 5:2 NIV). Vengeance fixes your attention at life's ugliest moments. Score-settling freezes your stare at cruel events in your past. Is this where you want to look? Will rehearsing and reliving your hurts make you a better person?

By no means. It will destroy you. An eye for an eye becomes a neck for a neck and a reputation for a reputation. When does it stop? It stops when one person imitates God.

ONE MORE THOUGHT

God knows what will happen if you fail to forgive. Bitterness will grow inside you like a weed on steroids. Worse, it will cut you off from God. He doesn't want that. You don't either. You don't have to forgive for the offender's sake. Do it for yours. Do it for God.

God Is Crazy About You

There are many reasons God saves you: to show his glory, to bring about his justice, to demonstrate his authority. But one of the sweetest reasons God saves you is because he is fond of you. He likes having you around. He thinks you are the hottest song he's seen on the charts in quite a while.

When you're crazy about another guy or gal, what do you do? You think about him all the time. Your heart skips a beat when you get a text from her. You can't wait to see him next. That's how God feels about you. If he had a refrigerator, your picture would be on it. If he had a wallet, your photo would be in it. He sends you flowers every spring and a sunrise every morning. Whenever you want to talk, he'll listen. He can live anywhere in the universe, and he chose your heart.

Face it, friend. He's crazy about you.

ONE MORE THOUGHT

You might think of God as a distant ruler, too busy to be much concerned about you. So not true! He's interested in everything about you. He even knows how many hairs you have on your head. What's that about? It's simple. He loves you.

> "So don't worry about tomorrow, for tomorrow will bring its own worries. Today's trouble is enough for today."
>
> [Matthew 6:34 NLT]

Face Challenges in Stages

An accomplished Ironman triathlete told me the secret of his success. "You last the long race by running short ones." Don't swim 2.4 miles; just swim to the next buoy. Rather than bike 112 miles, ride 10, take a break, and bike 10 more. Never tackle more than the challenge ahead.

Didn't Jesus offer the same counsel? "So don't ever worry about tomorrow. After all, tomorrow will worry about itself. Each day has enough trouble of its own" (Matthew 6:34 GOD'S WORD).

When asked how he managed to write so many books, Joel Henderson explained that he'd never written a book. All he did was write one page a day.[3]

Face challenges in stages. You can't control your temper forever, but you can control it for the next hour. Earning a high school or college degree can seem impossible, but studying one week at a time is doable. You last the long race by running the short ones.

ONE MORE THOUGHT

It's late. You're tired. And you only have an hour to write your English essay and beat the deadline. Believe me, I've been there! So don't try to write the whole essay at once. Pray. Then write a good opening sentence. And then

> Pray in the Spirit at all times with all kinds of
> prayers, asking for everything you need.
>
> [Ephesians 6:18 NCV]

Give Every Moment to God

How do I live in God's presence? How do I feel his unseen hand on my shoulder and hear his inaudible voice in my ear? How can you and I grow familiar with the voice of God? Here are a few ideas:

Give God your waking thoughts. Before you face the day, face the Father. Before you step out of bed, step into his presence.

Give God your waiting thoughts. Standing in line for the bus or lunch? Spend time with him in silence.

Give God your whispering thoughts. Consider every moment as a potential time of conversation with God.

Give God your waning thoughts. At the end of the day, let your mind settle on him. Conclude the day as you began it: talking to God.

ONE MORE THOUGHT

Talking to God all the time can become a holy habit. It shouldn't be a chore. Remember, he's eager to hear from you! He's the Father who's continually looking out for you, who'll never desert you, who always wants to know what you're thinking and feeling.

> Love does not delight in evil but rejoices with the truth.
>
> [1 Corinthians 13:6 NIV]

True Love

A guy dates a girl for three months. She says she's in love. He's not sure, but he knows he feels different when he's with her. He wonders if that's love. Maybe you've wondered too.

Want to know if you feel genuine love? Ask yourself this: *Do I encourage this person to do what is right?* For true love "takes no pleasure in other people's sins but delights in the truth" (1 Corinthians 13:6 TJB).

Here's an example. A young couple is on a date. His affection goes beyond her comfort zone. She resists. He tries the oldest line in the book: "But I love you. I just want to be near you. If you loved me . . ." That siren you hear? It's the phony-love detector. This guy doesn't love her. True love will never ask the "beloved" to do what he or she thinks is wrong.

Want to know if your love for someone is true? If your friendship is genuine? Ask if you influence this person to do what is right. If you answer yes, ask her out for lunch.

ONE MORE THOUGHT

Love has inspired more songs, books, movies, and bad poetry than any emotion you can think of. But what exactly is it? You'll find no better definition than Paul's words in 1 Corinthians 13. Check it out. I think you'll love it.

> So encourage each other and build each other up, just as you are already doing.
>
> [1 Thessalonians 5:11 NLT]

Uncommon Community

Something holy happens around a dinner table that will never happen in a church. In a church auditorium you see the backs of heads. Around the table you see the expressions on faces. In the auditorium one person speaks; around the table everyone has a voice. Church services are on the clock. Around the table there is time to talk.

Hospitality opens the door to uncommon community.

It's no accident that *hospitality* and *hospital* come from the same Latin word, for they both lead to the same result: healing. When you open your door to someone, you are sending this message: "You matter to me and to God." You may think you are saying, "Come over for a visit." But what your guest hears is, "I'm worth the effort."

Do you know people who need this message? A boy who's just moved to your school? A girl who always eats lunch alone? A classmate who's lost her mother? Some people pass an entire day with no meaningful contact with anyone else. Your hospitality can be their hospital.

ONE MORE THOUGHT

Left out. Not a good feeling, is it? People all around you feel this way every day. Maybe you're one of them. Why not invite one of these guys or gals to sit with you at lunch or have dinner at your home? They need your kind invitation more than you know.

> Anyone who wants to be a friend of the world becomes God's enemy.
>
> [James 4:4 NCV]

Set Apart

John the Baptist would never get hired to preach today. No church would touch him. He was a public relations disaster. He "wore clothes made from camel's hair, had a leather belt around his waist, and ate locusts and wild honey" (Mark 1:6 NCV). Who would want to look at a guy like that every Sunday?

His message was as rough as his dress: a no-nonsense, bare-fisted challenge to repent because God was on his way. John the Baptist set himself apart for one task: to be a voice of Christ. Everything about John centered on his purpose. His dress. His diet. His actions. His demands.

You don't have to be like the world to have an impact on the world. You don't have to be like the crowd to change the crowd. You don't have to lower yourself down to their level to lift them up to your level. Holiness doesn't seek to be odd. Holiness seeks to be like God.

ONE MORE THOUGHT

The world will pull you in ways you really don't want to go. Movies you don't need to see. Music you don't need to hear. Clothes and language that are all about trying to fit in. But should you fit in? John the Baptist didn't. He cared only about serving and being like God. Don't be afraid to be set apart.

> "Whoever comes to me will never be hungry, and whoever believes in me will never be thirsty."
>
> [John 6:35 NCV]

When God Says No

There are times when the one thing you want is the one thing you never get. A seat in the all-state band. A job at the corner shake stand. A date for homecoming. A clear map to your future.

You pray and wait. No answer. You pray and wait some more.

May I ask a very important question? What if God says no? What if the request is delayed or even denied? When God says no to you, how will you respond? If God says, "I've given you my grace, and that is enough," will you be content?

Content. That's the word. A state of heart in which you are at peace even if God gives you nothing more than he already has. He has his reasons for saying no. Our job is "being content in any and every situation" (Philippians 4:12 NIV). God's grace is always enough.

ONE MORE THOUGHT

What we need is so clear—at least *we* think so. We're like an ant stopping to pick up a crumb. We've got to have it! Too bad we're too small to see the elephant with the big feet headed our way. God is bigger than the ant or the elephant. He sees what's coming. And if he says no, it's better to leave the crumb behind.

> "For where two or three are gathered together in My
> name, I am there in the midst of them."
>
> [Matthew 18:20]

"I'm Depressed"

Years ago, my wife, Denalyn, battled a dark cloud of depression. Not just a bad mood, but deep dejection. Every day was gray. One Sunday, when the depression was suffocating, she armed herself with honesty and went to church. *If people ask me how I am doing, I'm going to tell them.* She answered each "How are you?" with a candid "Not well. I'm depressed. Will you pray for me?"

Casual chats became long conversations. Brief hellos became heartfelt moments of ministry. By the time she left the worship service, she'd signed up dozens of people to join with her in prayer. She traces the healing of her depression to that Sunday morning service. She found God's presence in the middle of God's people.

Are you struggling with depression? This is no time to be a hermit. Tell the people you trust: friends, parents, teachers, counselors. And tell God! No matter how bad life gets, he'll be with you. He wants you to know the joy found only in him.

ONE MORE THOUGHT

When life is so overwhelming that you feel you can't go on, talk about it—especially with God. He understands in a way no one else can. His power and love are your guide through the darkness to a brighter future.

All must give as they are able, according to the blessings
given to them by the LORD your God.

[Deuteronomy 16:17 NLT]

A Feast of Kindness

Leo Tolstoy, the great Russian writer, tells of the time he was walking down the street and passed a beggar. Tolstoy reached into his pocket to give the beggar some money, but his pocket was empty. Tolstoy turned to the man and said, "I'm sorry, my brother, but I have nothing to give." The beggar brightened and said, "You have given me more than I asked for—you have called me brother."

You may think you have nothing to offer those in need around you, but it's not true. For the discouraged and downhearted, the littlest thing—a smile or encouraging word—may be enough to lift their spirits. To the loved, a kind word is a crumb, but to the love-starved, a word of kindness can be a feast.

Look at the brothers and sisters around you. They may be hiding it, but I guarantee that some are hurting and hungry for the kindness only you can give.

ONE MORE THOUGHT

Write down the names of at least three people you don't usually talk to who could use a kind word. Now make it your mission to encourage them sometime in the next twenty-four hours. After all God has done for us, it's the least we can do.

Always be full of joy in the Lord. I say it again—rejoice!

[Philippians 4:4 NLT]

One Good Day

Rejoice *in* this day? God invites us to. As Paul rejoiced *in* prison; David wrote psalms *in* the wilderness; Jonah prayed *in* the fish belly; Paul and Silas sang *in* jail; and Jesus prayed *in* his garden of pain . . . Could we rejoice smack-dab *in* the middle of this day?

Imagine the difference if we could.

Suppose neck-deep in a terrible day you resolve to give it a chance. You choose not to complain or work or worry it away but give it a fair shake. You trust more. Stress less. Amplify gratitude. Mute grumbling. And what do you know? Before long the day is done and surprisingly decent.

So decent, in fact, that you resolve to give the next day the same fighting chance. It arrives with its hang-ups and bang-ups, computer crashes and homework hassles, but by and large, by golly, giving the day a chance works! You do the same the next day and the next. Days become a week. Weeks become months.

In such a fashion good lives are built. One good day at a time.

ONE MORE THOUGHT

Scripture says to be joyful *always*. That doesn't mean laughing when your dad yells at you or your favorite dog dies. It does mean remembering that God's power and love are bigger than any trouble you must tackle. Even in your worst moments, you can rest in God-inspired joy.

Time for God

How long has it been since you focused totally on God?

I mean, *really*. How long since you gave him complete, uninterrupted attention, time spent just listening for his voice? If you're anything like me, it's probably been too long.

Jesus didn't let that happen. Spend much time reading about the listening life of Christ and a distinct pattern emerges. He made a deliberate effort to devote regular time to God, praying and listening. Mark says, "Very early in the morning, while it was still dark, Jesus got up, left the house and went off to a solitary place, where he prayed" (Mark 1:35 NIV). For Jesus, God time apparently came before sleeping in, other appointments, checking for e-mails, and just about everything else.

Let me ask the obvious. If Jesus, the Son of God, the sinless Savior of humankind, thought it worthwhile to clear his calendar to pray, wouldn't we be wise to do the same?

ONE MORE THOUGHT

There's so much you have to do. School. Homework. Practice trombone. Chores. The basics of sleeping and eating. And then there's the stuff you really *want* to do: hang out with friends, play video games, check out the latest band. But if you squeeze God out of the schedule, guess what? The rest starts to feel as empty as a drum.

I can do all things through Christ, because he gives me strength.

[Philippians 4:13 NCV]

Big Brothers

Matt Stevens stands at the free throw line. His team is down by one point. Only a few seconds remain in the game. The crowd is quiet. The cheerleaders gulp. Does Matt even have a chance of making these shots? He's 0 for 6 on the day.

He's also blind.

How does a blind kid end up on the foul line? Because of his big brother. Joe Stevens spent a childhood helping Matt do the impossible: ride a bike, ice skate, play soccer. So, when Joe joined the basketball team, he brought his baby brother with him. Now, with the referees' permission, Joe taps the rim of the basket with a cane. Matt listens, pauses, and shoots. Swish! The game is tied! The crowd settles down so Matt can hear the click again. Swish number two! The game ends. Matt is the hero. All because of a big brother who made all the difference.[4]

You too have a big brother walking you through the rough patches of life, helping you do the impossible. Listen and you'll hear him tapping. His name is Jesus.

ONE MORE THOUGHT

Each of us is blind in one way or another. We can't see our way out of trouble, or we can't see who needs our help. We can't make it on our own. But as members of the family of God, we have a big brother who not only gets us through, he also allows us to do the impossible.

The grace of God that brings salvation has appeared.

[Titus 2:11]

Precious Grace

Grace is precious because Jesus is. Grace changes lives because he does. Grace secures us because he will.

To discover grace is to discover God's total devotion to you, his stubborn desire to give you a cleansing, healing, purging love that lifts the wounded back to their feet. Does he stand high on a hill and tell you to climb out of the valley? No. He bungees down and carries you out. Does he build a bridge and command you to cross it? No. He crosses the bridge and shoulders you over.

This is the gift that God gives. A grace that grants us first the power to receive love and then the power to give it. A grace that changes us, shapes us, and leads us to a life that is forever altered. Do you know this grace? Do you trust this grace? If not, you can. All God wants from us is faith. Put your faith in God.

ONE MORE THOUGHT

It's not so hard, is it? You have faith that you'll wake up tomorrow, that your room will still be here, that your school will still be there (even if you wish it weren't). So why not have faith in God? His grace is waiting for you.

Be What God Made You

Your father is a doctor. Your grandfather is a doctor. Everyone expects you to be a doctor. But you want to study music. Did you miss something?

No, I think you found something. People often say you can be anything you want if you work hard enough. A butcher. A sales rep. An ambassador. But can you? If God didn't pack within you the meat sense of a butcher, the people skills of a salesperson, or the world vision of an ambassador, can you be one? An unhappy, dissatisfied one perhaps. But a fulfilled one? Can an acorn become a rose, a whale fly like a bird, or lead become gold? No way. You can't be anything you want to be. But you can be everything *God* wants you to be.

God doesn't crank people out on an assembly line. You were uniquely crafted and carved. "I make all things new," he declares (Revelation 21:5). He didn't hand you your granddad's bag or your aunt's life; he personally and deliberately packed you. Live out of the bag God gave you. Enjoy making music.

ONE MORE THOUGHT

God gives each of us unique abilities and talents. When those connect with your passion and a mission that serves God, you're onto something exciting—and it just may be the calling that he had in mind for you when he created you.

Be wise in the way you act with people who are not believers.

[Colossians 4:5 NCV]

The World Is Watching

Those who don't believe in Jesus notice what we do. They make decisions about Christ by watching us. When we are kind, they assume Christ is kind. When we are gracious, they assume Christ is gracious.

But if we are arrogant or pushy, what will people think about our King? When we are dishonest, what assumption will an observer make about our Master? No wonder Paul says, "Be wise in the way you act with people who are not believers, making the most of every opportunity. When you talk, you should always be kind and pleasant so you will be able to answer everyone in the way you should" (Colossians 4:5–6 NCV). Courteous conduct honors Christ.

It also honors his children. When you surrender a place in line to someone, you honor him. When you return a borrowed book, you honor the lender. When you make an effort to greet everyone in the room, especially the ones others may have overlooked, you honor God's children.

ONE MORE THOUGHT

You can make the greatest speech ever about the love of Jesus, but if your actions don't show love, your words will be ignored. Think about your behavior over the past week—have people seen Christ in you? If not, what can you do this week to show his love to the world?

> God will bless you, if you don't give up when your faith is being tested.
>
> [James 1:12 CEV]

You'll Get Through This

I met a teenager at the café where she works. She's fresh out of high school. When she was fifteen, her divorced parents remarried, only to divorce again a few months ago. Recently her parents told her to make a choice: live with Mom or Dad. She got misty-eyed as she retold their announcement. If I see her again, here's what I will say: "You'll get through this. It won't be painless. It won't be quick. But God will use this mess for good. Don't be foolish or naïve. But don't despair either. With God's help, you will get through this."

Where do I get the nerve to speak such a promise into tragedy? From Jesus. He said, "In this world you will have trouble. But take heart! I have overcome the world" (John 16:33 NIV).

We *will* have trouble. No might or maybe about it. But we have every reason to be encouraged. Jesus has conquered the worst of this world. If we're with him, that means we will conquer too.

ONE MORE THOUGHT

Is anything more devastating than the divorce of your parents? How about the death of your mom, dad, brother, or sister? Jesus tells us we will have trouble, but that doesn't make it hurt less. Thankfully, he also offers himself. He is our hope and our healer. We can get through if we lean on him.

Kings like honest people; they value someone who speaks the truth.

[Proverbs 16:13 NCV]

God Loves the Truth

Our Master has a strict honor code. From Genesis to Revelation, the theme is the same: God loves the truth and hates deceit. "The LORD detests lying lips, but he delights in those who tell the truth" (Proverbs 12:22 NLT).

Truth-telling isn't always easy. You don't want to go out but don't want to hurt your friend's feelings. Can't you just say you have too much homework? You forgot the time and missed your curfew. Can't you just tell your parents the car wouldn't start?

Lies have no place among God's people. In 1 Corinthians 6:9–10, Paul lists the type of people who will not inherit God's kingdom. The gang includes those who sin sexually, worship idols, take part in adultery, sell their bodies, get drunk, rob people, and—there it is—lie about others.

Your fibbing stirs the same heavenly anger as adultery and aggravated assault? Apparently so. God loves the truth, so dishonesty is the opposite of everything he stands for.

ONE MORE THOUGHT

Telling the truth all the time may be hard, but it's so important. When our words are dishonest and lose their meaning in little things, we can't be trusted to speak and live out the truth in anything. Be like God. Love the truth.

> "Stockpile treasure in heaven, where it's safe from moth and rust and burglars."
> [Matthew 6:20 MSG]

God Owns It All

Your little brother just dropped your new cell phone, and you're having a major meltdown. I don't blame you for being upset, but here's a little tip that might help you keep things in perspective: it wasn't yours anyway.

What am I talking about? Try this, and you'll see what I mean. Grab some sticky notes and stick one on everything in your life that you won't be taking with you when you go to heaven someday. Go ahead—look in your bedroom, house, yard, garage. The clothes, the DVDs, the books, the game controllers, even the stuffed monkey you've had since you were two. Once you've finished, what's left? Your friends. Your church. The Word of God. Your family (including your little brother).

All that stuff? You don't get to keep it. *You never had it.* You own nothing. You are simply a caretaker of what God's given you. "The earth is the LORD's, and everything in it. The world and all its people belong to him" (Psalm 24:1 NLT). If he's not too concerned about a dropped cell phone, maybe you shouldn't be either.

ONE MORE THOUGHT

A funny thing about "stuff"—we think we own it, but it's more like the other way around. You buy a computer, and pretty soon it's demanding software upgrades, better security, internal cleanings, and external wipings. Who's really running the show? It's not you or your PC. It's God.

> A gossip goes around telling secrets, but those who
> are trustworthy can keep a confidence.
>
> [Proverbs 11:13 NLT]

Words That Wound

Do you ever talk about people behind their backs? It's called gossip. Perhaps you intend to hurt with your words, perhaps not; but that doesn't matter. Thanks to you, someone ends up on the floor because of a slur or slip of the tongue. And there the person lies, wounded and bleeding. Bruised feelings, punctured pride, broken heart.

Mary probably knew just what that felt like. An unmarried teen, pregnant. Stares and whispers when she walked by: "I guess Mary isn't the good girl we thought she was." But the gossipers didn't have all the facts. No one told them that Mary carried the Savior of the world.

You don't have all the facts either. So don't spread rumors or bad news or make accusations about others. Walk away when someone else does it. Make these words from Ephesians your motto: "Don't say anything that would hurt another person. Instead, speak only what is good so that you can give help wherever it is needed" (4:29 GOD'S WORD).

ONE MORE THOUGHT

Can you imagine Jesus hanging out with friends, sharing secrets about a disciple who isn't there? Can you imagine someone being inspired by your Christian example if *you* do it? When gossipers gab, everyone gets hurt.

MARCH

Trust in the LORD with all your heart,
And lean not on your own understanding.

[Proverbs 3:5]

God is being patient with you. He does not want anyone to be lost,
but he wants all people to change their hearts and lives.

[2 Peter 3:9 ncv]

A Father's Pride

If you welcome Jesus as your Savior, he promises you a new birth. "No one can see the kingdom of God unless they are born again" (John 3:3 niv). Does that mean your old nature will never reappear? Does that mean you will instantly be able to resist any temptation?

To answer that question, compare your new birth in Christ to a newborn baby. Can a newborn walk? Can he feed himself? Can he sing or read or speak? No, not yet. But someday he will.

It takes time to grow. But is the parent in the delivery room ashamed of the baby? Is the mom embarrassed that the infant can't spell . . . that the baby can't walk . . . that the newborn can't give a speech?

Of course not. The parents aren't ashamed; they are proud. They know that growth will come with time. So does God.

ONE MORE THOUGHT

Do you sometimes get frustrated with yourself? Do you feel your faith should be growing faster, your character stronger, your love for God deeper? Don't be too hard on yourself. Your Father doesn't expect instant maturity. Babies need time to grow up. So do Christians.

> It is no use for you to get up early and stay up late, working
> for a living. The LORD gives sleep to those he loves.
>
> [Psalm 127:2 NCV]

Hurry Up and Rest

I've been in a hurry my whole life. Hurrying to school, hurrying to finish homework. Pedal faster, drive quicker. I used to wear my wristwatch on the inside of my arm so I wouldn't lose the millisecond it took to turn my wrist. What insanity!

I wonder if I could have obeyed God's ancient command to keep the Sabbath holy. To slow life to a crawl for twenty-four hours? The Sabbath was created for frantic souls like me. People who need this weekly reminder: the world will not stop if you do.

Maybe you need the reminder too. Too many late nights of studying and Internet surfing? Is your schedule overflowing, leaving you drowning? This is why God insisted that we set aside a day for rest and time with him. He knows how much we need it, and how unlikely we are to take it. So hurry up and schedule it! Step away from insanity and into serenity.

ONE MORE THOUGHT

If you're tired all the time, your body is trying to tell you something—you need rest! Fatigue comes in more than one form, however. We need to renew emotionally and spiritually, not just physically. Instead of making time for everything else first, make time for God.

> GOD's loyal love couldn't have run out, his merciful love couldn't have dried up.
>
> [Lamentations 3:22 MSG]

New Love Every Morning

Jeremiah was depressed, as gloomy as a giraffe with a neck ache. Jerusalem was under siege, his nation threatened, his world collapsing like a sandcastle in a typhoon. He blamed God for his emotional distress and his physical problems. "He [God] turned me into a scarecrow of skin and bones, then broke the bones" (Lamentations 3:4 MSG).

Jeremiah realized how fast he was sinking, so he looked in a new direction. "There's one other thing I remember, and remembering, I keep a grip on hope: GOD's loyal love couldn't have run out, his merciful love couldn't have dried up. They're created new every morning. How great your faithfulness! I'm sticking with GOD (I say it over and over)" (vv. 21–24 MSG).

When depressed, Jeremiah rebooted his thoughts. He turned his eyes away from his stormy world and stared into the wonder of God and his promises: God's love never hits bottom. His mercy never ends. They're renewed every morning because he's so faithful.

Guess what? The storm didn't stop, but Jeremiah's discouragement did. So can yours.

ONE MORE THOUGHT

Feel like everyone's against you? God isn't. When you get dressed for school in the morning, try also "putting on" the loyal and merciful love he's created fresh, just for you. No matter what you're facing, you'll find it's more than enough.

In the beginning there was the Word. The Word
was with God, and the Word was God.

[John 1:1 NCV]

A Treasure Map

The Bible has been banned, burned, scorned, and ridiculed. Scholars have mocked it as foolish. Kings have branded it as illegal. A thousand times over its grave has been dug, but somehow the Bible never stays in the grave. Not only has it survived, it has thrived. It is the single most popular book in all of history. It has been and still is the best-selling book in the world!

There is no way on earth to explain it. Which perhaps is the only explanation. The answer? The Bible's durability is not found on earth; it is found in heaven. For the millions who have tested its claims and claimed its promises there is but one answer—the Bible is God's book and God's voice.

The purpose of the Bible is to proclaim God's plan and passion to save his children. That is the reason this book has endured through the centuries. It is the treasure map that leads us to God's highest treasure: eternal life.

ONE MORE THOUGHT

Pirates needed a map to find incredibly valuable treasure long buried. No map, no treasure. It's also true of us who seek spiritual treasure. God has provided us with the map: the Bible. Eternal riches await those wise enough to use it.

"The Son of Man did not come to be served, but to serve."

[Mark 10:45]

Jesus the Gentleman

I had never thought much about the courtesy of Christ before, but as I began looking, I realized that in the art of being a gentleman, Jesus is the grand master.

He always knocks before entering. He doesn't have to. He owns your heart. If anyone has the right to barge in, Christ does. But he doesn't. That quiet tap you hear? It's Christ. "Behold, I stand at the door and knock" (Revelation 3:20 NASB). And when you answer, he awaits your invitation to cross the threshold.

And when he enters, he always brings a gift. Some bring chocolate and daisies. Christ brings "the gift of the Holy Spirit" (Acts 2:38). And, as he stays, he serves. "For even the Son of Man did not come to be served, but to serve" (Mark 10:45 NIV). If you're missing your apron, you'll find it on him. He's serving the guests as they sit (John 13:4–5). He won't eat until he has offered thanks, and he won't leave until the leftovers are put away (Matthew 14:19–20).

ONE MORE THOUGHT

Christ holds the power of creation in his hands, yet he is as caring and careful with us as a mother with her newborn baby. His words contain truth that echoes throughout time, yet it is his loving acts that provide our model. He is courteous. He is kind. He serves. He is a gentleman.

> And he did rescue us from mortal danger, and he will rescue us again. We have placed our confidence in him, and he will continue to rescue us.

[2 Corinthians 1:10 NLT]

God's Best Work

Peter and his fellow storm riders knew they were in trouble that night on the Sea of Galilee. Their boat lurched and lunged like a kite in a March wind. Lightning sliced the blackness with a silver sword. Winds whipped the sails, leaving the disciples "in the middle of the sea, tossed by the waves" (Matthew 14:24). Maybe you can relate?

In the middle of flunking a class, tossed about by feelings of failure.

In the middle of a fight with a friend, tossed about by guilt.

In the middle of a breakup, tossed about by despair.

The disciples fought the storm for nine cold, skin-drenching hours. Then the unspeakable happened. Someone approached, walking on the water. "'A ghost!' they said, crying out in terror" (Matthew 14:26 MSG).

They didn't expect Jesus to come to them this way. Neither do we. We expect him to come in quiet worship songs and morning Bible studies. We never expect to see him in the middle of bitter feuds or broken relationships. But it is in storms that he does his best work, for it is in storms that he has our best attention.

ONE MORE THOUGHT

Funny how we do that—we expect to see Jesus at our "holy" times, but not the rest of the time. Only he's so much bigger than that. So call on him. Look for him. Not just when you worship. Not just when you pray. Anytime. Everywhere. Absolutely when you're in trouble. Because when you need him most, he's right there with you, ready to calm the craziest storm.

May the God of peace . . . equip you with all you need for doing his will.

[Hebrews 13:20–21 NLT]

Get Over Yourself

Here's an idea. *Get over yourself.*

Moses did. One of history's foremost leaders was "a very humble man, more humble than anyone else on the face of the earth" (Numbers 12:3 NIV). Mary did. When Jesus called her womb his home, she did not boast; she simply confessed: "I'm the Lord's maid, ready to serve" (Luke 1:38 MSG). Most of all, Jesus did. "Jesus . . . was given a position 'a little lower than the angels'" (Hebrews 2:9 NLT).

Jesus chose the servants' quarters. Can't we? We're important, but not essential. We have a part in the play, but we are not the main act. God is.

He did well before our birth; he'll do fine after our deaths. He started it all, sustains it all, and will bring it all to a glorious end. In the meantime, we have this high honor: to give up personal goals, do what's right even when there's no reward, deal with problems that others avoid, say no to selfishness, follow Christ, and make his plans our own.

ONE MORE THOUGHT

Sounds worse than chores, doesn't it? Give up your goals. Forget about rewards. Take on the tough problems. A funny thing about that, though—the more you do it, the closer you grow to God, and the more joy that flows into your heart. Try it. Less you, more God adds up to delight.

When we were unable to help ourselves, at the right time, Christ died for us.

[Romans 5:6 NCV]

When We Can't Pay

God did for us what I did for one of my daughters in the shop at a New York airport. The sign above the ceramic pieces read Do Not Touch. But the wanting was stronger than the warning, and she touched. And it fell. By the time I looked up, ten-year-old Sara was holding two pieces of a New York City skyline. Next to her was an unhappy store manager. Over them both was the written rule. Between them hung a nervous silence. My daughter had no money. He had no mercy. So I stepped in. "How much do we owe you?" I asked.

How was it that I owed anything? Simple. She was my daughter. And since she could not pay, I did.

Since you and I cannot pay, Christ did. We've broken so much more than souvenirs. We've broken God's heart. With the law on the wall and shattered commandments on the floor, Christ steps near (like a neighbor) and offers a gift (like a Savior).

ONE MORE THOUGHT

We often depend on others to pay for what we can't. While you're growing up, who puts up the cash to put food on your table? Who pays for the taxes and repairs on the home where you live? Jesus paid for even more than that. His gift took care of every mistake you ever made.

Jesus reached out his hand and touched the man and said, "I will. Be healed!"

[Matthew 8:3 NCV]

A Godly Touch

Have you felt the power of a godly touch? The doctor who treated you or the teacher who dried your tears? Was there a hand holding yours at a funeral? Another on your shoulder during a terrible day? A smile of welcome at a new class?

Can't we offer the same?

Maybe you already do. You have the master touch of the Physician himself, and you use your hands to serve too. Maybe they do so by typing encouraging e-mails or helping up the new kid on the team after he's fouled. Or you've used your hands to bake cookies for a church bake sale or to take juice to your mom when she's sick. You have learned the power of a touch.

But others of us tend to forget. Our hearts are good; it's just that our memories are bad. We forget how significant one touch can be. Aren't we glad Jesus didn't make the same mistake? He touched a man with leprosy and cured him instantly (Matthew 8:3). Jesus reminds us that we also have the power of a godly touch.

ONE MORE THOUGHT

Touch is powerful. It can do terrible things: abuse, violence. But when its motivation comes from the love of God, it can also do wonderful things: cheer up, heal, support, serve. Who do you know who needs a godly touch today?

He Is God Alone

To what can we compare God? Any pursuit of God's counterpart is vain. Any search for a godlike person or position on earth is futile. No one and nothing compares with him. No one advises him. No one helps him. It is he who "executes judgment, putting down one and lifting up another" (Psalm 75:7 ESV).

You and I may have power. But God *is* power. We may be lightning bugs, but he is lightning itself. Consider the universe around us. Unlike the potter who takes something and reshapes it, God took nothing and created something. God created everything that exists out of nothing. Prior to creation, the universe was not a dark space. The universe did not exist. God even created the darkness. "I create the light and make the darkness" (Isaiah 45:7 NLT).

Even God asks, "To whom will you compare me? Who is my equal?" (Isaiah 40:25 NLT). As if his question needed an answer, he gives one: "I alone am God! I am God, and there is none like me" (46:9 NLT).

ONE MORE THOUGHT

Ever feel as if God isn't up to the task of coping with your crises? That he's too distracted or tired or feeble to deal with your current disaster? Forget it! He is God. Our universe *is* because he breathed it into existence. One God. Alone.

> Hold on to what you have, so that no one will take your crown.
>
> [Revelation 3:11 NIV]

Your Day Is Coming

You may be one of the many who have never won a prize in their lives. Oh, maybe you kept statistics for your basketball team or handed out assignments for English class, but that's about it. You've never won much. You've watched the LeBron Jameses of this world carry home the trophies and walk away with the ribbons. All you have are "almosts" and "what ifs."

If that hits home, then you'll value this promise: "And when the Chief Shepherd appears, you will receive the crown of glory that will never fade away" (1 Peter 5:4 NIV).

Your day is coming. God has plans to honor you, to give you a reward that will last not for a season but for eternity. Nothing has more value than a crown from his kingdom. What the world has overlooked, your Father has remembered, and sooner than you can imagine, you will be blessed by him.

ONE MORE THOUGHT

It's tough to watch everyone else collect the awards and honors. But earthly trophies will soon rust and be forgotten. The prize that counts is heavenly glory awarded by the King of kings. It's a reward worth waiting for.

> We must pay the most careful attention . . . to what we
> have heard, so that we do not drift away.
>
> [Hebrews 2:1 NIV]

Failures

If you lose your faith, you will probably do so a little at a time. You will let a few days slip by without consulting your compass. Your sails will go untrimmed. Your rigging will go unprepared. And worst of all, you will forget to anchor your boat. And, before you know it, you'll be bouncing from wave to wave in stormy seas.

And unless you anchor deep, you could go down. How do you anchor deep? Look at the verse again: "We must pay the most careful attention . . . *to what we have heard*."

The most reliable anchor points are not recent discoveries. They are time-tested truths that have held their ground against the winds of change. Truths like: My life is not futile. My failures are not fatal. My death is not final.

Attach your soul to these boulders and no wave is big enough to wash you under.

ONE MORE THOUGHT

It's human nature to get excited about new ideas and trends. How else to explain our fascination with changing fashions? But when it comes to our faith, we should drop anchor on the truths that have always been. You'll find them in the Word of God.

We will find grace to help us when we need it.

[Hebrews 4:16 NLT]

Timely Help

God's help is timely. He helps us the same way a father gives plane tickets to his family. When I travel with my kids, I carry all our tickets in my satchel. When the moment comes to board the plane, I stand between the attendant and the child. As each daughter passes, I place a ticket in her hand. She, in turn, gives the ticket to the attendant. Each one receives the ticket in the nick of time.

What I do for my daughters, God does for you. He places himself between you and the need. And at the right time, he gives you the ticket. Wasn't this the promise he gave his disciples? "When you are arrested and judged, don't worry ahead of time about what you should say. Say whatever is *given you to say at that time*, because it will not really be you speaking; it will be the Holy Spirit" (Mark 13:11 NCV).

God leads us. He will do the right thing at the right time.

ONE MORE THOUGHT

Think back over your life. How many times have you received just what you needed, just when you needed it? The ticket that came through on the day of the concert. The perfect gift idea on the day before Mother's Day. Coincidence? Or maybe the helping hand of heaven.

> "He came to serve others and to give his life as a ransom for many people."
>
> [Mark 10:45 NCV]

One Task

One of the incredible abilities of Jesus was to stay on target. His life never got off track. As Jesus looked across the horizon of his future, he could see many targets. Many flags were flapping in the wind, each of which he could have pursued. He could have been a political revolutionary. He could have been content to be a teacher and educate minds. But in the end he chose to be a Savior and save souls.

Anyone near Christ for any length of time heard it from Jesus himself. "The Son of Man came to find lost people and save them" (Luke 19:10 NCV). The heart of Christ was relentlessly focused on one task. The day he left the carpentry shop of Nazareth he had one ultimate aim—the cross of Calvary.

You have a single task too. It's a response to the one Jesus chose. He called your task the first and greatest commandment: "Love the Lord your God with all your heart and with all your soul and with all your mind" (Matthew 22:37 NIV).

Are you on target?

ONE MORE THOUGHT

It's tough to set priorities when people are telling you a million things are important. So read Matthew 22:34–40, where Jesus cuts through the confusion. Love God. Everything else depends on this. Clear enough?

> "Today salvation has come to this house."
>
> [Luke 19:9]

A Changed Heart

If the New Testament has a con artist, Zacchaeus is the man. He never met a person he couldn't swindle or saw a dollar he couldn't hustle. He was a "chief tax collector" (Luke 19:2). First-century tax collectors cheated anything that walked. But when Jesus and his followers traveled through Jericho, even the local tax collector wanted a look. Jesus spotted him in a sycamore tree and said, "Zacchaeus, come down immediately. I must stay at your house today" (v. 5 NIV). Of all the homes in town, Jesus selected Zack's.

Zacchaeus was never quite the same. "Look, Lord! Here and now I give half of my possessions to the poor, and if I have cheated anybody out of anything, I will pay back four times the amount" (v. 8 NIV). Despite Zacchaeus's bad choices, despite his dishonest past, Jesus offered him kindness and a seat at heaven's table. Jesus offered him grace. And when that grace walked in the front door, selfishness scampered out the back. It changed the tax collector's heart.

Is grace changing yours?

ONE MORE THOUGHT

How about it—are you more like the cheating Zacchaeus or the changed Zacchaeus? If you don't like your answer, ask Jesus to show you how to fully embrace his grace. He's already reserved a seat at heaven's table just for you.

God is kind to you so you will change your hearts and lives.

[Romans 2:4 NCV]

More Like Jesus

Here's God's agenda for your day: to make you more like Jesus.

"God . . . decided from the outset to shape the lives of those who love him along the same lines as the life of his Son" (Romans 8:29 MSG). Do you see what God is doing? Shaping you "along the same lines as the life of his Son."

Jesus felt no guilt; God wants you to feel no guilt.

Jesus had no bad habits; God wants to do away with yours.

Jesus faced fears with courage; God wants you to do the same.

Jesus knew the difference between right and wrong; God wants us to know the same.

Jesus served others and gave his life for the lost; we can do likewise.

Jesus dealt with anxiety about death; you can too.

God's desire, his plan, his ultimate goal is to make you into the image of Christ.

ONE MORE THOUGHT

We have a model, an example of how we are to live out this gift of life we've been given. His name is Jesus. The next time you're confused or unsure about how to handle a situation, get out your Bible and read the history of Jesus. His example is always the right one.

Love . . . always protects.

[1 Corinthians 13:6–7 NIV]

A Cloak of Love

When Paul said, "Love always protects," he might have been thinking of a coat. One scholar believes he was.

The Theological Dictionary of the New Testament is known for its word study, not its poetry. But the scholar sounds poetic as he explains the meaning of *protect* as used in 1 Corinthians 13:7. The word conveys, he says, "the idea of covering with a cloak of love."

Remember receiving one? You were nervous about the test, but the teacher stayed late to help you. You were far from home and afraid, but your mother phoned to comfort you. You were innocent and accused, so your friend stood to defend you. Covered with encouragement. Covered with tender-hearted care. Covered with protection. *Covered with a cloak of love.*

This is how Christ covered you and me when he died on the cross. And this is how we need to cover the world.

ONE MORE THOUGHT

When you were a child, did you ever shiver so much that your mom or dad wrapped a coat around you? That simple act is a symbol of love that protects. There are a thousand ways to show such love, but each says, "I care for you, and I am watching over you."

> I pour out my problems to him; I tell him my troubles.
>
> [Psalm 142:2 NCV]

Pray Your Pain Out

isappointment. Rejection. Illness. Accident. You're hurting right now. *Pray your pain out.*

Go ahead, pound the table. March up and down the lawn. It's time for determined, honest prayers. Angry at God? Disappointed at his strategy? Ticked off at his choices? Let him know it. Let him have it! Jeremiah did. This ancient prophet pastored Jerusalem during a time of crisis. Unemployment. Disaster. Refugee camps. Hunger. Death. Jeremiah saw it all. His book in the Bible, Lamentations, could be summed up with one line: *this life is rotten!* So why would God include it? Maybe as an example for you?

Call out your complaints. God will not turn away at your anger. Even Jesus offered up prayers with "loud cries and tears" (Hebrews 5:7 NCV). It's better to shake a fist at God than turn your back to him. Words might seem hollow and empty at first. You will mumble your sentences, fumble your thoughts. But don't quit. And don't hide. God hears your list of hurts. He is ready to heal.

ONE MORE THOUGHT

The hardest part about being hurt is going through it alone. We so often try to hide it from everyone and pretend nothing happened. This isn't what God wants! He wants to hear from us, even when our words are little more than angry arrows. Talking about it is the first step to healing.

Anyone who doubts is like a wave in the sea, blown up and down by the wind.

[James 1:6 NCV]

Do You Doubt?

Doubt. He's a nosy neighbor. He's an unwanted visitor. He's an obnoxious guest.

He'll pester you. He'll irritate you. He'll criticize your judgment. His aim is not to convince you but to confuse you. He doesn't offer solutions; he only raises questions.

Had any visits from this fellow lately? If you find yourself going to church in order to be saved and not because you *are* saved, then you've been listening to him. If you find yourself doubting God could forgive you again for that, you've been sold damaged goods. If you are more skeptical about Christians than sincere about Christ, then guess who came to dinner?

I suggest you put a lock on your gate. I suggest you post a Do Not Enter sign on your door. "The fundamental fact of existence is that this trust in God, this faith, is the firm foundation under everything that makes life worth living" (Hebrews 11:1 MSG). Dismiss doubt. Trust your faith.

ONE MORE THOUGHT

The disciple Thomas is famous for his doubt. He didn't fully embrace his faith until the moment he saw and touched the wounds of the risen Jesus (John 20:27–28 NIV). Don't be a Thomas. You have the evidence in your heart. Be one of the blessed "who have not seen and yet have believed" (v. 29).

> You must choose for yourselves today whom you will serve.
>
> [Joshua 24:15 NCV]

You Decide

God's invitation is clear and unchangeable. He gives all, and we give him all. Simple and absolute. He is clear in what he asks and clear in what he offers. The choice is up to us. Isn't it incredible that God leaves the choice to us?

Think about it. There are many things in life we can't choose. We can't, for example, choose the weather. We can't choose whether or not we are born with a big nose or blue eyes or a lot of hair. Can't choose our parents either. We can't choose the school lunch menu. We can't even choose who will laugh at our jokes.

But we can choose where we spend eternity. The big choice, God leaves to us. It means more to him, and us, when we have the freedom to make up our own mind. Will you ever make a more important choice? It's the only decision that really matters.

ONE MORE THOUGHT

How do you make your most important decisions? Do you list pros and cons on a piece of paper? Ask your friends and parents? Flip a coin? The choice on whether or not to give your heart to God isn't like picking a color for your cell-phone case. It's the biggest decision you'll ever make.

> "The Son of Man did not come to be served. He came to serve others and to give his life as a ransom for many people."
>
> [Matthew 20:28 NCV]

Our Servant Master

As a young boy, I read a Russian fable about a master and a servant who went on a journey to a city. Many of the details I've forgotten but the ending I remember. Before the two men could reach the destination they were caught in a blinding blizzard. They lost their direction and were unable to reach the city before nightfall.

The next morning concerned friends went searching for the two men. They finally found the master, frozen to death, facedown in the snow. When they lifted him they found the servant—cold but alive. He survived and told how the master had voluntarily placed himself on top of the servant so the servant could live.

I hadn't thought of that story in years. But when I read what Christ said he would do for us, the story surfaced—for Jesus is the master who died for the servants.

ONE MORE THOUGHT

That story sums up our lives better than we realize. We're caught in a blizzard. We're lost. On our own, we can't get to where we're trying to go. Only through the sacrifice of our Master do we survive and reach the goal. He dies so we can live. One God. One plan. One life.

> "Watch and pray so that you will not fall into temptation."
>
> [Mark 14:38 NIV]

Watch and Pray

Watch." Warnings don't come any more practical than that. Watch. Stay alert. Keep your eyes open. When you see sin coming, duck. When you anticipate an awkward encounter, turn around. When you sense temptation, go the other way.

What Jesus was saying to the disciples and also to us is, "Pay attention." You know your weaknesses. You also know the situations in which your weaknesses are most vulnerable. Stay out of those situations. Backseats. Late hours. Offensive websites. Whatever it is that gives Satan a foothold in your life, stay away from it. Watch out!

Jesus also says, "Pray." Prayer isn't telling God anything new. There is neither a sinner nor a saint who would surprise him. What prayer does is invite God to walk the shadowy pathways of life with us. Prayer is asking God to watch ahead for falling trees and tumbling boulders and to bring up the rear, guarding our backside from the poison darts of the devil.

ONE MORE THOUGHT

Navigating the dangerous waters of life is a little like swimming at the beach with no lifeguard on duty—it's up to you to watch for trouble and make sure an undertow doesn't suck you in. Through prayer, you can invite a holy lifeguard to join you and protect you. He's always on duty.

> Come and see what our God has done, what awesome
> miracles he performs for people!
>
> [Psalm 66:5 NLT]

Good from Evil

Joseph's father favored him, and Joseph's brothers hated him for it. So they went nuclear on him. "They stripped Joseph of his tunic. . . . They took him and cast him into a pit" (Genesis 37:23–24). Joseph didn't climb out of bed that morning and think, *I better dress in padded clothing because this is the day I get tossed in a hole.* The attack caught him off guard.

So did yours. Joseph's pit came in the form of a cistern. Yours came in the form of a diagnosis, a foster home, a traumatic injury. Your pit feels like a kind of death. You wonder if you'll ever recover.

Joseph's story got worse before it got better. Yet he never gave up. Bitterness never staked its claim. He not only survived, he also thrived. By the end of his life, Joseph was the second most powerful man of his generation. How did he flourish in the middle of tragedy? Years later, Joseph explained it to his brothers. "You planned evil against me but God used those same plans for my good" (Genesis 50:20 MSG).

Trust God to do the same for you.

ONE MORE THOUGHT

When someone or something sneaks up from behind to give you a sucker punch, it sends you reeling. But not God. No one sneaks up on him. He always sees what's coming your way and is already planning his counterpunch. Invite him into the ring beside you, and get ready for his knockout.

> "I was hungry, and you fed me. I was thirsty, and you gave me a drink."
>
> [Matthew 25:35 NLT]

Love Them, Love Him

There are many reasons to help people in need. But for the Christian, none is higher than this: when we love those in need, we are loving Jesus. It is a mystery beyond science, a truth beyond statistics. But it is a message that Jesus made crystal clear: when we love them, we love him.

Many years ago I heard a woman discuss this work. Her sixty-nine years had bent her already small frame. But there was nothing small about Mother Teresa's presence. "Give me your unborn children," she offered. "Don't abort them. If you cannot raise them, I will. They are precious to God."

Who would have guessed this slight Albanian woman would change thousands of lives through the Missionaries of Charity, the order she founded in 1949? Shy and introverted as a child. Of fragile health. One of three children. Daughter of a generous but unremarkable businessman. Yet somewhere along her journey, she became convinced that Jesus walked in the "distressing disguise of the poor," and she set out to love him by loving them.

ONE MORE THOUGHT

Do you know the parable of the sheep and goats? If not, find your Bible and read Matthew 25:31–46. The hungry, the thirsty, the unwelcome, the unclothed, the sick, the imprisoned—somehow these are Jesus himself. When we care for them, we love him.

> Perfect love expels all fear.
>
> [1 John 4:18 NLT]

Courage from Grace

Paul wrote, "Don't copy the behavior and customs of this world" (Romans 12:2 NLT). Easier to say than do, right? It takes courage to defend someone whom everyone else is picking on or to say at a party, "No, I don't do that." So where does our courage come from?

Grace. As Paul also wrote, to Titus, "God's readiness to give and forgive is now public. Salvation's available for everyone! . . . Tell them all this. Build up their *courage*" (Titus 2:11, 15 MSG). Do you know God's grace? Then you can love boldly, live robustly. You can swing from trapeze to trapeze; his safety net will break your fall. Nothing fosters courage like a clear grasp of grace.

The world wants you to wear what everyone else wears, say what everyone else says, believe what everyone else believes. Be brave enough to be different. Grace gives you the courage to stand up for God.

ONE MORE THOUGHT

When you start paying attention to it, you realize it's everywhere—pressure to fit in. People resist when you go against the culture. But isn't that what Jesus' life was all about? Remember God's grace, and you'll find the strength to go his way.

Happy is the person whose sins are forgiven, whose wrongs are pardoned.

[Psalm 32:1 NCV]

Owning Up

If we are already forgiven, then why does Jesus teach us to pray, "Forgive us our debts" (Matthew 6:12)?

The very reason your parents want you to do the same. If I tell one of my daughters to be home by a certain time and she disobeys by intentionally staying out late, I don't disown her. I don't kick her out of the house or tell her to change her last name. But I do expect her to be honest and apologize. And until she does, the tenderness of our relationship will suffer. The nature of the relationship won't change. I'll still be Dad, and she'll still be my daughter. But the intimacy between us will be blocked.

The same happens in our spiritual life. Confession does not create a relationship with God; it simply nourishes it. If you are a believer, owning up to your mistakes does not change your position before God, but it does increase your peace with God.

ONE MORE THOUGHT

Did you ever make a really bad mistake and refuse to say you were sorry? It probably gave you more indigestion than a triple-burger binge. Confession clears all that up. Better relationships on the outside. More peace on the inside.

People harvest only what they plant.

[Galatians 6:7 NCV]

The Greenhouse of the Heart

Think for a moment of your heart as a greenhouse. Green vines instead of valves and veins. Divided into sections of beans and tomatoes instead of atria and ventricles. What do a greenhouse and your heart have in common? Both have to be managed.

Consider for a moment your thoughts as seed. Some thoughts become flowers. Others become weeds. Sow seeds of hope and enjoy optimism. Sow seeds of doubt and expect insecurity.

The proof is everywhere you look. Ever wonder how some people resist negative ideas and remain patient, optimistic, and forgiving? Could it be that they daily sow seeds of goodness and are able to enjoy the harvest? Ever wonder why others have such a gloomy attitude? You would too if your heart were a greenhouse of weeds and thorns.

Jesus is the master gardener. He knows when to cut back a vine and when to uproot the whole thing and throw it away. Is it time to let him go to work in the greenhouse of your heart?

ONE MORE THOUGHT

Plants in a greenhouse don't do well without loving care. Ignore them and they die. The same is true of your cat, your goldfish, or any living thing—including your heart. So allow the master gardener inside. Sow seeds of goodness. And watch your garden grow.

> The soul of Jonathan was knit to the soul of David,
> and Jonathan loved him as his own soul.
>
> [1 Samuel 18:1]

Best Friends

Jonathan and David were best friends. "The soul of Jonathan was knit to the soul of David, and Jonathan loved him as his own soul" (1 Samuel 18:1). As if the two hearts were two fabrics, God "needle and threaded" them together. So interwoven that when one moved, the other felt it.

Do you have a friend like Jonathan? Someone who protects you, who seeks nothing but your interests, wants nothing but your happiness? An ally who lets you be you? A person you feel safe with? God gave David such a friend.

He gave you one as well. Has Jesus not made a promise to you? "I am with you always, even to the end of the age" (Matthew 28:20). Has he not clothed you? He offers you "white garments, that you may be clothed" (Revelation 3:18). Christ dresses you in clothing suitable for heaven.

Make a mental list of all the ways he shows you his kindness. Everything from sunsets to salvation—look at what you have. Allow Jesus to be knit to your soul. Let him be your best friend.

ONE MORE THOUGHT

A personal relationship with Jesus is a bit different from your other friendships. For one thing, you can't physically *see* him. Yet he's certainly there, speaking to you through his words in the Bible, encouraging you through the actions of others. So talk to him. Pray to him. Worship him. He can truly be your best friend.

God raised the Lord and will also raise us up by his power.

[1 Corinthians 6:14 ESV]

Fill Up on Faith

You're overworked. Under-energized. Burned out. What do you do when you run out of gas? The answer isn't to push the car yourself, yet that's just what you do. Stopping for gas is for wimps.

If you're putting in extra hours each day just to keep up, you need to fill yourself with some high-test fuel. Try some promises from Philippians—six promises from a premium-grade book:

"I am certain that God, who began the good work within you, will continue his work until it is finally finished" (1:6 NLT). "To me, to live is Christ, and to die is gain" (1:21). "Don't try to impress others. Be humble, thinking of others as better than yourselves" (2:3 NLT). "I gave up all that inferior stuff so I could know Christ personally, experience his resurrection power, be a partner in his suffering" (3:10 MSG). "I press on to reach the end of the race and receive the heavenly prize" (3:14 NLT). "I can do everything through Christ, who gives me strength" (4:13 NLT).

Fill your tank with verses like these, and stop trying to push yourself around. God is able to do what you can't.

ONE MORE THOUGHT

You know you're in trouble if you decide you're too busy to pray or read your Bible. We need this "faith fuel"—it's what keeps us going. Try to go without it and you'll soon find yourself stranded on the side of life's highway.

> The Spirit produces the fruit of love, joy, peace, patience.
>
> [Galatians 5:22 NCV]

The Fruit of Patience

Teachers seem to drone on forever. The weekend never arrives soon enough. The computer takes too darn long to boot up!

If patience is hard for you, you might ask this question: How filled are you with God's patience? You've heard about it from your parents. Studied it at a Sunday school class. Maybe underlined Bible verses about it. But have you received it? The proof is in your patience. Patience that is deeply received results in patience that is freely offered.

God does more than demand patience from us; he offers it to us. Patience is a fruit of his Spirit. It hangs from the tree of Galatians 5:22: "The Spirit produces the fruit of love, joy, peace, patience" (NCV). Have you asked God to give you some fruit? *Well, I did once, but* . . . But what? Did you, ahem, grow impatient? Ask him again and again and again. He won't grow impatient with your pleading, and you will receive patience in your praying.

ONE MORE THOUGHT

In our fast-paced world, patience is almost a lost art. Not to God, though. He includes it in the gifts offered to us by the Holy Spirit. Must be important, right? Come to think of it, my life goes a lot better when I practice patience. How about yours?

> The world and all its wanting, wanting, wanting is on the way
> out—but whoever does what God wants is set for eternity.
>
> [1 John 2:17 MSG]

A Perfect Place

In heaven you will be at your best forever. Even now you have your moments. Occasional glimpses of your heavenly self. When you change your baby sister's diaper, forgive your friend's temper, or wash your dad's car, you display traces of saintliness. It's the other moments that sour life. Tongue, sharp as a razor. Moods as menacing as Frankenstein's monster. Those parts wear you out.

But God bars imperfections at heaven's gate. His light silences the wolf man within. "Nothing that is impure will enter the city" (Revelation 21:27 GNT). Pause and let this promise drench you. Can you envision your sinless existence?

You will be you at your best forever! And you'll enjoy everyone else at their prime! Christ will have completed his redemptive work. All gossip and jealousy extracted. The last drop of grumpiness suctioned. You'll love the result. No one will doubt your word, question your motives, or speak evil behind your back.

Heaven is a perfect place of perfected people with our perfect Lord.

ONE MORE THOUGHT

On the days when nothing seems to go right—flat tires, forgotten homework, frustrating friends—it's nice to know that all this is temporary. A better, in fact perfect, place stands ready for us. I don't know about you

APRIL

For I know the thoughts that I think toward
you, says the Lord, thoughts of peace and not
of evil, to give you a future and a hope.

[Jeremiah 29:11]

You made my whole being; you formed me in my mother's body.

[Psalm 139:13 NCV]

Knit Together with Love

In my closet hangs a sweater that I seldom wear. It's too small. I should throw that sweater away. But love won't let me.

It's the creation of a devoted mother expressing her love. *My* mother. Each strand was chosen with care. Each thread was selected with affection. It is valuable not because of its function but because of its maker.

That must have been what the psalmist had in mind when he wrote, "You knit me together in my mother's womb" (Psalm 139:13 NIV). Think on those words. You were knitted together. You aren't an accident. You weren't mass-produced. You aren't an assembly-line product.

You're no April fool. You were deliberately planned, specifically gifted, and lovingly positioned on this earth by the Master Craftsman. When he gazes upon you, he doesn't see an ordinary lump of clay. He sees a beautiful work of art, uniquely molded and shaped according to his loving design.

ONE MORE THOUGHT

Think about something you worked really, really hard on. A piece of pottery. An essay. A song. After putting so much of yourself into it, doesn't it mean that much more to you? That's how God feels about you. He crafted you with great love and care.

Be sure that no one pays back wrong for wrong, but always try
to do what is good for each other and for all people.

[1 Thessalonians 5:15 NCV]

"I Will Call You Friends"

Friends. There's nothing quite like good times with best buddies. Your friends can be the glue that gets you through the day, sticking by you when the world seems against you. But when those relationships turn sour, everything seems wrong. It hurts when friends don't get along.

Jesus understands the challenge. He came to build relationships with people. He came to take away the hostile feelings, conflict, and isolation that existed between God and man. Once he overcame that, he said, "I have called you friends" (John 15:15).

In repairing a relationship, it's essential to realize that no friendship is perfect and no person is perfect. If you decide that you're going to make a relationship work, you can develop peace treaties of love and acceptance and harmony to change a difficult situation into something beautiful. Jesus was misunderstood and rejected, yet he patiently persisted at forming relationships with his followers. Can't you and I do the same?

ONE MORE THOUGHT

What is it that you like most about your best friends? Their loyalty? Willingness to listen? Upbeat attitude? Crazy sense of humor? Whatever it is, remember those qualities when you find yourselves fighting. A good friendship isn't something to throw away.

For your sake we face death all day long.

[Romans 8:36 NIV]

The Voice of Adventure

There is a rawness and a wonder to life. Pursue it. Hunt for it. Sell out to get it. Your goal is not to live long; it's to live.

Jesus says the options are clear. On one side there is the voice of safety. You can build a fire in the hearth, stay inside, and stay warm and dry. You can't fall if you don't take a stand, right? You can't lose your balance if you never climb, right? So don't try it. Take the safe route.

Or you can hear the voice of adventure—God's adventure. Instead of building a fire in your hearth, build a fire in your heart. Follow God's impulses. Talk to the girl no one talks to. Volunteer at the senior center. Try out for the play or team. Lead a Bible study. Run for school president. Make a difference. Sure, it isn't safe, but what is?

Jesus didn't play it safe. He died on a cross for you. Allow him to lead you into your own God-inspired destiny.

ONE MORE THOUGHT

Remember when you were little, exploring every shelf you could reach? We're all born with a God-given need to stretch and learn and discover. Sadly, many of us grow out of it. But we don't have to—and we shouldn't. Taking risks for God's sake brings him glory.

> The eyes of the Lord watch over those who do right,
> and his ears are open to their prayers.
>
> [1 Peter 3:12 NLT]

Let's Talk to Jesus

What do you do when you run out of gas? Maybe you haven't had this problem, but all of us run out of something. You need kindness, but the gauge is on empty. You need hope, but the needle is in the red. You want five gallons of solutions but can only muster a few drops.

My first thought when I run out of fuel is, *How can I get this car to a gas pump?* Your first thought when you have a problem should be, *How can I get this problem to Jesus?*

Let's get practical. You and a good friend are about to battle it out again. The thunderstorm looms on the horizon. Both of you need patience, but both tanks are empty. What if one of you calls, "Time-out"? What if one of you says, "Let's talk to Jesus before we talk to each other. In fact, let's talk to Jesus until we can talk to each other"?

Couldn't hurt. After all, he broke down the walls of Jericho. Perhaps he could do the same for yours.

ONE MORE THOUGHT

Doesn't it make sense? Jesus already knows what you're facing. He has a bit of experience dealing with people and their problems. He loves you and wants to help. Why not talk to him about every dilemma and crisis? He's listening right now.

He has filled them with skill.

[Exodus 35:35]

Packed for a Purpose

You were born prepacked. God looked at your entire life, determined your assignment, and gave you the tools to do the job.

Before going out, you do something similar. You consider the demands of the journey and pack accordingly. Cold weather? Bring a jacket. Class project? Carry the laptop. Time with your friend who's a running fanatic? Better take some sneakers and a bucketful of water.

God did the same with you. *Joe will research animals . . . install curiosity. Meagan will lead a private school . . . an extra dose of management. I need Eric to comfort the sick . . . include a healthy share of compassion. Denalyn will marry Max . . . instill a double portion of patience.*

God has a wonderful plan in mind for you. But he wouldn't send you on this expedition without the proper preparation. He packed you on purpose for a purpose.

ONE MORE THOUGHT

How has God packaged your life? Write down some of the "tools" he's given you. How might you use your talents and gifts to serve his purposes? Talk about it with a parent or friend; then pray about it with God.

He is in charge of it all, has the final word on everything.
At the center of all this, Christ rules the church.

[Ephesians 1:22 MSG]

Center of the Universe

Tapping the collective shoulder of humanity, God points to the Son—his Son—and says, "Behold the center of it all."

When God looks at the center of the universe, he doesn't look at you. When heaven's stagehands direct the spotlight toward the star of the show, I need no sunglasses. No light falls on me.

Lesser orbs, that's us. Appreciated. Valued. Loved dearly. But central? Essential? Pivotal? Nope. Sorry. The world does not revolve around us. Our comfort is not God's priority. If it is, something's gone wrong. If we are the marquee event, how do we explain flat-earth challenges like death, disease, slumping economies, or rumbling earthquakes? If God exists to please us, then shouldn't we always be pleased?

Could a cosmic shift be in order? Perhaps our place is not at the center of the universe. God does not exist to make a big deal out of us. We exist to make a big deal out of him. It's not about you. It's not about me. It's all about him.

ONE MORE THOUGHT

We have a bit of trouble with this, don't we? We want the spotlight. We want the full attention of our family and friends—and God's too, come to think of it. But who created whom? Might be a good idea, right now, to get on your knees and worship the One at the center of the universe.

Remember Jesus Christ, who was raised from the
dead. . . . This is the Good News I preach.

[2 Timothy 2:8 NCV]

Remember Jesus

Paul was in prison in Rome and knew his execution was near. In a letter written within earshot of the sharpening of the blade that would sever his head, Paul urged Timothy to remember. You can almost picture the old warrior smiling as he wrote the words. "Remember Jesus Christ, who was raised from the dead. . . . This is the Good News I preach" (2 Timothy 2:8 NCV).

When times get hard, remember Jesus. When people don't listen, remember Jesus. When tears come, remember Jesus. When disappointment is your partner, remember Jesus.

Remember the sick who were healed with his callused hands. Remember the dead called from the grave with a Galilean accent. Remember the eyes of God that wept human tears. Remember Jesus, the reason a prisoner could talk about Good News just before his execution—and the reason we can talk about Good News no matter what crisis we face.

ONE MORE THOUGHT

When bad news or bad times hit, our minds typically turn to mush. Memories go missing along with everything else. If you can remember one thing during your worst moment, let it be this: the Good News that Jesus Christ went to the cross for you.

Brag About That!

Demanding respect is like chasing a butterfly. Chase it, and you'll never catch it. Sit still, and it may land on your shoulder. Those who talk about their need for respect sound like people with a head bigger than their hat size. Their efforts to boost their standing come off as empty bragging.

The French philosopher Blaise Pascal asked, "Do you wish people to speak well of you? Then never speak well of yourself." Maybe that's why the Bible says, "Don't praise yourself. Let someone else do it."

Do you feel a need for affirmation? Does your self-esteem need attention? You don't need to drop names or show off. You need only pause at the base of the cross and be reminded of this: the maker of the stars would rather die for you than live without you. And that is a fact. So if you need to brag, brag about that.

ONE MORE THOUGHT

Have you been around people who always talk about themselves? Who are always trying to make themselves look good to others? Don't be one of those. You have a Lord who loves you for eternity. Boast about him, and

May the Lord lead your hearts into God's love and Christ's patience.

[2 Thessalonians 3:5 NCV]

Take Heart!

The majority is not always right. If the majority had ruled, the children of Israel never would have left Egypt. They would have voted to stay in bondage. If the majority had ruled, David never would have fought Goliath. His brothers would have voted for him to stay with the sheep. What's the point? Instead of listening to the majority, you must listen to your own heart and do what you know is right.

God says you're on your way to becoming a disciple when you can do right and keep a pure heart. "Who may stand in his holy place? The one who has clean hands and a pure heart" (Psalm 24:3–4 NIV).

Do you ever wonder if everything will turn out right as long as you do everything right? Do you ever try to do something right and yet nothing seems to turn out like you planned? Take heart. When people do what is right—no matter what the majority says—God remembers.

ONE MORE THOUGHT

We do it all the time—we raise our hands or cast our votes to make a decision or express an opinion. Sometimes, though, our hearts don't agree with the majority's choice. Is that a big deal? Only when the majority goes against God's standards. He is the majority of One.

> "I will talk to the Father, and he'll provide you another Friend
> so that you will always have someone with you."
>
> [John 14:16 MSG]

Our Holy Helper

The way we panic at the sight of change, you'd think bombs were falling.

"Run for your lives! Graduation is coming!"

"Load the women and children into the bus, and head north. Our favorite burger place is going out of business!"

Change trampolines our lives, and when it does, God sends someone special to stabilize us. On the eve of his death, Jesus gave his followers this promise: "When the Father sends the Advocate as my representative—that is, the Holy Spirit—he will teach you everything and will remind you of everything I have told you. I am leaving you with a gift—peace of mind and heart. And the peace I give is a gift the world cannot give" (John 14:26–27 NLT).

As a departing teacher might introduce the classroom to her replacement, so Jesus introduces us to the Holy Spirit. And what a ringing endorsement he gives. Jesus calls the Holy Spirit his "representative." The Spirit comes in the name of Christ, with equal authority and identical power.

We don't face change alone. The Spirit is our holy helper.

ONE MORE THOUGHT

So what exactly is the Holy Spirit? He is, well . . . spirit. Think of him as you think of Jesus—someone who loves you, guides you, gives his all for you. Someone holy, of God and with God. He is a teacher and friend who brings peace of mind—that's some gift!

Work as if you were serving the Lord, not as if you
were serving only men and women.

[Ephesians 6:7 NCV]

Working to Please God

What if everyone worked with God in mind? Suppose no one worked to satisfy self or to make the most money but everyone worked to please God.

Many occupations would instantly cease: drug trafficking, thievery, prostitution, nightclub and casino management. Certain careers, by their nature, cannot please God. These would end. Certain behaviors would end too. If I'm repairing a car for God, I'm not going to overcharge his children. If I'm painting a wall for God, you think I'm going to use paint thinner to cheapen the job? Nope.

Imagine if everyone worked as if God were watching. Every teacher, hopeful. Every boss, thoughtful. Every officer, careful. Every coach, insightful. Every salesperson, delightful. Every lawyer, skillful. Imagine if you went through your day with the same approach. Perhaps you'd work a little harder, speak a little kinder.

Impossible? Not entirely. All we need is someone to start a worldwide revolution. Might as well be us.

ONE MORE THOUGHT

God *is* watching what we say and do, not as a stern judge but as a loving Father. After all he's done for us, would it hurt to try to please him? To bring a smile to his face? Give it a try. You'll find it the most satisfying service of all.

When you talk, do not say harmful things, but say what people need—words that will help others become stronger.

[Ephesians 4:29 NCV]

Encouraging Words

In many houses discouragement is the language everyone speaks. The home is a war zone, and the warriors have nicknames like Stupid, Idiot, Dummy, and Little Pain in the Neck. Bullets and shrapnel litter their lives.

In other homes, families follow the spirit of the Western tune "Home on the Range." There, a discouraging word is seldom heard. People hide their hurts with smiles on their faces. Maybe the reason discouragement is seldom heard is because words are seldom heard. Silence is deadly.

Other homes flourish with encouragement. Everyone believes in one another, supports one another, builds up, refreshes. Pats on the back. Notes in the lunch boxes. Love letters under the pillows. Hearts expressed. Prayers.

Which home would you rather live in?

You can be the first person to allow the sweet-smelling flowers of love to bloom in your house. It starts with returning a cranky comment with a few encouraging words.

ONE MORE THOUGHT

Words are powerful. If you've been on the other end of stinging criticism, you know what I mean. Will one positive remark transform your family? Probably not. But keep it up. No one can resist the power of encouragement

He is despised and rejected by men, a Man of sorrows and acquainted with grief.

[Isaiah 53:3]

Never More Human

The scene is very simple; you'll recognize it quickly. A grove of twisted olive trees. Ground cluttered with large rocks. A low stone fence. A dark, dark night.

See that solitary figure? Flat on the ground. Face stained with dirt and tears. Fists pounding the hard earth. Eyes wide with a stupor of fear. Hair matted with salty sweat. Is that blood on his forehead?

That's Jesus. Jesus in the Garden of Gethsemane (Luke 22:44).

We see an agonizing, straining, and struggling Jesus. We see a "man of sorrows." We see a man struggling with fear, wrestling with commitments, and yearning for relief.

Seeing God like this does wonders for our own suffering. God was never more human than at this hour. God was never nearer to us than when he hurt. Like us, he was looked down on and rejected. He understands the agonies we go through because he's been through them himself.

ONE MORE THOUGHT

We often tell friends we understand what they're going through, but do we really? Unless your own dad has lost his job, can you know how a family feels when their income is suddenly cut off? Yet Jesus does understand. He's felt every sorrow you have, and he's walking with you in yours right now.

I've got my eye on the goal, where God is beckoning us onward—
to Jesus. I'm off and running, and I'm not turning back.

[Philippians 3:13–14 MSG]

Stay in the Race

In 1952, Florence Chadwick attempted to swim the chilly ocean waters between Catalina Island and the California shore. She swam through foggy weather and choppy seas for fifteen hours. Her muscles began to cramp, and her resolve weakened. She begged to be taken out of the water, so aides lifted her into a boat. They paddled a few more minutes, the mist broke, and Florence discovered that the shore was less than a half mile away. "All I could see was the fog," she later explained. "I think if I could have seen the shore, I would have made it."[5]

Take a long look at the shore that awaits you. Don't be fooled by the fog. The finish may be only strokes away. God may be, at this moment, lifting his hand to conduct a victory song. Angels may be assembling, saints gathering, demons trembling. Stay at it! Stay in the water. Stay in the race. Stay in the fight. Forgive, one more time. Be generous, one more time. Study for one more test, encourage one more friend, swim one more stroke.

ONE MORE THOUGHT

We all have times when we're misled by "mist" that hides good news just beyond our vision. The next time you're fogged in, get out your Bible, and list some of God's promises to you. A better, God-filled future may already be on your horizon.

Christ's love is greater than anyone can ever know, but
I pray that you will be able to know that love.

[Ephesians 3:19 NCV]

It Wasn't Fair; It Was Love

It makes you mad when life isn't fair. When someone cuts in line. When the coach favors one player over another. When the cheater gets an A and you don't.

Come to think of it, it wasn't fair when spikes pierced the hands that formed the earth. And it wasn't fair that the Son of God was forced to hear the silence of God. It wasn't fair, but it happened.

While Jesus was on the cross, God sat on his hands. He turned his back. He ignored the screams of the innocent. He sat in silence while the sins of the world were placed upon his Son. And he did nothing while a cry echoed in the black sky: "My God, my God, why have you forsaken me?"

Was it right? No. Was it fair? No. Was it love? Yes. Life may be unfair, but God's love for us overwhelms the most unfair thing we can think of. Jesus knows unfair. He conquers it with love.

ONE MORE THOUGHT

Think about the times you've been treated unfairly. Kind of makes you furious, right? Makes you want to teach someone a lesson, yes? But think about how Jesus responded to the most unfair event in history. Was he furious? Did he respond with revenge? No. His response was love.

For God presented Jesus as the sacrifice for sin.

[Romans 3:25 NLT]

"Christ Died for Me"

Barabbas had been thrown into jail for rebellion and murder, but the Roman governor declared he would let one prisoner go free. When the crowd clamored for Jesus to be executed, Barabbas became the pardoned prisoner. We're not told how Barabbas responded to the gift of freedom. Maybe he scorned it out of pride or refused it out of shame. We don't know. But you can determine what to do with yours. Personalize it.

As long as the cross is God's gift to the world, it will touch you but not change you. Satisfying as it is to shout, "Christ died for the world!" even sweeter it is to whisper, "Christ died for *me*." "He took *my* place on the cross." "He carried *my* sins, *my* cold and cruel heart." "Through the cross he claimed, cleansed, and called *me*." "He felt *my* shame and spoke *my* name."

Thank God for the day grace happened to you. Thank Jesus for giving his life for yours—the best trade you'll ever make.

ONE MORE THOUGHT

You make trades all the time. With your friends, one pair of earrings for another. With the store clerk, your fifty dollars for his video game. Few of these trades will change you. None will mean more than the one Jesus offers—his life on earth for your life in heaven. It's the one deal you don't want to miss.

John said, "Look, the Lamb of God, who takes away the sin of the world!"

[John 1:29 NCV]

No Accident

Jesus was born crucified. Whenever he became aware of who he was, he also became aware of what he had to do. The cross-shaped shadow could always be seen. And the screams of people imprisoned by sin could always be heard.

This explains the determination on his face as he turned to go to Jerusalem for the last time. He was on his death march (Luke 9:51). This explains the firmness in the words, "The Father loves me, because I give up my life, so that I may receive it back again. No one takes my life from me. I give it up willingly!" (John 10:17–18 CEV).

So call it what you wish: An act of grace. A martyr's sacrifice. But whatever you call it, don't call it an accident. Things did not just "happen" to Jesus. By following God's will, he changed our history. It was God's plan from the beginning.

ONE MORE THOUGHT

Our lives can feel awfully random at times. Stuff, as they say, happens. But there's nothing random about the death of Jesus on the cross and what it means for our future with him. No one can change the plans of God.

When he saw the crowds, he felt sorry for them because they
were hurting and helpless, like sheep without a shepherd.

[Matthew 9:36 NCV]

He Understands

I can't understand it. I honestly cannot. Why did Jesus die on the cross? Oh, I know, I know. I have heard the official answers. "To satisfy the old law." "To fulfill prophecy." And these answers are right. They are. But there is something more here. Something very compassionate. Something yearning. Something personal.

What is it?

Could it be that his heart was broken for all the people who cast despairing eyes toward the dark heavens and cry the same "Why?" Could it be that his heart was broken for the hurting?

I imagine him bending close to those who hurt. I imagine him listening. I picture his eyes misting and a pierced hand brushing away a tear. He who also was once alone understands.

ONE MORE THOUGHT

The next time you're hurting or reeling from a broken heart—maybe you're there right now—talk to Jesus about it. Allow him to wipe your tears. If anyone knows about rejection, betrayal, pain, and a heart that needs healing, it's him.

> "Seek God's kingdom, and all your other needs will be met as well."
>
> [Luke 12:31 NCV]

What We Need

Sometimes God is so touched by what he sees that he gives us what we need and not simply what we ask for. It's a good thing. For who would have ever thought to ask God for what he gives? Which of us would have dared to say, "God, would you please hang yourself on a tool of torture as a substitution for every mistake I have ever committed?" And then have the nerve to add, "And after you forgive me, could you prepare me an awesome place in heaven to live forever?"

And if that wasn't enough: "And would you please live within me and protect me and guide me and bless me with more than I could ever deserve?" Honestly, would we have the gall to ask for that?

Jesus already knows what we need. He knows the cost of grace. He already knows the price of forgiveness. It's everything. But he offers it anyway.

ONE MORE THOUGHT

God is like this. We ask for the pain to go away after a breakup, and he gives us a lifelong friend to share every struggle. We ask for one good day, and he offers us eternal life with him. More than we ask for. All that we need

"He is risen from the dead. . . . Come, see where his body was lying."

[Matthew 28:6 NLT]

The Empty Tomb

Following Christ demands faith, but not blind faith. Take a look at the vacated tomb. Did you know the opponents of Christ never challenged that it was empty? No Pharisee or Roman soldier ever led a group back to the burial site and declared, "The angel was wrong. The body is here. It was all a rumor."

They would have if they could have. Within weeks, disciples occupied every Jerusalem street corner, announcing a risen Christ. What quicker way for the enemies of the church to shut them up than to produce a cold and lifeless body? But they had no cadaver to display.

No wonder there was a Jerusalem revival. When the apostles argued for the empty tomb, the people looked to the Pharisees to deny it. They never did. As A. M. Fairbairn put it long ago, "The silence of the Jews is as eloquent as the speech of the Christians!"

ONE MORE THOUGHT

Doesn't it all come down to this? Jesus said he would rise again on the third day. He was publicly crucified on a cross, his body sealed in a tomb. And on the third day, he got up to meet again with his friends. Does your faith need more than this?

God put the wrong on him who never did anything
wrong, so we could be put right with God.

[2 Corinthians 5:21 MSG]

God's Sacrifice

When was the last time you sacrificed? Maybe you gave up a movie night to fill in as babysitter for a friend? Or gave your lunch to someone who forgot his? Most of our sacrifices don't cost us much. God, on the other hand, gave up what he loved most.

When God gave us his Son, his Son gave up heaven. Try to imagine that sacrifice. What if you left your home to become homeless or left the human race to become a mosquito? Would that be comparable to God's becoming human?

Then there is Christ on the cross. Although he was without sin, he paid the price for our sin by taking it on himself. We've always been sinners, so can any of us understand this sacrifice?

I've never given my child to evil people. I might give part of myself to help evil people. But sacrifice one of my daughters? No way. Even if I knew I would see her again, I wouldn't do it. But God did. Seems to me that God gave more than we could ever ask.

ONE MORE THOUGHT

Think about this for a minute. Could you give up those you love most? Just being apart from them would hurt. Then add in their terrible suffering and pain. That's sacrifice. That's God's enormous, unending love for us.

Everyone who is a child of God conquers the world.

[1 John 5:4 NCV]

Do What's Right

You get impatient with your own life, trying to conquer algebra or control your gossiping—and in your frustration begin to wonder where the power of God is. Be patient. God is using today's difficulties to strengthen you for tomorrow. He is *preparing* you. The God who makes all things grow will help you grow too.

Think about the fact that God lives within you. Think about the power that gives you life. Knowing that God is in you may change the places you want to go and the things you want to do today.

Do what is right this week, whatever it is, whatever comes down the path, whatever problems and dilemmas you face—just do what's right. Maybe no one else is doing what's right, but you do what's right. You be honest. You take a stand. You be true. After all, regardless of what you do, God does what is right: he saves you with his grace.

ONE MORE THOUGHT

Patience. Power. Character. It's an incredible combination. Mix them with a heavy dose of faith in a grace-giving God, and you'll be a conqueror, well on your way to fulfilling his plan for you. Just remember that it might not all happen today.

> "Peace be with you."
>
> [John 20:19 NCV]

Jesus Offers Peace

The church of Jesus Christ began with a group of frightened men in a second-floor room in Jerusalem.

They'd marched with Jesus for three years. But now that he was crucified, they gathered quietly, afraid of being found out as followers of Christ. They were timid soldiers, reluctant warriors, speechless messengers. Daring to dream that the master had left them some word, some plan, some direction, they came back. But little did they know their wildest dream wasn't wild enough. Just as someone mumbles, "It's no use," they hear a noise. They hear a voice: "Peace be with you."

The one betrayed sought his betrayers. What did he say to them? Not "What a bunch of flops!" Not "I told you so." No "Where-were-you-when-I-needed-you?" speeches. But simply one phrase, "Peace be with you." The very thing they didn't have was the very thing he offered: peace.

He offers the same to us.

ONE MORE THOUGHT

When are you most afraid? When the teacher hands out the test? When the popular people walk your way? When you think about the future? Even in your most fearful moments, Jesus is with you, offering a peace you can't

The person who shows mercy can stand without fear at the judgment.

[James 2:13 NCV]

Just Be There

Nothing takes the place of your presence. E-mails are nice. Phone calls are special. But being there in the flesh sends a message.

After Albert Einstein's wife died, his sister, Maja, moved in. For fourteen years she cared for him, allowing his valuable research to continue. In 1950 she suffered a stroke and lapsed into a coma. Thereafter, Einstein spent two hours every afternoon reading aloud to her. She gave no sign of understanding his words, but he read anyway. If she understood anything by his gesture, she understood this—he believed that she was worth his time.

Do you believe in your family? Then show up. Show up at your brother's games and sister's plays. Do you believe in your friends? Then show up. Show up at their concerts when they play a solo and at their bedside when they've had a wreck. You want to bring out the best in someone? Then show up.

After all, that's what Jesus did. When we needed him most, he was there, in the flesh.

ONE MORE THOUGHT

Do you notice when people come to your special occasions? Of course you do. Will they notice when you do the same? You can count on it. So be someone they can count on. Show up, just as God shows up every moment for us.

> [God] has not punished us as our sins should be punished.
>
> [Psalm 103:10 NCV]

Soaked in Mercy

Do you really think you haven't done things that hurt Christ? Have you ever been dishonest with his money? That's cheating. Ever gone to church to be seen rather than to see him? Hypocrite. Ever broken a promise you've made to God? Ever misused his name?

Don't you deserve to be punished? And yet, here you are. Reading this book. Breathing. Still witnessing sunsets and hearing babies gurgle. Still watching the seasons change. There are no lashes on your back or hooks in your nose or shackles on your feet. Apparently God hasn't kept a list of your wrongs.

Listen. You have not been sprinkled with forgiveness. You have not been spattered with grace. You have not been dusted with kindness. You have been *soaked* in it. "The LORD is compassionate and merciful, slow to get angry and filled with unfailing love" (Psalm 103:8 NLT).

You are submerged in mercy. You are a minnow in the ocean of his mercy. Let it change you!

ONE MORE THOUGHT

We sometimes complain that life isn't fair, that we didn't get what we deserved. That's messed up. If someone tallied up all our mistakes, all our wrongs, all our offenses against God, we wouldn't want what we deserve. Let's be grateful that God gives us mercy instead.

Promise me, O women of Jerusalem, by the gazelles and wild deer, not to awaken love until the time is right.

[Song of Solomon 3:5 NLT]

God Is Enough

May I offer a bit of free advice? When it comes to romance and love: *be careful.*

Before you get into an exclusive dating relationship, take a good long look around. Make sure this is God's intended place for you. And, if you suspect it isn't, get out. Don't force what is wrong to be right. Be careful.

And, until love is stirred, let God's love be enough for you. There are seasons when God allows us to feel the frailty of human love so we'll appreciate the strength of his love. Didn't he do this with David? Saul turned on him. Michal, his wife, betrayed him. Jonathan and Samuel were David's friends, but they couldn't follow him into the wilderness. Betrayal and circumstances left David alone. Alone with God. And, as David discovered, God was enough. That's why David wrote these words in a desert: "Your unfailing love is better than life itself. . . . You satisfy me more than the richest feast" (Psalm 63:3, 5 NLT).

ONE MORE THOUGHT

We all want to be loved. And when that cute guy or gal you've admired for so long actually asks you out, who wouldn't be interested? Just be careful. Infatuation isn't the same as real love. Let God's genuine love be your standard for every relationship.

With my mouth will I make known Your faithfulness to all generations.

[Psalm 89:1]

Why Worship?

During our summer vacation I signed up for a sailing lesson. Ever puzzled by the difference in leeward, starboard, and stern, I asked the crew a few questions. After a while the captain offered, "Would you like to sail us home?" He assured me I would have no trouble. "Target that cliff," he instructed. "Set your eyes and the boat on it."

I found the instruction hard to follow. Other sights invited my attention: the rich mahogany of the deck, the rich foam cresting on the waves. I wanted to look at it all. But if I looked too long, I risked losing the course. The boat stayed on target as long as I set my eyes ahead where they needed to be.

Worship helps us do this in life. It lifts our eyes off the boat with its toys and passengers and sets them "on the realities of heaven, where Christ sits in the place of honor at God's right hand" (Colossians 3:1 NLT). If you want to sail home, focus on the target of heaven.

ONE MORE THOUGHT

Have you ever tried worshiping not just on Sundays, but every day? For the next week, see what happens if you set aside a short time each morning to praise God. Thank him for all that he is and all he does in your life. I predict you'll do a much better job of keeping your life on course.

> "Good people have good things in their hearts."
> [Matthew 12:35 NCV]

People Who Change Lives

Name the ten wealthiest men in the world. Name eight people who have won the Nobel or Pulitzer prize.

How did you do? I didn't do well either. With the exception of you trivia hounds, none of us remember the headliners of yesterday too well. Surprising how quickly we forget, isn't it? And what I've mentioned above are no second-rate achievements. These are the best in their fields. But the applause dies. Awards tarnish. Achievements are forgotten.

Here's another quiz. See how you do on this one. Name ten people who have taught you something worthwhile. Name five friends who have helped you in a difficult time.

Easier? It was for me too. The lesson? The people who change lives are not the ones with the credentials, but the ones with the concern. "My children, we should love people not only with words and talk, but by our actions and true caring" (1 John 3:18 NCV).

ONE MORE THOUGHT

How do you want to be remembered for your time on this planet? You can pile up all the awards and achievements you want, but if you want to leave a lasting legacy, show one person at a time that you care by your words

Though He was crucified in weakness, yet He lives by the power of God.

[2 Corinthians 13:4]

The Intersection of Love

The cross. Can you turn any direction without seeing one? Perched atop a chapel. Carved into a graveyard headstone. Engraved in a ring or suspended on a chain. The cross is the universal symbol of Christianity. "Carrying his own cross, Jesus went out to a place called The Place of the Skull, which in the Hebrew language is called Golgotha" (John 19:17 NCV).

An odd choice, don't you think? Strange that a tool of torture would come to represent a movement of hope.

Why is the cross the symbol of our faith? To find the answer look no further than the cross itself. Its design couldn't be simpler. One beam horizontal—the other vertical. One reaches out—like God's love. The other reaches up—as does God's holiness. One represents the width of his love; the other reflects the height of his holiness. The cross is the intersection. The cross is where God forgave his children without lowering his standards.

ONE MORE THOUGHT

What could be wider than God's wonderful love? What could be higher than his holiness? When you look at the cross, remember the horror of Jesus' crucifixion. But also remember why he endured it, and how his end was only the beginning.

These little troubles are getting us ready for an eternal glory
that will make all our troubles seem like nothing.

[2 Corinthians 4:17 CEV]

Getting Ready

Who can find a place in life's puzzle for a child devastated by cancer or a city devastated by an earthquake? When your dad loses his job or your friend's family loses their home . . . do such moments serve a purpose?

They do if we see them from an eternal perspective. I have proof: you in the womb. In that prebirth season, your bones solidified, your eyes developed, the umbilical cord transported nutrients into your growing frame . . . for what reason? Womb time equipped you for earth time.

Some of your new features went unused before birth. You grew a nose but didn't breathe. Eyes developed, but could you see? Your tongue, toenails, and crop of hair served no function then. But aren't you glad you have them now?

Certain chapters in this life seem so unnecessary, like nostrils on the preborn. Suffering. Loneliness. Disease. Heartbreak. But what if this earth is the womb? Might these challenges serve to prepare us for the world to come? As Paul wrote, "These little troubles are *getting us ready* for an eternal glory" (2 Corinthians 4:17 CEV).

ONE MORE THOUGHT

You won't have to look far to find people with troubles. You may be one of them. Be encouraged knowing this: God isn't wasting your tough times. They will serve a purpose—if not in this life, then certainly in the next.

MAY

_____

Your word is a lamp to my feet and a light to my way.

[Psalm 119:105]

Forgive as the Lord forgave you.

[Colossians 3:13 NIV]

If Hurts Were Hairs

If hurts were hairs, we'd all look like grizzlies. After all, aren't there so many? When friends mock the way you dress, their insults hurt. When teachers ignore your work, their neglect hurts. When your mom embarrasses you, when your girlfriend snubs you, when your boyfriend drops you, it hurts. So how will you respond?

Build a prison of hate if you want, each brick a hurt. Design it with one cell and a single bunk. (You won't attract roommates.) Hang large video screens on each of the four walls so recorded images of the offense can play over and over. Appealing? No, appalling. It will leave you bitter, bent, and angry.

Instead, give the grace you've been given. You don't approve of the deeds of your offender when you do. Jesus didn't approve your sins by forgiving you. Grace is not blind. It sees the hurt full well. But grace chooses to see God's forgiveness even more. Where grace is lacking, bitterness abounds. Where grace abounds, forgiveness grows.

ONE MORE THOUGHT

In this life, pain is as sure as the summer sun. You can't avoid it, but you can control what you do about it. So don't let hurt poison your heart. Ask God to help you forgive. It's not about forgetting the bad stuff. It's about remembering the good stuff.

The just shall live by faith.
[Romans 1:17]

The Wrong Plane

At the moment I don't feel too smart. I just got off the wrong plane that took me to the wrong city and left me at the wrong airport. I went east instead of west and ended up in Houston instead of Denver.

It didn't look like the wrong plane, but it was. I walked through the wrong gate, dozed off on the wrong flight, and ended up in the wrong place. Do you know the feeling?

Paul says we've all done the same thing. Not with airplanes and airports, but with our lives and God. He tells the Roman readers, "There is none righteous, no, not one" (Romans 3:10). "All have sinned and fall short of the glory of God" (v. 23).

We are all on the wrong plane, he says. All of us. Gentile and Jew. Rich and poor. Tall and short. Every person has taken the wrong turn. And we need help. The wrong solutions are pleasure and pride; the correct solution is Christ Jesus (Romans 3:21–26).

ONE MORE THOUGHT

Have you ever taken a wrong turn and ended up in the wrong place? A room, a class, a party? Some of our decisions and attitudes can be wrong turns too. That's why we need to rely on Jesus as our pilot. When he's at the controls, we're guaranteed to arrive at the right place.

> "I am the LORD your God, who holds your right hand, and
> I tell you, 'Don't be afraid. I will help you.'"
>
> [Isaiah 41:13 NCV]

No Fears at All

Could you use some courage? Are you backing down more than you're standing up? You sound like one of the disciples of Jesus.

We need to remember that Peter, John, Matthew, and the rest were common men given an incredible task. Before they were the stained-glassed saints in the windows of cathedrals, they were somebody's next-door neighbors trying to make a living and raise a family. They weren't standout students from seminaries or super-heroes of faith. They struggled to follow Jesus, sometimes literally walking on water, sometimes falling in. But they were an ounce more devoted than they were afraid and, as a result, did some extraordinary things. Things that changed the world: "You gave them to me and they have obeyed your word" (John 17:6 NIV).

What in this world are you afraid of? Failure? Someone making fun of you? Answer the big question of eternity and you'll realize that earthly fears are no fears at all.

ONE MORE THOUGHT

You aren't the first to wonder if you can do it—or the first to wonder about this Jesus fellow. The disciples know how you feel. They literally walked with God and still had trouble! But they overcame their fear and followed him into history and heaven. You can do the same.

You should know that your body is a temple for the Holy Spirit who is in you. You have received the Holy Spirit from God. So you do not belong to yourselves.

[1 Corinthians 6:19 NCV]

Your Body Belongs to God

You will live forever in this body. It will be different, mind you. What is now crooked will be straightened. What is now faulty will be fixed. Your body will be different, but you won't have a different body. You will have this one. Does that change the view you have of it? I hope so.

God has a high regard for your body. You should as well. Forget all those ads saying you need to be this size or wear this makeup. Just respect the body that God gave you. I did not say worship it. I did not say show it off to get the attention of others. But I did say respect it. It is after all the temple of God. Be careful how you feed it, use it, and maintain it. You wouldn't want anyone trashing your home; God doesn't want anyone trashing his. After all, it is his, isn't it?

ONE MORE THOUGHT

When you accept the idea that your body belongs to God, it changes things. You're less likely to stuff it with greasy fries. You're more likely to exercise. You're more aware of showing too much skin. You're better at avoiding crazy risks. God sees your body as highly valuable—along with the person

All things are worth nothing compared with the
greatness of knowing Christ Jesus my Lord.

[Philippians 3:8 NCV]

He Did It for You

Want to know the coolest thing about Christ's coming?

Not that the One who hung the galaxies gave it up to be a carpenter, hanging doorjambs for a cranky client who wanted everything yesterday but couldn't pay for anything until tomorrow. Not that he refused to defend himself when blamed for every sin of every jerk and Jezebel since Adam. Not even that after three days in a dark hole he stepped into the Easter sunrise with a smile and a swagger and a question for lowly Lucifer—"Is that your best punch?"

That was cool, incredibly cool.

But want to know the coolest thing about the One who gave up the crown of heaven for a crown of thorns? Here's a hint: he loves you as his own. "See what great love the Father has lavished on us, that we should be called children of God!" (1 John 3:1 NIV).

The coolest thing? He did it for you. Just for you.

ONE MORE THOUGHT

We tend to think that Christ died for "humanity," for the millions who have put their trust in him, for the unknowable masses. That statement is true—but it misses the personal. Jesus knows and loves your individual heart. He didn't give his life just for a crowd. He gave it specifically for you.

The Lord sees the good people and listens to their prayers.

[1 Peter 3:12 NCV]

Prayer: Privilege and Power

You and I live in a loud world. To get someone's attention is no easy task. He must be willing to set everything aside to listen: turn down the music, turn away from the monitor, turn the corner of the page and set down the book. When someone is willing to silence everything else so he can hear us clearly, it is a privilege. A rare privilege, indeed.

Yet your prayers are honored in heaven in just this way. God drops whatever he's doing to hear your thoughts. He pushes aside all obstacles to hear your message. Your words are like a high-priority text to heaven. They go directly to the very throne of God.

Your words do more than get God's attention. Your prayer on earth activates God's power in heaven, and "God's will is done on earth as it is in heaven." Your prayers move God to change the world. You may not understand the mystery of prayer. You don't need to. But this much is clear: Actions in heaven begin when someone prays on earth.

ONE MORE THOUGHT

Prayer truly is a mystery. Although God can do anything, he desires to hear our dreams and desires, and he allows us to influence his hand on history. When offered a privilege like that, don't you think prayer is a good idea?

We have stopped evaluating others from a human point of view.

[2 Corinthians 5:16 NLT]

Label Them or Love Them?

Categorizing others creates distance. It gives us a convenient excuse for avoiding them.

Jesus took an entirely different approach. He was all about including people, not excluding them. "The Word became flesh and blood, and moved into the neighborhood" (John 1:14 MSG). Jesus touched lepers and loved foreigners and spent so much time with partygoers that people called him a "lush, a friend of the riff-raff" (Matthew 11:19 MSG). Racism couldn't keep him from the Samaritan woman; demons couldn't keep him from the demon-possessed. His Facebook friends would have included financial schemers and women of questionable reputations.

God calls us to be like Jesus, to change the way we look at people. Not to see them as jocks or geeks, preps or techs, insiders or outsiders. Not to label.

Let's view people as we do ourselves. Blemished, perhaps. Unfinished, for certain. In our lifetimes you and I are going to come across people tossed out of the "in" crowd. And we get to choose. Neglect or rescue? Label them or love them? We know Jesus' choice. Just look at what he did with us.

ONE MORE THOUGHT

Have you ever been labeled? I'm guessing it didn't feel too great. When people put you in a box, they stop seeing the real person inside. Do you know someone who's in a box right now? What can you do today to tear off the label?

When your faith is tested, your endurance has a chance to grow.

[James 1:3 NLT]

Testing

A couple of days ago, Denalyn and I had a disagreement. We had agreed to sell our house, but we couldn't agree on a realtor. Back and forth we went. A pleasant day turned sour. The time came for me to preach at morning worship services. I gave Denalyn a quick goodbye. "We'll deal with this later," I said.

But God wanted to deal with me immediately. The drive to church is only five minutes, but that's all it took for God to prick my conscience. It was a test. Would I pout or apologize? Would I ignore the tension or take care of it? Before the service began, I called Denalyn, apologized for my stubbornness, and asked for her forgiveness. Later that night, we reached a decision on a realtor, had a prayer, and put the matter to rest.

If you see your troubles as nothing more than hassles and hurts, you'll be bitter and mad. Yet if you see your troubles as tests, used by God for his glory and your growth, you'll pass with flying colors.

ONE MORE THOUGHT

Every day God tests us through people, pain, or problems. Can you identify your tests of today? Friends who act like jerks? Teachers who pile on homework? Acne and an aching head? An overloaded schedule? Whatever they are, remember that God has a purpose for your problems.

He gave up his place with God and made himself nothing.

[Philippians 2:7 NCV]

Give Up Your Life

G od will give you an uncommon life if you surrender your common one. "If you try to hang on to your life, you will lose it. But if you give up your life for my sake, you will save it" (Matthew 16:25 NLT).

Jesus did. He "made himself nothing by taking the very nature of a servant, being made in human likeness. . . . He humbled himself by becoming obedient to death" (Philippians 2:7–8 NIV).

No one in Nazareth saluted him as the Son of God. He did not stand out in his elementary-classroom photograph, demanded no glossy page in his high school yearbook. Friends knew him as a woodworker, not star hanger. His looks turned no heads; his position earned him no credit. "He gave up his place with God and made himself nothing."

God hunts for those who will do likewise. These are the people he uses to bring Christ to the world.

ONE MORE THOUGHT

Give up. Surrender. Abandon. Submit. They are words we resist, words that hint at failure. Yet nothing could be further from the truth. It is only when we let go of life as we know it that we discover true life—the glorious plan laid out by God.

> "Blessed are the pure in heart, for they will see God."
> [Matthew 5:8 NIV]

Purity Today

Heaven is no place for the unholy. "Nothing that is impure will enter the city" (Revelation 21:27 GNT). All the sin that blackened our hearts will be washed clean. All the razor-sharp comments that filled our minds checked at the door. What's left? A better, brighter, and purer child of God.

But here's the thing—we don't have to die to enjoy some of heaven's blessings here on earth. What it takes is pure minds and bodies. "Flee also youthful lusts; but pursue righteousness, faith, love, peace with those who call on the Lord out of a pure heart" (2 Timothy 2:22). That gorgeous guy in second period? Those images of women on the Internet? Turn your gaze and thoughts in a new direction. God wants you to see them not as appetizers for the eyes but as his cherished children.

Easier said than done? You know it. But the payoff of purity today is peace of mind and a heart that is ready for heaven.

ONE MORE THOUGHT

Whether you crave someone's body or someone's new iPhone, lust is trouble. The longer you allow those thoughts to hang around, the harder it is to delete them from your mind. God will help you. Pursue purity and you'll enjoy peace for a lifetime—and more.

We hope for something we have not yet seen, and we patiently wait for it.

[Romans 8:25 CEV]

A Mother Must Wait

For Mary, the future mother of Jesus, it was the shock of her life. The angel Gabriel told her that she would become pregnant. The announcement stirred a torrent of questions in her heart. How would she become pregnant? What would the people think? What would her fiancé, Joseph, say? Gabriel explained some of it. But to find out for sure, Mary would have to wait.

To wait, biblically speaking, is not to assume the worst, worry, make demands, or take control. Nor is waiting doing nothing. It is a sustained effort to stay focused on God through prayer and belief. To wait is to "rest in the LORD, and wait patiently for Him" (Psalm 37:7).

It seems that's just what Mary did. And God worked as she waited. He sent a message to Joseph. He prompted Caesar to declare a census. He led the family to Bethlehem. "God is always at work for the good of everyone who loves him" (Romans 8:28 CEV). Mary learned a lesson all of us would be wise to learn—how to mix patience with total trust in God.

ONE MORE THOUGHT

Mothers know all about patience. Yours had to wait months just to see your face (today might be a good day to thank her for that). We all have to wait sometimes. So how will we do it? Stressed out and ready to scream? Or calm and confident, trusting in God? Let's follow the example of the mother of Jesus.

A friend loves you all the time.

[Proverbs 17:17 NCV]

What Friends Do

One gets the impression that to John, Jesus was above all a loyal companion. Messiah? Yes. Son of God? Indeed. Miracle worker? That too. But more than anything, Jesus was a pal. Someone you could go camping with or bowling with or count the stars with.

So what do you do with a friend like that? Well, that's rather simple. You stick by him. Maybe that's why John is the only one of the twelve who was at the cross. He came to say good-bye. By his own admission he hadn't quite put the pieces together yet. But that didn't really matter. As far as he was concerned, his closest friend was in trouble, and he came to help.

Dying on the cross, Jesus asked John, "Can you take care of my mother?" John must have said yes because "from that time on, this disciple took her into his home" (John 19:27 NIV).

Of course he did. That's what friends are for.

ONE MORE THOUGHT

Of all his friends and disciples, John was the one Jesus trusted to take care of his mother. Are you that kind of friend, someone who would be trusted with what others cherish most? If not, what can you do to become the kind of friend who always loves and is always trusted?

I will praise You, for I am fearfully and wonderfully made.

[Psalm 139:14]

Something Special

How would you answer this multiple-choice question?
I am:

(a) a coincidental collision of particles.
(b) an accidental evolution of molecules.
(c) soulless matter in the universe.
(d) "fearfully and wonderfully made."

Don't dull your life by missing this point: you are more than statistical chance, more than a product of your genes and experience, more than a combination of inherited chromosomes and childhood trauma. More than a walking weather vane whipped about by the cold winds of fate. Thanks to God you can say, "You shaped me first inside, then out. . . . Body and soul, I am marvelously made! . . . You know exactly how I was made, bit by bit, how I was sculpted from nothing into something" (Psalm 139:13–15 MSG).

Because of your Maker, that "something" is something special.

ONE MORE THOUGHT

Read Psalm 139. How does it reject the idea that our existence is an accident? What does it say about how we should respond to our Maker? If you are made by a God who can do all this, what does it say about you?

Now we see a blurred image in a mirror. Then we will see very clearly.

[1 Corinthians 13:12 GOD'S WORD]

Mirror, Mirror

Mirror, mirror, on the wall, who is the most faithful one of all?

When I stand in front of a mirror, I see the face of a failure. A man who let down his Maker. Again. I promised I wouldn't, but I did. I was quiet when I should have been bold. I took a seat when I should have taken a stand. If this were the first time, it would be different. But it isn't. How many times can one fall and expect to be caught?

Your eyes look in the mirror and see the same. A failure. A promise-breaker. But when you look through the eyes of faith, everything changes. You look in the mirror and see a robed rebel bearing the ring of grace on your finger and the kiss of your Father on your face.

Your eyes see your faults. Your faith sees your Savior. Your eyes see your guilt. Your faith sees his sacrifice for you.

ONE MORE THOUGHT

There's more to the Christian than meets the eye. On the outside, we look like just another guy or gal stumbling through our days, trying to figure everything out. But if we could see deeper, we'd discover so much more—a Savior inside of us, full of mercy, power, and love.

"Since I, the Lord and Teacher, have washed your
feet, you ought to wash each other's feet."

[John 13:14 NLT]

Washing Judas's Feet

On the night before his crucifixion, Jesus gets up from a table, picks up a towel and water basin, and prepares to wash the feet of each of his disciples. Even Judas's feet, you ask? The lying, conniving, greedy rat who sold Jesus down the river for a pocket of cash? Jesus won't wash his feet, will he? Sure hope not. If he washes the feet of *his* Judas, you'll have to wash the feet of yours. *Your* betrayer. Your lowlife, good-for-nothing villain. Jesus' Judas walked away with thirty pieces of silver. Your Judas walked away with your reputation, idea, virginity, trust, best friend.

You expect me to wash his feet and let him go?

Most people don't want to. They use the villain's photo as a dart target. Most people keep a pot of anger on low boil. But you aren't "most people." Look at your feet. They are wet, grace soaked. Jesus has washed the grimiest parts of your life. Your toes and arches and heels have felt the cool basin of God's grace.

ONE MORE THOUGHT

Picture the "villain" in your life, the person you just can't stand. Could you wash his feet—maybe not literally, but could you show him kindness and compassion? This is what Jesus did, and what he asks of you. This is grace in action.

Happy is he who has the God of Jacob for his help,
whose hope is in the LORD his God.

[Psalm 146:5]

Hope Filled

If you look hard enough and long enough, you'll find something to complain about. Adam and Eve did. Surrounded by all they needed, they set their eyes on the one thing they couldn't have—forbidden fruit. They found something to complain about.

What about you? What are you looking at? The one fruit you can't eat? Or the million you can? His plan or your problems? Each a gift or a grind?

> And now, dear brothers and sisters, one final thing. Fix your thoughts on what is true, and honorable, and right, and pure, and lovely, and admirable. Think about things that are excellent and worthy of praise. (Philippians 4:8 NLT)

When we see as God wants us to see, we see heaven's hand in the middle of sickness, the Holy Spirit comforting a broken heart. We see not what is seen, but what is unseen. We see with faith and not flesh, and since faith leads to hope, we of all people are hope filled. For we know there is more to life than what meets the eye.

ONE MORE THOUGHT

What's really bugging you right now? Take a moment to look past the problem. Can you see God's hand in it? Can you see how he might use your struggle as part of his plan? Think about what's excellent in your life. Now look again—hope is on your horizon.

If you hide your sins, you will not succeed.

[Proverbs 28:13 NCV]

Honest with God

Our high school baseball coach had a firm rule against chewing tobacco. We had a couple of players who were known to sneak a chew, and he wanted to call it to our attention. He got our attention, all right. Before long we'd all tried it. A sure test of manhood was to take a chew when the pouch was passed down the bench. I had barely made the team; I sure wasn't going to fail the test of manhood.

One day I'd just popped a plug in my mouth when one of the players warned, "Here comes the coach!" Not wanting to get caught, I did what came naturally and swallowed. I added new meaning to the scripture, "I felt weak deep inside me. I moaned all day long" (Psalm 32:3 NCV). I paid the price for hiding my disobedience.

My body was not made to ingest tobacco. Your soul was not made to ingest sin.

May I ask a blunt question? Are you keeping any secrets from God? Take a pointer from a nauseated third baseman. You'll feel better if you get it out.

ONE MORE THOUGHT

Take a look at your life over the last twenty-four hours, the last month, the last year. Is there anything you're trying to keep hidden from God? You realize he already knows about it. He's just waiting for you to confess so he can forgive and bless you.

> "I tell you the truth, whoever hears what I say and believes
> in the One who sent me has eternal life."
>
> [John 5:24 NCV]

One Option

When you accept God as Creator, you will admire him. When you recognize his wisdom, you will learn from him. When you discover his strength, you will rely on him. But only when he saves you will you worship him.

It's a "before-and-after" deal. Before your rescue, you could easily keep God at a distance. Sure, he was important, but so was a lot of stuff. Friends. Family. Grades. Swim team. Spanish club.

Then came the storm . . . the rage . . . the fight . . . the ripped moorings. . . . Despair fell like a fog; your bearings were gone. In your heart, you knew there was no exit. Did you turn to your friends and family for help? They could only do so much. Lean on your skills for strength? The storm wasn't impressed with your talent.

Suddenly you were left with one option. The One worthy of your love and praise. The One who deserves your worship. Who is it? The One and only God.

ONE MORE THOUGHT

Nothing gets our attention quite like a crisis. When families fracture or when a disease like cancer strikes, we suddenly realize there are few places to turn. So where do we run? To the One who rescues. Don't wait for a crisis to notice God. Worship him now!

Use your whole body as an instrument to do what is right for the glory of God.

[Romans 6:13 NLT]

Respect God's Body

When it comes to our bodies, the Bible declares that we don't own them. "You are no longer your own. God paid a great price for you. So use your body to honor God" (1 Corinthians 6:19–20 CEV).

Use your body to grab attention? Too-tight tops and shorter-than-short shorts? No. Use your body to honor God. "Use your whole body as an instrument to do what is right for the glory of God" (Romans 6:13 NLT). Your body is God's instrument, intended for his work and for his glory.

Use your body for short-term pleasures with long-term consequences? Doughnuts for dinner every evening? Drinking parties on weekends? No. Maintain God's instrument. Feed it. Care for it. Rest it. When he needs a sturdy implement—a servant who is rested enough to serve, fueled enough to work, alert enough to think—let him find one in you.

Your body, God's tool. Maintain it. Your body, God's temple. Respect it. "God owns the whole works. So let people see God in and through your body" (1 Corinthians 6:20 MSG).

ONE MORE THOUGHT

If there's anything we see as ours, it's our own bodies, right? The Bible says otherwise. Our arms, legs, brains, and belly buttons, along with everything else, belong to God. Think about this. Pray about it. You might start treating your home of skin and bones with more respect.

> The wisdom that comes from God is first of all pure,
> then peaceful, gentle, and easy to please.
>
> [James 3:17 NCV]

A Cure for Heart Trouble

Do you have heart trouble? Is yours filled with anger and anxiety? Jesus is your cure.

His heart was pure. The Savior was adored by thousands, yet content to live a simple life. He was cared for by women (Luke 8:1–3), yet never accused of lustful thoughts; rejected by the people he created, but willing to forgive them before they even asked. Peter, who traveled with Jesus for three and a half years, described him as a "pure and perfect lamb" (1 Peter 1:19 NCV).

His heart was peaceful. The disciples fretted over the need to feed thousands, but not Jesus. He thanked God for the problem. The disciples shouted for fear in the storm, but not Jesus. He slept through it. Peter drew his sword to fight soldiers coming for his master. Not Jesus. He lifted his hand to heal. His heart was at peace.

You too can know purity and peace. Allow Jesus into your heart. He's the surgeon-Savior who knows just what to do.

ONE MORE THOUGHT

Some days it seems like your troubles are more permanent than a tattoo. Jesus is your answer. Talk with him. Pray to him. Worship him. He will calm and clean your heart. When he's done, you and Jesus will be ready to tackle

"Whoever lives and believes in Me shall never die."

[John 11:26]

Whoever

I love to hear my wife say "whoever." Sometimes I detect my favorite fragrance wafting from the kitchen: strawberry cake. Soon I'm standing over the just-baked, just-iced pan of pure pleasure. Yet I've learned to hold my fork until Denalyn gives clearance. "Who is it for?" I ask. She might break my heart. "It's for a birthday party, Max. Don't touch it!" Or she might throw open the door of delight. "Whoever."

Who isn't a *whoever*? The word sledgehammers racial fences and dynamites social classes. It bypasses gender borders and surpasses outdated traditions. *Whoever* makes it clear: God's grace is meant for the world. For those who attempt to restrict it, Jesus has a word.

"*Whoever* acknowledges me before others, I will also acknowledge before my Father in heaven" (Matthew 10:32 NIV). "*Whoever* does God's will is my brother and sister and mother" (Mark 3:35 NIV). "*Whoever* believes and is baptized will be saved, but whoever does not believe will be condemned" (Mark 16:16 NIV).

We lose much in life—friends, dreams, chances. We lose at love. But we never lose our place on God's "whoever" list.

ONE MORE THOUGHT

All those "whoevers" in the Bible should create a picture in our minds. There is Jesus, not so far away. He's smiling—at us. His eyes glow with warmth. His arms are open wide, welcoming. Now he's waving us to come closer. Can you see him? Will you go?

My goal was to spread the Good News where the name of Christ was not known.

[Romans 15:20 GOD'S WORD]

Spread the Good News

Salvation isn't the most comfortable lunchtime topic. You don't often hear, "Could you hand me a napkin, and by the way, are you going to heaven or hell?" Yet God is counting on you to spread his Good News.

You don't have to put a collar around your neck or preach long, boring sermons to be a minister. According to Paul, ministers talk about the gospel everywhere they go and about what God is doing in their lives. It's not always easy to live your faith out loud, but your courage now can make a difference for eternity.

When you arrive in heaven, I wonder if Christ might say these words to you: "I'm so proud that you let me use you. Because of you, others are here today. Would you like to meet them?" Friends, neighbors, even family members all step forward.

Are you a minister? You bet. Are you making a difference? Absolutely.

ONE MORE THOUGHT

Think you don't influence your friends? Think again! They're listening to you and watching every move. If you're a believer and they aren't, this isn't the time to keep it a secret. Let them know of your love for God—and back it up with your actions.

The Lord has assigned to each his task.

[1 Corinthians 3:5 NIV]

Decisions

You have two options but can make only one choice. Work this summer for your parents or for your aunt on the coast? Serve with an inner-city youth ministry or a short-term mission in Mexico? Music camp or Young Life camp? How do you decide?

Like a pilot before takeoff, I always go over my preflight checklist before any trips into the unknown. I ask myself three questions: *Where has God taken me before?* I remember all the places God sent me in the past, the experiences I faced, the cultures I embraced, the lifestyles I encountered. God uses past experiences to overcome present problems. *What people and places excite me?* We all have different passions and burdens. Some like to serve in foreign countries. Others like to help their neighbors. *What am I good at?* We each have at least one unique talent, and we are expected to do that one thing well.

Once you've been through your checklist, talk to God about it. He'll help you decide. Then you'll be ready to fly!

ONE MORE THOUGHT

When you have to make a big decision, listen closely to God. His way is always right. If you don't sense a strong push in one direction, it may mean that either choice is great. We learn from new adventures and opportunities no matter where they take us.

> Jesus looked at them and said, "With man this is impossible, but with God all things are possible."
>
> [Matthew 19:26 NIV]

Paul, Superhero

Peer into the prison and see Paul for yourself: bent and frail, shackled to the arm of a Roman guard as he awaits trial. Behold the apostle of God. Dead broke. No family. No property. Nearsighted and worn out.

No Superman, Batman, or Spider-Man is Paul. He doesn't look anything like a superhero.

Doesn't sound like one either. He introduced himself as the worst sinner in history. He was a Christian-killer before he was a Christian leader. At times his heart was so heavy, Paul could barely drag his pen across the page. "What a miserable man I am! Who will save me from this body that brings me death?" (Romans 7:24 NCV).

Only heaven knows how long he stared at the question before he found the courage to defy logic and write, "I thank God for saving me through Jesus Christ our Lord!" (Romans 7:25 NCV). Paul became a superhero of the Christian faith only when he put his faith and trust in Christ.

ONE MORE THOUGHT

Do you admire the fictional superheroes in the comic books and on the movie screens? They display powers and deeds of daring that real people can only dream of. Yet you *do* have the opportunity to be a superhero. When you join your life to Jesus, you connect to a power that makes made-up superheroes look tame.

God never changes his mind about the people he
calls and the things he gives them.

[Romans 11:29 NCV]

Trust Your Destiny

We tend to define ourselves by our disasters. Don't make this mistake. Think you have lost it all? You haven't. "God's gifts and God's call are under full warranty—never canceled, never rescinded" (Romans 11:29 MSG).

Here's how it works. Your boyfriend dumps you. All those promises about taking you to the prom melted the moment he met the new girl on the track team. Now you feel flatter than trash under a steamroller. The jerk. The bum. The no-good pond scum. You're tempted to get even. But wait! You have a warranty. God is calling you to a different life. And so you choose to ponder your destiny. "I am God's child. My life is more than this life . . . more than this broken heart. This is God's promise and, unlike that sorry excuse for a guy, God won't break a promise."

Bingo. You just redefined your life according to God's dictionary. You just trusted your destiny.

ONE MORE THOUGHT

Is anything worse than a broken promise? It leaves us feeling betrayed and beaten down. God won't do that to you. He's created a plan for your life and given you talents to help you achieve it. Keep following him and you'll find the future you were meant for.

Give thanks to GOD—he is good and his love never quits.

[1 Chronicles 16:34 MSG]

The Grateful Heart

At a banquet, a wounded soldier was presented with the gift of a free house. He nearly fell over with gratitude. He bounded on to the stage with his one good leg and threw both arms around the presenter. "Thank you! Thank you! Thank you!" He hugged the guitar player in the band and the big woman on the front row. He thanked the waiter, the other soldiers, and then the presenter again. Before the night was over, he thanked me! And I didn't do anything.

Shouldn't we be equally grateful? Jesus is building a house for us (John 14:2). Our deed of ownership is every bit as certain as that of the soldier.

And God gives us so much more. A zillion diamonds sparkle in the sky every night. *Thank you, God.* A miracle of muscles enables eyes to read these words and your brain to process them. *Thank you, God.* Brave men and women, like the wounded soldier, fight for our freedoms. *Thank you, Lord.* The grateful heart is like a magnet, sweeping over the day, collecting reasons for gratitude.

ONE MORE THOUGHT

We take so much for granted. The roof over your head and the pillow under it. Food to share and friends who care. We should always thank God for these things. Even if we're having a bad week, we know how the story ends. We should be grateful for a room reserved in heaven.

We take every thought captive so that it is obedient to Christ.

[2 Corinthians 10:5 GOD'S WORD]

Manage Your Thoughts

You've got to admit, some of our hearts are trashed out. Let any riffraff knock on the door, and we throw it open. Anger shows up, and we let him in. Revenge needs a place to stay, so we have him pull up a chair. Pity wants to have a party, so we show him the kitchen. Lust rings the bell, and we set up the guest room. Don't we know how to say no?

Many don't. For most of us, thought management is, well, unthought of. We think much about time management, weight management, course-load management, skin management. But what about thought management? Shouldn't we be as concerned about managing our thoughts as we are managing anything else?

The Bible says, "Keep your minds on whatever is true, pure, right, holy, friendly, and proper. Don't ever stop thinking about what is truly worthwhile and worthy of praise" (Philippians 4:8 CEV). Another way to say it? Don't let in the trash.

ONE MORE THOUGHT

What have you been thinking about lately? Do you control your thoughts, or do your thoughts control you? Every kind of garbage is knocking on the door of your mind, trying to get in and make itself at home. Keep the door locked by thinking about what is true and pure and giving God the key.

Finding Good in the Bad

It would be hard to find someone worse than Judas. Some say he was a good man with a backfired strategy. I don't buy that. The Bible says, "Judas . . . was a thief" (John 12:6 NCV). The man was a crook. Somehow he was able to live in the presence of God and experience the miracles of Christ and remain unchanged.

In the end he decided he'd rather have money than a friend, so he sold Jesus for thirty pieces of silver. Judas was a scoundrel, a cheat, and a bum. How could anyone see him any other way?

I don't know, but Jesus did. Only inches from the face of his betrayer, Jesus looked at him and said, "Friend, do what you came to do" (Matthew 26:50 NCV). What Jesus saw in Judas as worthy of being called a friend, I can't imagine. But I do know that Jesus doesn't lie, and in that moment he saw something good in a very bad man.

Jesus modeled what we must do to those who hurt us. Because he does the same for you and me.

ONE MORE THOUGHT

I'll bet you can think of a few people you're not fond of. People who have harassed and hurt you. People you'd never call "friend." Yet Jesus loves these very same people. He looks at them and, despite their flaws, sees the good in them. Maybe we can too.

The LORD is my shepherd; I have everything I need.
[Psalm 23:1 NCV]

We Need a Shepherd

Sheep aren't smart. They tend to wander into running creeks for water, then their wool grows heavy and they drown. They need a shepherd to lead them to "calm water" (Psalm 23:2 NCV). They have no natural defense—no claws, no horns, no fangs. They're helpless. Sheep need a shepherd with a "rod and . . . shepherd's staff" to protect them (v. 4 NCV). They have no sense of direction. They need someone to lead them "on paths that are right" (v. 3 NCV).

So do we. We like to talk about how smart we are, how strong we are, how independent we are. But we, too, tend to be swept away by waters we should have avoided. We have no defense against the evil lion that prowls about seeking someone to devour. We, too, get lost.

We need a shepherd. We need a shepherd to care for us and to guide us. And we have One.

ONE MORE THOUGHT

Aren't there days when you feel as silly and defenseless as a sheep? Moving but not sure where you're going. Sensing trouble but realizing it's too late. Grades and talent and popularity don't help much in such moments. Only a shepherd will do.

> "My true brother and sister and mother are those who do what God wants."
>
> [Mark 3:35 NCV]

Family

I t may surprise you to know that Jesus had a family. He did. And it may surprise you to know that his family was less than perfect. They were. If your family doesn't appreciate you, take heart; neither did Jesus'. Christ himself said, "A prophet is honored everywhere except in his hometown and with his own people and in his own home" (Mark 6:4 NCV).

There was a time when Jesus' brothers and sisters were seen with him in public. Not because they were proud of him but because they were ashamed of him. "His family . . . went to get him because they thought he was out of his mind" (Mark 3:21 NCV). Jesus' siblings thought their brother was a lunatic. They were embarrassed!

Maybe you know the feeling? Maybe your family is more drama than delight, more crazy than kind? I can't say that your family will ever understand or bless you, but I know God will. Let God give you what your family doesn't. If your earthly family doesn't support you, then let your heavenly one take its place.

ONE MORE THOUGHT

We can't choose our families. If your father is a jerk, you can be the world's best child and he still won't tell you so. It's an unfair game with unfair rules. Jesus didn't play it. You shouldn't either. Take your place in God's family. Accept him not only as Lord and Savior but also as your Father.

God, why have you rejected us for so long?

[Psalm 74:1 NCV]

God Invites Our Questions

Thomas came with doubts. Did Christ turn him away? Moses had his reservations. Did God tell him to go home? Job had his struggles. Did God avoid him? Paul had his hard times. Did God abandon him?

No. God never turns away the sincere heart. Tough questions don't stump God. He invites our probing.

Maybe you're wondering why God seems to stand aside when so many terrible things happen. Why he allows temptation. Why he seemed to disappear last month when you needed him. Whether you can *truly* trust and believe in him.

Mark it down. God never turns away the honest seeker. "If any of you needs wisdom, you should ask God for it" (James 1:5 NCV). Go to God with your questions. Read his Word. If you're patient, he will point you to the answers you seek. The bonus will be a deeper, richer, stronger faith.

ONE MORE THOUGHT

Any teacher will tell you that questions are part of the process of learning. So don't worry about asking God questions—he can handle it! A mature faith doesn't come with age. It comes with seeking and growing in Jesus day by day.

JUNE

What we see will last only a short time, but
what we cannot see will last forever.

[2 Corinthians 4:18 NCV]

We are like clay, and you are the potter; your hands made us all.

[Isaiah 64:8 NCV]

Your Heart Can Change

God wants us to be just like Jesus.

Isn't that good news? You aren't stuck with today's personality. You aren't condemned to "grumpydom." You are tweakable. Even if you've worried each day of your life, you needn't worry the rest of your life. So what if you were born a snob? You don't have to die one.

Where did we get the idea we can't change? Where did statements such as "It's just my nature to worry" or "I'll always be pessimistic. I'm just that way" come from? Would we say that about our bodies? "It's just my nature to have a broken leg. I can't do anything about it." Of course not. If our bodies malfunction, we seek help. Shouldn't we do the same with our hearts? Shouldn't we seek help for our sour attitudes? Can't we request treatment for our selfish tirades?

Of course we can. Jesus can change our hearts. He wants us to have a heart like his.

ONE MORE THOUGHT

Ever get frustrated with yourself? Wish you could adjust your attitude? Jesus is your answer. If you doubt it, remember that he changed the entire world. If he can do that, don't you think he can change you?

The battle is the LORD's.

[1 Samuel 17:47]

Take a Swing at Your Giant

David runs toward the army to meet Goliath (1 Samuel 17:48). Goliath throws back his head in laughter, just enough to shift his helmet and expose a square inch of flesh. David spots the target and seizes the moment. His sling swirls. The stone torpedoes through the air and into the skull; Goliath crumples to the ground and dies. David yanks Goliath's sword from its sheath, shish-kebabs the Philistine, and cuts off his head.

You might say that David knew how to get *a head* of his giant.

When was the last time you did the same? How long since you ran toward your challenge? We tend to retreat, ducking behind a pile of homework or slipping into the distraction of party life. For a time we feel safe, comfortable, but then the work runs out or the parties end, and we hear Goliath again. Booming. Bombastic.

Try a different tack. Rush your giant with a God-soaked soul. *Giant of depression? You won't conquer me. Giant of alcohol, drugs, insecurity . . . you're going down.* How long since you loaded your sling and took a swing at your giant?

ONE MORE THOUGHT

Sometimes it's the bold who carry the day. You may not feel too bold at the moment, but God will make up the difference. Ask him now for strength, for courage, for power to topple the giant in your life. You can do it—go!

161

> You will keep him in perfect peace, whose mind is
> stayed on You, because he trusts in You.
>
> [Isaiah 26:3]

Fix Your Thoughts on God

Goliaths still roam our world. Disaster. Deceit. Disease. Divorce. Depression. Supersized challenges still swagger and strut, still steal sleep and hinder joy. But they can't dominate you. You know how to deal with them. You face giants by facing God first.

Paul, the apostle, wrote, "Prayer is essential in this ongoing warfare. Pray hard and long" (Ephesians 6:18 MSG). Prayer spawned David's successes. How do you survive a fugitive life in the caves? David did with prayers like this one: "Be good to me, God—and now! I've run to you for dear life. I'm hiding out under your wings until the hurricane blows over. I call out to High God, the God who holds me together" (Psalm 57:1–2 MSG).

Mark well this promise: "[God] will keep in perfect peace all who trust in [God], all whose thoughts are fixed on [God]!" (Isaiah 26:3 NLT). God promises not just peace, but perfect peace. To whom? To those whose minds are "fixed" on God. Forget an occasional text. Peace is promised to the one who fixes thoughts and desires on the King.

ONE MORE THOUGHT

God hears every prayer from the children he loves, but which kind do you think pleases him most? Random, fleeting words, more of a wave and "Hi, God, how are you?" Or sit-down, in-depth, intimate conversations? Paul says, "Pray hard and long." Sounds like good advice for the people of God.

> I do not live anymore—it is Christ who lives in me.
>
> [Galatians 2:20 NCV]

Give God Your Hands

You have an essay to finish writing. A trumpet solo to practice. A garbage can to dump. Simply put, you have things to do.

So does God. Grandmas need hugs. Shut-ins need company. The hungry need a food drive. Stressed-out students need hope. God has work to do. And he uses our hands to do it.

What the hand is to the glove, the Spirit is to the Christian. God gets into us. At times, we barely notice. Other times, we can't miss it. God gets his fingers into our lives, inch by inch reclaiming the territory that is rightfully his.

Your tongue? He claims it for his message. Your feet? He summons them for his purpose. Your mind? He made it and intends to use it for his glory. Your eyes, face, and hands? Through them he will weep, smile, and touch. He has work to do. Give God your hands (and the rest of you) and watch them change lives.

ONE MORE THOUGHT

God won't settle for using part of you to accomplish his purposes. What good is half a hammer? He wants all your heart, all your mind, all your faith, so you can participate fully and he can complete his perfect and

Why Worry?

Two words sum up Christ's opinion of worry: *irrelevant* and *irreverent.*

"Can all your worries add a single moment to your life?" (Matthew 6:27 NLT). Of course not. Worry is irrelevant. It changes nothing. When was the last time you solved a problem by worrying about it? Imagine someone saying, "I got behind in my homework, so I decided to worry my way out of it. And, you know, it worked! A few sleepless nights, a day of puking and hand wringing, and— glory to worry—the finished assignments just appeared on my desk."

It doesn't happen! Worry changes nothing. You don't add one day to your life or one bit of life to your day by worrying. Your anxiety earns you a stomachache, nothing more.

Ninety-two percent of our worries are needless. Not only is worry irrelevant, doing nothing; worry is irreverent, distrusting God.

ONE MORE THOUGHT

Read the words of Jesus in Matthew 6:25–34. Isn't he telling us that God will give us what we need whether we worry or not? Isn't he saying that we should focus on today and that worrying about tomorrow is wasted energy? Let's show our faith and leave worry behind.

Two Choices

Pilate, the Roman governor confronted with a prisoner who agreed that he was a king, had a question. It is the question that rings throughout history: "What should I do with Jesus, the one called the Christ?" (Matthew 27:22 NCV).

Perhaps you, like Pilate, are curious about this one called Jesus. What do you do with a man who claims to be God yet hates religion? What do you do with a man who calls himself the Savior yet condemns systems? What do you do with a man who knows the place and time of his death yet goes there anyway?

You have two choices. You can reject him. That is an option. You can, as have many, decide that the idea of God's becoming a carpenter is too weird—and walk away.

Or you can accept him. You can journey with him. You can listen for his voice amid the hundreds of voices and follow him.

ONE MORE THOUGHT

What will you do with Jesus? You're curious enough to be reading this devotional. Maybe you've already spoken of your faith in Christ, but you're still holding something back. You can't keep going that way. Reject him? Or totally accept him? It's time to choose.

The Father has loved us so much that we are called children of God. And we really are his children.

[1 John 3:1 NCV]

Who Am I?

Life can be so confusing. Figuring out what you're supposed to do. Discovering what you're good at (and not so hot at). Finding what you believe. It can leave your head spinning faster than a jet-powered merry-go-round. You start wondering, *Just who am I?*

Let me tell you who you are. In fact, let me proclaim who you are. You are part of God's family and will inherit his kingdom with Christ (Romans 8:17). You are eternal, like an angel (Luke 20:36). You have a crown that will last forever (1 Corinthians 9:25). You are a holy priest (1 Peter 2:5), a treasured possession (Exodus 19:5).

But more than any of the above—more significant than any title or position—is the simple fact that you are God's child. "We really are his children" (1 John 3:1 NCV). As a result, if something is important to you, it's important to God. You belong to him.

ONE MORE THOUGHT

We have so many roles to play. Son or daughter. Brother or sister. Student. Friend. Teammate. Yet there's one that counts above all the rest: child of God. This is the role that gives you status. This is the part that gives you peace and love forever. Never forget who you are.

"You must be compassionate, just as your Father is compassionate."

[Luke 6:36 NLT]

Curing the Boredom Blues

I'll bet you've used this line once or twice: "Mom, I'm bored." There are days when life seems to drag. When teachers drone. When the most exciting thing around is watching the clock tick off another minute.

Want a cure for the boredom blues? Do an outrageous deed. A caring act beyond reimbursement. Kindness without compensation. Do a deed for which you cannot be repaid. I'm talking about cleaning up an elderly neighbor's yard when she's not home. Washing your dad's car when he's out of town. Inviting the guy with no friends over to play video games. Inviting the new girl to your church youth group. Bringing cookies to a shut-in or a homeless person.

Jesus said, "Help and give without expecting a return. You'll never—I promise—regret it" (Luke 6:36 MSG). When you see the joy that results from your gift of love and time, it will blow away your boredom and replace it with breathtaking.

ONE MORE THOUGHT

Funny thing about being bored—the focus is all on you and how you feel. When you dare to do a kind deed for someone, it shifts your attention. You start noticing what's going on around you instead of what's inside you. That's not boring. That's exciting.

The LORD hates what evil people do, but he loves those who do what is right.

[Proverbs 15:9 NCV]

The Fire of Anger

Perhaps the wound is old. A parent abused you. A teacher slighted you. A friend betrayed you. And you are angry. Or perhaps the wound is fresh. The buddy who owes you money just rode by on his new bike. The boyfriend who made so many promises last week has forgotten how to pronounce your name. And you are hurt.

Part of you is broken, and the other part is bitter. Part of you wants to cry, and part of you wants to fight. There is a fire burning in your heart. It's the fire of anger.

And you are left with a decision. "Do I put the fire out or heat it up? Do I get over it or get even? Do I release it or resent it? Do I let my hurts heal, or do I let hurt turn into hate?"

Hate is wrong. Revenge is bad. But the worst part of all is that without forgiveness, bitterness is all that's left.

ONE MORE THOUGHT

You probably know someone whose anger has turned to bitterness. What is that person like? More frowns than fun? More words that cut instead of encourage? Is that who you want to be? Give your broken heart to God. Let the fire go out. Forgive.

"Those people who keep their faith until the end will be saved."

[Matthew 10:22 NCV]

Be a Finisher

Are you close to quitting? Please don't do it. Are you discouraged about your future? Hang in there. Are you weary with doing good? Do just a little more. Are you pessimistic about the loyalty of your friends? Give them another chance. No communication with your parents? Try one more time.

Remember, a finisher is not one with no wounds or weariness. Quite to the contrary, he, like the boxer, is scarred and bloody. Mother Teresa is credited with saying, "God didn't call us to be successful, just faithful." The fighter, like our Master, is pierced and full of pain. Like Paul, he may even be bound and beaten. But he keeps going.

The Land of Promise, says Jesus, awaits those who endure. It is not just for those who make the victory laps or drink champagne. No, sir. The Land of Promise is for those who simply remain to the end. Your arrival will start a celebration like no other.

ONE MORE THOUGHT

God honors those who finish. Job suffered through terrible loss and misery yet never lost his faith, and God blessed him almost beyond measure. The same could be said for Joseph and countless others. Trouble making you want to quit? Don't give in. You can't imagine what God has waiting for those who finish.

> "Life is not defined by what you have, even when you have a lot."
>
> [Luke 12:15 MSG]

The Prison of Want

Are you in prison? You are if you feel better when you have more and worse when you have less. You are if delight is one delivery away, one award away, or one makeover away. If your happiness comes from something you deposit, drive, drink, digest, or download, then face it—you are in prison, the prison of want.

That's the bad news. The good news is, you have a visitor. And your visitor has a message that can get you paroled. Make your way to the receiving room. Take your seat in the chair, and look across the table at the psalm writer, David. He motions for you to lean forward. "I have a secret to tell you," he whispers, "the secret of satisfaction. 'The LORD is my shepherd; I shall not want'" (Psalm 23:1).

It's as if he is saying, "What I have in God is greater than what I don't have in life."

You think you and I could learn to say the same?

ONE MORE THOUGHT

We are born wanting. As babies, we want milk, we want attention, we want to be changed—and we want it now! But as we grow, we learn that what we want is not the same as what we need. Faith leaves want behind. Need is met by God.

> You are my place of safety and protection. You are my God and I trust you.
>
> [Psalm 91:2 NCV]

God Wrote Your Story

Have bad things *really* happened to you? You and God may have different definitions for the word *bad*. Maybe your dictionary defines it as "pimple on nose" or "pop quiz in geometry." "Dad, this is really bad!" you say. Dad, having been around the block a time or two, thinks differently. He understands that pimples pass.

What you and I might rate as an absolute disaster, God may rate as a pimple-level problem that will pass. He views your life the way you view a movie after you've read the book. When something bad happens, you feel the air sucked out of the theater. Everyone else gasps at the crisis on the screen. Not you. Why? You've read the book. You know how the good guy gets out of the tight spot. God views your life with the same confidence. He's not only read your story . . . he wrote it.

ONE MORE THOUGHT

Think back to your last bad day. How bad was it? Will you remember it five years from now? Ten? Your problems are real. I understand that. But it may help to remember that God has seen the rest of your story, and it has a happy ending.

The ways of God are without fault.

[Psalm 18:30 NCV]

The Cure for Disappointment

When God doesn't do what we want, it's not easy. Never has been. Never will be. But faith is the conviction that God knows more than we do about this life and he will get us through it. Our disappointment is cured by rearranged expectations.

I like the story about the fellow who went to the pet store in search of a singing parakeet. Seems he lived alone and his house was too quiet. The store owner had just the bird for him, so the man bought it.

The next day the bachelor came home from work to a house full of music. He went to the cage to feed the bird and noticed for the first time that the parakeet had only one leg. He felt cheated that he'd been sold a one-legged bird, so he called and complained.

"What do you want," the store owner responded, "a bird who can sing or a bird who can dance?" Good question for times of disappointment.

ONE MORE THOUGHT

We're a lot like the man with the new parakeet. We get what we need, then complain about it. Is God providing for you? Has he given you hope for today and hope for heaven? We'll dodge disappointment if we trust God to give us what we need.

Jesus said, "Come follow me."

[Matthew 4:19 NCV]

God's Favorite Word

Invitations make us feel special. Whether it's a card in the mail requesting we come to a birthday party or a personal offer to go to the dance, an invitation is a moment to celebrate.

Our God is an inviting God. He invited Mary to birth his Son, the disciples to fish for men, the woman who committed adultery to start over, and Thomas to touch his wounds. God is the King who prepares the palace, sets the table, and invites his subjects to come in. In fact, it seems his favorite word is *come*.

"*Come*, let us talk about these things. Though your sins are like scarlet, they can be as white as snow." "All you who are thirsty, *come* and drink." "*Come* to me all, all of you who are tired and have heavy loads, and I will give you rest."

God is a God who invites. He's asking you, right now, to talk with him so you can both get to know each other better. What do you say?

ONE MORE THOUGHT

The invitations from God keep coming. He asks you to check him out. He asks you to read his Word and see if it's true. He asks you to give your heart to him. He asks you to grow more and more like Christ. He asks you to spend forever with him. Each invitation is incredible. Won't you say yes?

My children, listen to your father's teaching; pay attention so you will understand.

[Proverbs 4:1 NCV]

A Father's Lesson

A father passes on many lessons to his children. One of my most important came near the end of my father's life. He had just retired. He and Mom had saved their money and made their plans. They wanted to visit every national park in their travel trailer. Then came the diagnosis: amyotrophic lateral sclerosis (Lou Gehrig's disease), a cruel degenerative disease of the muscles.

At the time, my wife, Denalyn, and I were preparing to do mission work in Brazil. When we got the news, I offered to change my plans. After all, how could I leave the country while he was dying? Dad's written reply was immediate. "In regards to my disease and your going to Rio. That is really an easy answer for me and that is 'GO.' . . . I have no fear of death or eternity . . . so don't be concerned about me. Just 'GO.' Please him."

Dad reminded me that when facing trouble or even death, there is still just one answer. Be brave. Please God. My father's lesson was that doing the will of the Father always matters most.

ONE MORE THOUGHT

What are the lessons your parents have passed on to you? If you're able, why don't you thank them today for their guidance? While you're at it, thank your heavenly Father for his guidance too—and remember to keep pleasing him.

You made us a little lower than you yourself, and you
have crowned us with glory and honor.

[Psalm 8:5 CEV]

Correct Your I-Sight

Are you too hard on yourself? Expect too much of yourself? Feel like you can't do anything right? Do you have poor I-sight?

Remember that your identity isn't about what you do but who you are. You're a child of God, created by the Master for his plans and glory. When you see yourself through his lens, your "I can't do anything" turns into "I can do all things through Christ who strengthens me" (Philippians 4:13). God is bigger than your shyness, your fears of rejection, your past failures. He wants you to reach out to others in his name. You may not see it yet, but he is preparing you to change the world.

To fully belong to God means to throw away feelings of insecurity. You are part of his family, forged to play a role in a holy future—and he does not make mistakes.

ONE MORE THOUGHT

Maybe you don't measure up to your standards. Maybe your performance lately feels pitiful. God doesn't care about that. He loves and values you because he made you. He has plans for you that you can't even imagine. Trust him. Love him. He gave his life for something precious—you.

Simplify Your Faith

There are some who position themselves between you and God. There are some who suggest the only way to get to God is through them. There is the great teacher who has the final word on Bible teaching. There is the father who must bless your acts. There is the spiritual leader who will tell you what God wants you to do. Jesus' message for complicated religion is to remove these middlemen. "You have only one Master, the Christ" (Matthew 23:10 NCV).

He's not saying that you don't need teachers, elders, or counselors. He is saying, however, that we are all brothers and sisters and have equal access to the Father. Simplify your faith by seeking God for yourself. No confusing ceremonies necessary. No mysterious rituals required. No complicated channels of command or levels of access.

You have a Bible? You can study. You have a mind? You can think. You have a heart? You can pray. And God welcomes it.

ONE MORE THOUGHT

It's one of the wonderful paradoxes of the Christian faith—incredible, life-changing power in a simple message. Jesus asks us to confess our sin and believe in him. Having a relationship with him is just as simple. Study his Word. Think about what it means. Talk to him in prayer.

> "I was without clothes, and you gave me something to wear."
>
> [Matthew 25:36 NCV]

What Love Does

What if you were given the privilege of Mary? What if God himself were placed in your arms as a naked baby? Would you not do what she did? "She wrapped the baby with pieces of cloth" (Luke 2:7 NCV). The baby Jesus, still wet from the womb, was cold and chilled. So this mother did what any mother would do; she did what love does: she covered him.

Wouldn't you cherish an opportunity to do the same? You have one. Such opportunities come your way every day. The homeless man shivering on the street corner—could you hand him your coat? The lonely outcast two grades below you—could you offer her an encouraging word?

Jesus said, "I was without clothes, and you gave me something to wear. . . . I tell you the truth, anything you did for even the least of my people here, you also did for me" (Matthew 25:36, 40 NCV). You can cover just about anything with love.

ONE MORE THOUGHT

If someone handed you a cold and shivering baby, of course you would cover and take care of him. But we can't always see the cold that people are feeling inside. Almost everyone you meet is shivering from some kind of hurt. When you care for them, you're also caring for Jesus.

The LORD chose me and gave me a name before I was born.

[Isaiah 49:1 CEV]

Making Good

Christine Caine was abandoned, unnamed, by the mother and father who conceived and bore her. Could anything be worse? Actually, yes. She was sexually abused by members of her new family. They turned her childhood into a horror story of one encounter after another. Twelve years of ugly evil.

Yet, what they intended for evil, God used for good. Christine chose to focus on the promise of her heavenly Father and not the hurts of her past. Years later, when she heard of the plight of girls caught in the sex-slave industry, she knew she had to respond. This unnamed, abused girl set out to rescue the nameless and abused girls of her day. Now she travels the world meeting with cabinets, presidents, and parliaments. Satan's plan to destroy her actually strengthened her resolve to help others. With God as her helper, she will see sex slavery brought to its knees.[6]

No evil is beyond God's reach. He will make good out of your mess too. That's his job.

ONE MORE THOUGHT

In one form or another, you've seen evil. You know what the devil can do. But God's call on you is greater than Satan's worst scheme. Rely on the Lord's power and promise. Let it strengthen your resolve to overcome evil and fulfill his plan to make amazing good.

> Depend on the LORD; trust him, and he will take care of you.
>
> [Psalm 37:5 NCV]

He Meets Our Needs

God is committed to caring for our needs. Paul tells us that a man who won't feed his own family is worse than an unbeliever (1 Timothy 5:8). How much more will a holy God care for his children? After all, how can we carry out his mission for us unless our needs are met? How can we teach or help or tell others about Jesus unless we have our basic needs satisfied? Will God enlist us in his army and not provide meals? Of course not.

"I pray that the God of peace will give you every good thing you need so you can do what he wants" (Hebrews 13:21 NCV). Hasn't that prayer been answered in our lives? We may not have had a feast, but haven't we always had food? (Yes, school lunches count as food.) Perhaps there was no banquet, but at least there was bread. And many times there was so much more. God takes care of us every day.

ONE MORE THOUGHT

What if you wrote out a list of everything you wanted? Be honest—would the paper stretch taller than you? How about what we need? Much shorter list. Food. Shelter. Clothing. Love. God knows exactly what we need, and he's committed to giving it to us.

My God, I want to do what you want. Your teachings are in my heart.

[Psalm 40:8 NCV]

What Ignites Your Heart?

Want to know God's will for your life? Then answer this question: What ignites your heart? Forgotten orphans? Untouched nations? The inner city? The outer limits? Honor the fire within you!

Do you have a passion to sing? Then sing! Are you stirred to manage? Then manage! Do you ache for the sick? Then treat them! Do you hurt for the lost? Then teach them! Maybe your dream is to be a diver, a dancer, a veterinarian, a ventriloquist. Go for it!

As a young man I felt the call to preach. Unsure if I was correct in my reading of God's will for me, I sought the counsel of a minister I admired. His advice still rings true. "Don't preach," he said, "unless you *have* to." As I pondered his words I found my answer: "I have to. If I don't, the fire will consume me."

God may very well be the source of your passion. What is the fire that consumes you?

ONE MORE THOUGHT

Your gifts and dreams are not random. God gives each of us unique abilities and desires for our future. What seems silly or impractical to someone else may be exactly what God has planned for you. If he opens the door, don't be afraid to walk through it.

> He who overcomes, and keeps My works until the end,
> to him I will give power over the nations.
>
> [Revelation 2:26]

What If God Weren't Here?

Think for a moment about this question: What if God weren't here on earth? You think people can be cruel now, imagine us without the presence of God. You think we are brutal to each other now, imagine the world without the Holy Spirit. You think there is loneliness and despair and guilt now, imagine life without the touch of Jesus.

What would your family and friends be like without him shaping their character? What would *you* be like? No forgiveness. No hope. No acts of kindness. No words of love. No more food given in his name. No more songs sung to his praise. No more deeds done in his honor. If God took away his angels, his grace, his promise of eternity, and his servants, what would the world be like?

In a word, hell.

Let's thank God now and every day that he is here with us.

ONE MORE THOUGHT

How is your imagination? Do you ever create stories and worlds in your head? I like to think I have a pretty good imagination, but there are some things I'd rather not picture. One is a world without God. I'm grateful I don't have to think about it. I'll bet you are too.

> "I have found David the son of Jesse, a man after
> My own heart, who will do all My will."
>
> [Acts 13:22]

The Heart God Loves

God called David "a man after my own heart." One might read David's story and wonder what God saw in him. The fellow fell as often as he stood, stumbled as often as he conquered. He stared down Goliath yet ogled Bathsheba, defied God-mockers in the valley yet joined them in the wilderness. He could lead armies but couldn't manage a family. Raging David. Weeping David. Bloodthirsty. God-hungry.

A man after God's own heart? That God saw him that way gives hope to us all. Straight-A souls find David's story disappointing. The rest of us find it reassuring. We ride the same roller coaster. We alternate between swan dives and belly flops, savory steaks and burnt toast.

We need David's story. Some note the absence of miracles in his story. No Red Sea openings, chariots flaming, or dead Lazaruses walking. No miracles. But there is one. David is one. The God who made a miracle out of David stands ready to make one out of you.

ONE MORE THOUGHT

Can you relate to David? Maybe not the king part, but probably the success-then-stumble pattern of his life. His actions didn't always merit applause, but his heart was usually in the right place. That's a good starting point for all of us. Set your heart on God and you're going to be just fine.

God . . . forgave all our sins. He canceled the debt,
which listed all the rules we failed to follow.

[Colossians 2:13–14 NCV]

The Gift We Call Grace

All the world religions can be placed in one of two categories: legalism or grace. You are saved based on your deeds or you are saved based on the gift of Christ's death.

A legalist believes the supreme force behind salvation is you. If you look right, speak right, and belong to the right group, you will be saved. The responsibility doesn't lie within God; it lies within you. The result? Everything looks great on the outside. The talk is good and the step is true. But look closely. Listen carefully. Something is missing. What is it? Joy. What's there? Fear. (That you won't do enough.) Arrogance. (That you have done enough.) Failure. (That you have made a mistake.)

Spiritual life is not a human effort. It's not a test to study for or a grade to earn. You don't achieve salvation by building up extra credit points. Your life of faith is rooted in and coordinated by the Holy Spirit. Every spiritual achievement is created and energized by God. Including salvation, the gift we call grace.

ONE MORE THOUGHT

It goes against everything we've been taught. If you want something big, something important, you have to work for it, right? Not this time. The most important achievement of all—a reserved seat in heaven—can't be earned

"It gives your Father great happiness to give you the Kingdom."

[Luke 12:32 NLT]

He Loves to Give

God loves to give. He "gives generously to all without finding fault" (James 1:5 NIV). He *lavishes* us with love (1 John 3:1). He is rich in "kindness, forbearance and patience" (Romans 2:4 NIV). His grace is "exceedingly abundant" (1 Timothy 1:14) and "indescribable" (2 Corinthians 9:15). He turned a few bread loaves and fish into food for five thousand, changed water at a wedding into wine, and overflowed the boat of Peter with fish, twice. He healed all who sought health, taught all who wanted instruction, and saved all who accepted the gift of salvation.

Picture him at the center of the circle, a huge smile on his face, teaching you the latest dance step. When God gives, he dances for joy. He strikes up the band and leads the giving parade.

God dispenses his goodness not with an eyedropper but a fire hydrant. You simply can't contain it all. So let it bubble over. Spill out. Pour forth. And enjoy the flood.

ONE MORE THOUGHT

Today, try giving an unexpected gift to someone you know. It might be that scarf your sister likes or the picked-up bedroom your mom keeps talking about. Notice the smile it triggers on her face. Notice the pleasure it triggers in you. It's a tiny glimpse of the joy God feels when he gives to you.

Therefore, if anyone is in Christ, he is a new creation; old things
have passed away; behold, all things have become new.

[2 Corinthians 5:17]

"We Can Fix This"

One of my Boy Scout assignments was to build a kite. One of
my blessings as a Boy Scout was a kite-building dad. We fash-
ioned a sky-dancing masterpiece: red, white, and blue and shaped
like a box. We launched our creation on the back of a March wind.
But after some minutes, my kite caught a downdraft and plunged. I
did all I could to maintain elevation. But it was too late.

Envision a redheaded, heartsick twelve-year-old standing over
his collapsed kite. Envision a square-bodied man with ruddy skin
placing his hand on the boy's shoulder. My dad surveyed the heap
of sticks and paper and assured, "It's okay. We can fix this." I
believed him. Why not? He spoke with authority.

So does Christ. To all whose lives feel like a crashed kite, he
says, "It's okay. We can fix this." Your world may look like a pile of
worthless sticks. Take heart. The hand of Jesus is on your shoulder.
You are blessed with a life-building Savior.

ONE MORE THOUGHT

God once told Jeremiah, "Like clay in the hand of the potter, so are you in
my hand" (Jeremiah 18:6 NIV). He is the master of reshaping broken pieces
and lumpy lives. Trust him. His hand is on your shoulder. He's ready to go
to work.

> "You shall be witnesses to Me in Jerusalem, and in all Judea and Samaria, and to the end of the earth."
>
> [Acts 1:8]

Spread the News

The tall one in the corner—that's Peter. Galilee thickened his accent. Fishing nets thickened his hands. Stubbornness thickened his skull. The guy picked to lead the next great work of God knows more about bass and boat docks than he does about Roman culture or Egyptian leaders. And his cronies: Andrew, James, Nathanael. Do they have any formal education?

In fact, what do they have? Humility? They argued over who would be Jesus' top assistant. Sound theology? Peter told Jesus to forget the cross. Loyalty? When Jesus was arrested, they ran. Yet look at them six weeks later, acting like they'd just won tickets to the World Cup Finals. High fives and wide eyes. Wondering about Jesus' final commission: "You will be my witnesses . . . to the ends of the earth" (Acts 1:8 NIV).

You hillbillies will be my witnesses. *You* uneducated and simple folk will be my witnesses. *You* who once called me crazy, who doubted me in the Upper Room. *You* will be my witnesses.

He's speaking to the disciples. He's also speaking to us.

ONE MORE THOUGHT

There's a point behind Jesus' pick of the twelve disciples. These boys were not the cool, cultured guys. If you think you need special training to spread the Good News of God, think again. He wants you to use what you've got to talk about him. You're already ready.

> "Stay alert, be in prayer, so you don't enter the
> danger zone without even knowing it."
>
> [Mark 14:38 MSG]

No Part of Poison

Joseph was twenty-seven years old when he crashed into a sand-bar of sexual temptation. When his brothers sold him into slavery, they probably thought they'd doomed him to hard labor and an early death. Instead, an Egyptian named Potiphar put Joseph in charge of his household. People noticed him, including Mrs. Potiphar. Before long, she made her play: "Come to bed with me!" (Genesis 39:7 NIV).

Far from home, rejected by his family, stressed from work, Joseph could have justified it. So can you. You've been dumped, bruised, and burned. Few friends and fewer solutions. A guy or gal sends you a text: "Meet me tonight." Or a friend slides you a beer. A classmate offers some drugs. Excuses pop up like weeds after a summer rain. *No one would know. I won't get caught. It won't hurt anyone.* Except that isn't true. You'd be hurting the people who care about you. Not to mention God. Not to mention yourself.

Joseph turned Mrs. Potiphar down. He wanted no part of her poison. Put yourself in Joseph's shoes and do the same.

ONE MORE THOUGHT

Temptations slither into our lives in many forms. Some are obvious. Some are sneaky. When you find one hissing at you, do what Jesus did and repeat verses from the Bible. Or simply follow the advice of Proverbs 3:7 (MSG): "Run to GOD! Run from evil!" Temptation can't get you if it can't catch you.

> "Father, forgive them, for they do not know what they are doing."
>
> [Luke 23:34 NIV]

Our Compassionate Christ

Have you ever wondered how Jesus kept from striking back at the mob that killed him? Have you ever asked how he kept control? Here's the answer. It's this statement: "for they do not know what they are doing." Look carefully. It's as if Jesus considered this bloodthirsty, death-hungry crowd not as murderers, but as victims. It's as if he saw in their faces not hatred but confusion. It's as if he regarded them not as a militant mob but, as he put it, "sheep without a shepherd" (Mark 6:34 NIV).

"They don't know what they are doing." When you think about it, they didn't. They were mad at something they couldn't see so they took it out on—of all people—God.

Maybe you know someone like this. Someone who wants to harm you, filled with anger and hate. Maybe you can see this person as Jesus does. Someone lost, a sheep without a shepherd. Someone who doesn't know what he or she is doing. Someone loved by God.

ONE MORE THOUGHT

When someone is insulting you, shouting at you, or even trying to hit you, it's pretty tough to keep from striking back. The trick is to see what's behind the attack. Is it fear? Lack of faith? Just plain ignorance? Whatever the case, Jesus loves this person just as much as he loves you.

> If we confess our sins, he will forgive our sins, because
> we can trust God to do what is right.
>
> [1 John 1:8–9 NCV]

Full, Honest Confession

Confess. Admit. Come clean. Fess up. The words all mean the same thing—but what is that exactly?

Confession isn't telling God what he doesn't know. Impossible. Confession isn't complaining. If I just repeat my problems and woes, I'm whining. Confession isn't blaming. Pointing fingers at others without pointing any at me feels good, but it doesn't bring healing.

Confession is so much more. Confession is a radical reliance on grace. A declaration of our trust in God's goodness. If our understanding of grace is small, our confession will be small: reluctant, hesitant, incomplete, buried in excuses and qualifications. You know the kind. "Hey, Sis, sorry that I read your diary, but you really shouldn't have left it open on your bed."

Wild, overflowing grace, on the other hand, creates a full and honest confession. Like the one of the son who took his inheritance money, left home, blew it all, and returned in shame to say, "Father, I have sinned against heaven and before you. I am no longer worthy to be called your son" (Luke 15:21 ESV).

ONE MORE THOUGHT

You blew it—we've all been there. Now is not the time to hold back! Take it to God. Confess every last detail, not because he doesn't already know but because you need to get it out. Sure, it's hard, but trust him. His life-changing forgiveness is right around the corner.

JULY

"Peace I leave with you, My peace I give to you;
not as the world gives do I give to you. Let not
your heart be troubled, neither let it be afraid."

[John 14:27]

We can make our plans, but the LORD determines our steps.

[Proverbs 16:9 NLT]

Who's in Charge?

Can you imagine what would have happened if your parents, when you were six years old, honored each of your requests? Your room would be overflowing with toys. Your belly would be bloated from all the ice cream.

Can you imagine the chaos if God granted each of our requests today?

"For God has not *destined* us for wrath, but to obtain salvation through our Lord Jesus Christ" (1 Thessalonians 5:9 ESV).

Note God's destiny for your life: salvation.

God's core desire is that you reach that destiny. His itinerary includes stops that encourage your journey. He frowns on stops that deter you. When his supreme plan and your earthly plan collide, a decision must be made. Who's in charge of this journey?

If God must choose between your earthly satisfaction and your heavenly salvation, which do you hope he chooses?

Me too.

ONE MORE THOUGHT

When was the last time you really wanted something and it didn't happen for you—maybe yesterday? How did you handle that moment? It may help to remember that God has a plan for us we can't always see. He's in charge—and that's a good thing.

These trials make you partners with Christ in his suffering, so
that you will have the wonderful joy of seeing his glory.

[1 Peter 4:13 NLT]

Hurting for a Purpose

It's so hard to see the people you love hurting. Maybe your best
friend is freaking out because her parents are getting divorced.
Maybe another friend's mother is fighting cancer. What can you tell
them?

Tell them that God uses struggles for his glory. The last three
years of my dad's life were scarred by ALS (amyotrophic lateral
sclerosis). A healthy mechanic became a bed-bound paralytic. He
lost his voice and his muscles, but he never lost his faith. Visitors
noticed. Not so much in what he said but more in what he didn't
say. Never outwardly angry or bitter, Jack Lucado suffered with
dignity.

His faith led another man to faith. After my dad's funeral this
man sought me out and told me. Because of my dad's example, he
became a Jesus follower.

Did God allow my father's illness for that very reason? Knowing
the value God places on one soul, I wouldn't be surprised. And imagining the wonder of heaven, I know my father's not complaining.

ONE MORE THOUGHT

We may not always see it or understand it, but God is able to bring good
out of our pain and struggles. We also can't see, today, how he blesses in
heaven those who suffer and stay faithful while on earth. Be confident that
the reward far outweighs the hurt.

"Because you were loyal with small things, I will let you care for
much greater things. Come and share my joy with me."

[Matthew 25:21 NCV]

Little Things

Remember Joseph and Mrs. Potiphar? When Joseph refused her advances, the master's wife made up a story and had Joseph thrown into prison. The warden put Joseph in charge of his cellmates. Joseph could have sat in a corner and mumbled, "I've learned my lesson. I'm not running anything for anybody." But he didn't complain, didn't criticize. He displayed a willing spirit with the prisoners. He even interpreted their dreams. Little things, really. But God took notice.

God is watching how you handle the little things too. If you are faithful over a few matters, he will set you over many (Matthew 25:21). God allowed Joseph to rise to a powerful position, where his wisdom saved the lives of thousands. The reward of good work is greater work.

Do you aspire to great things? Excel in the small things. Show up on time. Finish your work early. Don't complain. Let others grumble in the corner of the prison cell. Not you. You know how God shapes his servants. Today's prisoner may become tomorrow's prime minister. When you are given a task, take it.

ONE MORE THOUGHT

Great artists and composers are remembered for their sweeping, stunning works. Michelangelo and the ceiling of the Sistine Chapel. Beethoven and his Fifth Symphony. Yet each masterpiece was created through the repeated excellence of a single brushstroke and a single note. Greatness is found in the little things.

> "Come to me, all of you who are tired and have
> heavy loads, and I will give you rest."
>
> [Matthew 11:28 NCV]

Depend on Jesus

We often celebrate our independence as individuals and as a nation, but independence in our faith means no faith at all. Following Jesus means depending on him.

As long as you can carry your burdens alone, you don't need a burden bearer. As long as your situation brings you no grief, you will receive no comfort. And as long as you can take him or leave him, you might as well leave him, because he won't be taken half-heartedly. When Jesus is one of many options, he is no option.

But when you are full of sadness and sorrow over your mistakes, when you admit that you have no other choice but to give all your problems to him, and when there is truly no other name that you can call, then go ahead. Tell him all your troubles. Give all your problems to him. He is waiting in the middle of the storm with the answers you need. You can—you must—depend on him.

ONE MORE THOUGHT

Independence Day has long been a national holiday. But for you and me, every day is "Dependence Day" on Jesus. He's the One we need when everything around us is falling apart. He's the One who holds today and tomorrow in his hands. He is our only option.

Do not be overcome by evil, but overcome evil with good.

[Romans 12:21]

God's Math

Captain Sam Brown was serving in Afghanistan when an improvised explosive device turned his Humvee into a Molotov cocktail. Before Sam passed out, he caught a glimpse of his singed face in the mirror. He didn't recognize himself.

By the time I met Sam in 2011, he'd undergone dozens of surgeries. The pain chart didn't have a number high enough to register the agony he felt. Yet, in the midst of the horror, beauty walked in. He gathered the courage to ask out his dietician, Amy Larsen. The two continued to see each other. Sam talked to Amy about God's mercy and led her to Christ. Soon thereafter they were married. And as I write these words, they are the parents of a seven-month-old baby boy. Sam directs a program to aid wounded soldiers.

The physical and emotional stress has taken its toll on their marriage at times. Yet Sam and Amy have come to believe that God's math works differently than ours: *War + near-death + agonizing rehab = wonderful family and hope for a bright future.* In God's hand, intended evil is eventual good.

ONE MORE THOUGHT

We all go through experiences that are a bit like Sam Brown's—calm interrupted by an explosion, leaving us scarred, unable to recognize ourselves. Who can see a bright future at such moments? God can. Despair + God = amazing possibilities.

He'll calm you with his love and delight you with his songs.

[Zephaniah 3:17 MSG]

Love Without Limit

Several hundred feet beneath my chair is a lake, an underground cavern of crystalline water known as the Edwards Aquifer. We South Texans know much about this aquifer. We know its length (175 miles). We know its layout. We know the water is pure. Fresh. It irrigates farms, waters lawns, fills pools, and quenches thirst.

But for all the facts we do know, there is an essential one we don't. We don't know its size. The depth of the cavern? A mystery. Number of gallons? Unmeasured.

"We estimate," a water conservationist said. "We try to measure. But the exact quantity? No one knows."

Bring to mind another unmeasured pool? It might. Not a pool of water but a pool of love. God's love. Aquifer fresh. Pure as April snow. One swallow satisfies the thirsty throat and softens the crusty heart. Dunk a life in God's love, and watch it emerge cleansed and changed. We know the impact of God's love.

But the volume? No person has ever measured it.

ONE MORE THOUGHT

God's love is without limit. Think you care for your dog? God loves you more. Think you love sausage and mushroom pizza? God tops that. Think you love your friends, your parents, your brother and sister? God loves you even more than this. Face it—you can't outlove God.

Let us, then, feel very sure that we can come before
God's throne where there is grace.

[Hebrews 4:16 NCV]

Let Your Kingdom Come

Jesus tells us, "This is how you should pray: 'Our Father in heaven, let your name be kept holy. Let your kingdom come'" (Matthew 6:9–10 GOD'S WORD).

When you say, "Let your kingdom come," you are inviting the Messiah himself to walk into your world. "Come, my King! Take your place as our ruler. Be present in my heart. Be present in my classroom. Come into my family. Be Lord of my friendships, my fears, and my doubts." This is no feeble request; it's a bold appeal for God to occupy every corner of your life. It is saying you understand that coaches, teachers, principals, and presidents do not have ultimate authority. Only him.

Who are you to ask such a thing? Who are you to ask God to take control of your world? You are his child, for heaven's sake! And so you can ask boldly.

ONE MORE THOUGHT

Ever wonder how you should talk to God? Read Matthew 6:5–14. It is specific instruction on how you should pray. When you talk to him, invite him to rule your life as your King. Be bold in your request. After all, your King commands it.

Do not say to your neighbor, "Come back tomorrow and I'll give it to you"—
when you already have it with you.

[Proverbs 3:28 NIV]

Now, Not Later

When Jesus lands on the shore of Bethsaida, he leaves the Sea of Galilee and steps into a sea of humanity (Mark 6:34). Keep in mind, he has crossed the sea to get away from the crowds. He longs to relax with his followers. He needs anything but another crowd of thousands to teach and heal. But his love for people overcomes his need for rest.

We often procrastinate, putting off homework or chores. We also postpone serving others. Yet the Bible tells us, "Do not withhold good from those to whom it is due, when it is in your power to act" (Proverbs 3:27 NIV). Have you followed up with the gal you prayed with last week? Have you visited the grandfather you promised last month to see?

Can you imagine Jesus telling the crowd, "Come back tomorrow, I'll heal you then"? He saw the need and met it that moment. That's a wise approach for me and you as well.

ONE MORE THOUGHT

When we put things off, it usually ends up creating stress and hurt for not only ourselves but also the people around us. That's true for tasks and appointments. It also applies to relationships. When the Holy Spirit nudges you to encourage or help someone, don't wait. Deal with it in the moment, just as Jesus did.

"After I rise from the dead, I will go ahead of you into Galilee."

[Matthew 26:32 NCV]

The Only Explanation

Remember the fear of Christ's followers at his arrest? They ran. Scared as cats in a dog pound.

But fast-forward forty days. Bankrupt traitors have become a force of life-changing fury. Peter is preaching in the very precinct where Christ was arrested. Followers of Christ defy the enemies of Christ. Whip them and they'll worship. Lock them up and they'll launch a jailhouse ministry. As bold after the resurrection as they were cowardly before it.

There must be an explanation. Greed? They made no money. Power? They gave all the credit to Christ. Popularity? Most were killed for their beliefs.

Only one explanation remains—a resurrected Christ and his Holy Spirit. The courage of these men and women was forged in the fire of the empty tomb. You can call on this same courage. Whether you're giving an oral report on Romania or telling the world about Christ, his strength is always with you.

ONE MORE THOUGHT

Nobody makes a comeback like Christ. Old rock stars and ballplayers sometimes surprise us with a performance that seems beyond their years, but rising from the dead is reserved for Jesus only. The next time you need courage for a comeback, remember what Christ did. His power is in you.

"Give us each day the food we need."

[Luke 11:3 NLT]

Give Today a Chance

My friend and I went on a hill-country bicycle trek. A few minutes into the trip I began to tire. Within a half hour my thighs ached and my lungs heaved like a beached whale. I could scarcely pump the pedals. I'm no Tour de France contender, but neither am I a newcomer, yet I felt like one. After forty-five minutes I had to dismount and catch my breath. That's when my partner spotted the problem. Both rear brakes were rubbing my back tire! Rubber grips contested every pedal stroke.

Don't we do the same? Guilt presses on one side. Dread drags the other. No wonder we get so tired. We sabotage our day, wiring it for disaster, lugging along yesterday's troubles, downloading tomorrow's struggles. Regret over the past, stress over the future. We aren't giving the day a chance.

What can we do? Here's my proposal: consult Jesus. Entrust your day to his oversight. "Give us day by day our daily bread" (Luke 11:3). Leave yesterday behind. Let tomorrow wait. Give today a chance.

ONE MORE THOUGHT

Sometimes you feel as if the world and its problems are crushing you. Don't pick up that load—it's too heavy! Ask God to provide what you need for today. Let him worry about the rest. When you do, you'll enjoy the journey a whole lot more.

> "Anything you did for even the least of my people here, you also did for me."
>
> [Matthew 25:40 NCV]

To See God

When Francis of Asissi turned his back on wealth to seek God in simplicity, he took off his robes and walked out of the city. He soon encountered a leper on the side of the road. He passed him, then stopped and went back and hugged the diseased man. Francis then continued on his journey. After a few steps he turned to look again at the leper, but no one was there.

For the rest of his life, he believed the leper was Jesus Christ. He may have been right.

Jesus lives in the forgotten. He has taken up residence in the ignored. He has made a mansion in the middle of the sick. Do you know of anyone who's forgotten, ignored, or sick? An elderly neighbor? A teen who seems to have no friends? A friend's mom, dealing with cancer? If you want to see God, you must go among the broken and beaten, and there you will see him.

ONE MORE THOUGHT

Read the words of Jesus in Matthew 25:31–46. It would seem that Christ is all around us. If he is telling us that the homeless stranger at the side of the road is Jesus, what should we do the next time we see him?

Christ was offered once to bear the sins of many.
[Hebrews 9:28]

We Need a Savior

Y ou can't forgive me for my sins nor can I forgive you for yours. Two kids in a mud puddle can't clean each other. They need someone clean. Someone spotless.

We need someone clean too. That's why we need a savior.

Trying to make it to heaven on our own goodness is like trying to get to the moon on a moonbeam; nice idea, but try it and see what happens.

Listen. Quit trying to take care of your own guilt. You can't do it. There's no way. Not with drugs or drama or great grades or perfect church attendance. Sorry. I don't care how bad you are. You can't be bad enough to forget it. And I don't care how good you are. You can't be good enough to overcome it.

You need the One who came to earth specifically for you. You need the only One who can wash away every mistake with a holy bath. You need a Savior.

ONE MORE THOUGHT

Can you hit a home run in every at-bat? Throw a touchdown pass on every attempt? Bowl a strike in every frame? No one does that. We can't perform well enough to earn forgiveness. So don't try. God sent a solution. A Savior.

It is not our love for God; it is God's love for us. He sent
his Son to die in our place to take away our sins.

[1 John 4:10 NCV]

God's Dream

What great deeds have you attempted? Running for a school
record on the track? Winning the state spelling bee? Organizing a multi-school food drive? Dancing for twenty-four hours
straight?

When it comes to our relationship with God, we have attempted
to reach the moon but barely made it off the ground. We tried
to swim the Atlantic, but couldn't get beyond the reef. We've
attempted to scale the Everest of salvation, but we have yet to leave
the base camp, much less make it up the slope. The quest is simply
too great. We don't need more supplies or muscle or technique; we
need a helicopter.

Can't you hear it hovering?

"God has a way to make people right with him" (Romans 3:21
NCV). We need to understand this truth. God's highest dream
is not to make us rich, not to make us successful or popular or
famous. God's dream is to make us right with him.

ONE MORE THOUGHT

We all dream of great triumphs at one time or another. Deeds that will make
us famous, even legends—at least in our neighborhood! God has different
dreams, however. He wants you and I, his children, to be close to him for
eternity.

Wear Christ's Character

Clothing can symbolize character. The Bible often describes our behavior as the clothes we wear. Peter urges us to be "clothed with humility" (1 Peter 5:5). David speaks of evil people who clothe themselves "with cursing" (Psalm 109:18).

What character are you wearing? Who are you when no one is looking? Do you adjust your character wardrobe to fit in with the crowd you happen to be with, or are you the same person in each situation? People of good and godly character are truthful, faithful, trustworthy, kind, helpful, and respectful no matter who they're with or where they are.

What does this look like? The life of Jesus. The character of Christ never changed, even when he faced execution. We know that Jesus wore a tunic that was "seamless, woven in one piece from top to bottom" (John 19:23 NLT). It matched his character. Seamless. Coordinated. Unified. He was like his robe: uninterrupted perfection. The perfect model for us.

ONE MORE THOUGHT

Are you wearing the character of Christ? If not, put on the Word of God each morning. When getting into the Bible becomes as routine as getting dressed, you'll find your character matching the model of Jesus.

Honor your father and mother . . . that it may go well with you.

[Ephesians 6:2–3 NIV]

Honor Your Parents

Parents. They've controlled your life for so long. They still do. But now you're older, wiser, more mature. You need them to let go a little. You want to honor them, but they're driving you crazy!

I am a son and a parent, so I see both sides of the coin. As a son, I too wanted more freedom and the chance to make my own decisions. As a parent, I understand fearing that our children will make the wrong decisions and longing to protect them from the mean ol' world. So what do you do?

The Bible says, "Children, obey your parents in the Lord, for this is right" (Ephesians 6:1 NIV). As long as your mom and dad aren't asking you to go against what God desires, you are called to obedience. Tough sometimes, but true.

This doesn't mean you can't talk to them about your concerns and frustrations. They were teens once themselves. After a bit of gentle prodding, they may remember—and let go just a little more.

ONE MORE THOUGHT

Obeying your parents isn't always easy when you don't agree with their decisions. I get that. Here's another way to look at it: God gave you your mom. He provided your dad. When you obey and please them, you're doing his will. You're obeying and pleasing God.

> When it's sin versus grace, grace wins hands down.
>
> [Romans 5:21 MSG]

Overcoming Guilt with Grace

Satan never shuts up. The apostle John called him the accuser: "For the Accuser of our brothers and sisters has been thrown down to earth—the one who accuses them before our God day and night" (Revelation 12:10 NLT). He gets people to peddle his poison. Friends dredge up your past: "Remember that time you cheated on the test?" Preachers proclaim all guilt and no grace: "You don't measure up to God's standards." Your parents own a travel agency that specializes in guilt trips: "Why can't you grow up?" "Would it kill you to work a little harder?" "You could be so pretty. When are you going to lose a little weight?"

Jesus overcomes the devil's guilt with grace. You are who your Creator says you are: *Spiritually alive. Connected to God. Awake to your potential. An honored child.*

Remember, when God looks at you, he sees Jesus first. It boils down to this choice: Do you trust your Advocate or your accuser?

ONE MORE THOUGHT

Words, words, words . . . we're bombarded by them every day. Texts from friends. Lectures by teachers. Ads on the Internet. Lyrics on the iPod. Ever feel overwhelmed? Try tuning in to a single voice, the one that counts the most. It's the one that whispers of grace.

God is my strength and power, and He makes my way perfect.

[2 Samuel 22:33]

"Yes, You Can"

Two types of thoughts continually compete for your attention. One says, "Yes, you can." The other says, "No, you can't." One says, "God will help you." The other lies, "God has left you." One proclaims God's strengths; the other lists your failures. One tries to build you up; the other seeks to tear you down.

And here's the great news: you select the voice you hear. Why listen to the mockers? Why heed their voices? Why give ear to pea brains and hecklers when you can, with the same ear, listen to the voice of God?

A young woman fights her anxiety by memorizing long sections of Scripture. A young man unplugs the Internet after checking his e-mail so he won't be tempted by pornography. A student tires of her negative, gossiping friends and starts eating lunch with classmates she barely knows.

Turn a deaf ear to the old voices. Open a wide eye to the new choices.

ONE MORE THOUGHT

The decision is always ours. God does not force us to believe in him, nor does he make us listen to him. We always have the choice to turn to him or to the tantalizing voices that surround us. I vote for his voice. What is he saying to you right now?

By humility and the fear of the LORD are riches and honor and life.

[Proverbs 22:4]

Think of Yourself Less

God hates arrogance. He hates to see his children fall. God hates what pride does to his children. He doesn't dislike arrogance. He hates it. Could he state it any clearer than Proverbs 8:13: "I hate pride and arrogance" (NIV)? And then a few chapters later: "GOD can't stomach arrogance or pretense; believe me, he'll put those upstarts in their place" (16:5 MSG).

You don't want God to do that. It's far wiser to climb down the mountain than to fall from it.

Pursue humility. Humility doesn't mean you think less of yourself but that you think of yourself less. "Don't cherish exaggerated ideas of yourself or your importance, but try to have a sane estimate of your capabilities by the light of the faith that God has given to you" (Romans 12:3 PHILLIPS).

Resist the place of celebrity. "Go sit in a seat that is not important. When the host comes to you, he may say, 'Friend, move up here to a more important place.' Then all the other guests will respect you" (Luke 14:10 NCV).

Wouldn't you rather be invited up than put down?

ONE MORE THOUGHT

Humility. Think of yourself less. When you're blessed with a pile of birthday presents, remember those who aren't. When you earn a spot on the varsity team, comfort those who tried and fell short. God hates pride, but he loves the humble.

> "Unless a person is born from above, it's not possible to see what I'm pointing to—to God's kingdom."
>
> [John 3:3 MSG]

New Birth

Jesus motions for his guest to sit. Nicodemus does and initiates the most famous conversation in the Bible: "Rabbi, we know that You are a teacher come from God; for no one can do these signs that You do unless God is with him" (John 3:2).

Nicodemus begins with what he "knows." *I've done my homework*, he implies. *Your work impresses me.* Nicodemus expects some hospitable chitchat. None comes. Jesus makes no mention of Nicodemus's VIP status, good intentions, or academic credentials. To Jesus, they don't matter. He simply issues this proclamation: "Unless one is born again, he cannot see the kingdom of God" (v. 3).

Behold the Grand Canyon of Scripture. Nicodemus stands on one side, Jesus on the other, and Christ pulls no punches about their differences. Nicodemus inhabits a land of good efforts and hard work. Give God your best, his philosophy says, and God does the rest.

Jesus' response? Your best won't do. Your works don't work. Your finest efforts don't mean squat. Unless you decide to live your life for Christ, you can't even see what God is up to.

ONE MORE THOUGHT

Joining Jesus isn't about trying really hard or piling up enough extra credit points. It's about our new birth—about confessing all sin and choosing to believe in and follow him. We try to complicate it, but it's that simple. New birth. New life.

For God all things are possible.

[Mark 10:27 NCV]

God in a Box?

When you think about God, don't try to reduce him to your limited imagination. Don't put him in a box. He's so much more than that.

Our questions show how little we understand him: How can God be everywhere at one time? (Who says God is bound by a body?) How can God hear all the prayers that come to him? (Perhaps his ears are different from ours.) How can God be the Father, the Son, and the Holy Spirit? (Could it be that heaven has a different set of physics than earth?) If people down here won't forgive us, how much more are we guilty before a holy God? (Oh, just the opposite. God is always able to give grace when we humans can't—he invented it.)

The moment you begin to think *God wouldn't . . . God won't . . . God can't*, stop and think again. He's bigger, stronger, more power-ful, and more loving than you'll ever know. Put him in the largest box you can imagine? Not a chance. He'll never fit.

ONE MORE THOUGHT

We're used to measuring our world with numbers. Seven classes a day. Sixty-four inches tall. Two thousand songs in the iPod. But can we measure the grains of sands on a beach? The stars in the sky? Planets in the universe? Nope. Can we measure God? Nope again. He'll never be reduced to a number.

"All people will know that you are my followers if you love each other."

[John 13:35 NCV]

Footprints

Watch a small boy follow his dad through the snow. He stretches to step where his dad stepped. Not an easy task. His small legs extend as far as they can so his feet can fall in his father's prints. The father, seeing what the son is doing, smiles and begins taking shorter steps, so the son can follow.

It's a picture of discipleship. In our faith we follow in someone's steps. A parent, a teacher, a hero—none of us are the first to walk the trail. All of us have someone we follow.

In our faith we leave footprints to guide others. A younger sister, a friend, a new Christian. They look up to us. They see that we have something they want and need. We do all we can to help them follow. Nobody should be left to walk the trail alone.

ONE MORE THOUGHT

You will have many chances in life to disciple someone—to show them the path to Jesus. Try to take advantage of every one. No effort is more important. Who is watching you today, ready to walk in your footprints?

With God everything is possible.

[Matthew 19:26 NLT]

God Can Handle It

Nature is God's workshop. The sky is his résumé. The universe is his business card. You want to know who God is? See what he has done. You want to know his power? Take a look at his creation. Curious about his strength? Pay a visit to his home address: 1 Billion Starry Sky Avenue.

Our atmosphere of sin can't reach him. The timeline of history can't contain him. The weariness of our bodies has no effect on him.

What controls you doesn't control him. What troubles you doesn't trouble him. What fatigues you doesn't fatigue him. Is an eagle disturbed by traffic? No, he rises above it. Is the whale perturbed by a hurricane? Of course not, he plunges beneath it. Is the lion flustered by the mouse standing directly in his way? No, he steps over it. How much more is God able to soar above, plunge beneath, and step over the troubles of the earth!

Think he can handle our puny problems? Of course he can. He's God.

ONE MORE THOUGHT

Read the first chapter of Genesis. What kind of being can create . . . everything? A spiritual One. A holy One. The One and only God. We try to think of him in human terms, but we can never really comprehend him. He's always been. And he'll always be more than enough for you and me.

"Be still, and know that I am God."

[Psalm 46:10]

God Works While You Wait

We don't like to wait. We are the giddyup generation. We frown at the person who takes eleven items into the ten-item express checkout. We drum our fingers while the song downloads or the microwave heats our burrito. "Come on, come on." We want six-pack abs in ten minutes and minute rice in thirty seconds. We don't like to wait. Not on the doctor, the traffic, the pizza.

Not on God?

You may be waiting for a new room, a new job, a new friend, a new direction. If so, here is what you need to know. *While you wait, God works.* "My Father is always at his work," Jesus said (John 5:17 NIV). God never twiddles his thumbs. He never stops. He takes no vacations. He rested on the seventh day, but got back to work on the eighth and hasn't stopped since. Just because you are idle, don't assume God is. He knows just what you need and just when you need it.

ONE MORE THOUGHT

The world is God's waiting room. We wait on him to give, to heal, to help. And because we can't see what he's up to, we get impatient. But like a play director who prepares all the actors and sets backstage, God is preparing events according to his perfect plan. Just wait and see.

God the Father knew you and chose you long ago.

[1 Peter 1:2 NLT]

You Are First Choice

You are God's child. He saw you, picked you, and placed you. "You did not choose Me, but I chose you" (John 15:16). Before you are a butcher, baker, or computer maker; male, female, Asian, or black, you are God's child. Replacement or fill-in? Hardly. You are his first choice.

Such isn't always the case in life. A groom once leaned over to me, just minutes before I officiated his wedding, and said, "You weren't my first choice." "I wasn't?" "No, the preacher I wanted couldn't make it." "Oh." "But thanks for filling in." "Sure, anytime." I considered signing the marriage license: "Substitute."

You'll never hear such words from God. He chose you. He selected you because he wanted to. He walked onto the auction block where you stood and proclaimed, "This child is mine." And he bought you with the "precious blood of Christ, as of a lamb without blemish and without spot" (1 Peter 1:19).

Remember it. You are God's first choice, now and forever.

ONE MORE THOUGHT

In elementary school, did you ever line up in front of two captains who picked teams for a game? Were you ever humiliated to be one of the very last chosen? Won't happen with God. He's the ultimate captain, and he picks you first every time.

I can do all this through him who gives me strength.

[Philippians 4:13 NIV]

The Bounce-Back Clown

I was about eight years old when, at a neighborhood party, I met the bounce-back clown. He was pear-shaped, narrower at the top than the bottom. Inflated and Bozo-like. As tall as I was. He didn't make music at the touch of a button or recite lines at the pull of a string. He didn't do anything, except this: bounce back.

Knock him down, he popped right up. Clobber him with a bat, pop him in the nose, give him a swift kick to the side, and he would fall down, but not for long. We did our best to level the clown. One punch after the other, each more vicious than before. None of us succeeded. Only later did I learn Bozo's secret: a three-pound counterbalance at his base.

Life comes at us, too, with a fury of flying fists: right hook of rejection, sucker punch of loss. It's a slugfest out there. We too need a counterbalance. It turns out we have one. Not a piece of iron, but a deeply felt faith in God's power and authority.

ONE MORE THOUGHT

When you're fighting off one punch after another, just standing up is a challenge, let alone bouncing back. But you have a secret weapon. You know who has the power, who's in control. You know who wins in the end. So don't be a clown. Call for God's help, and bounce back.

> "I am with you always, to the very end of the age."
>
> [Matthew 28:20 NIV]

He Gives Us Himself

The story is told of a man on an African safari deep in the jungle. The guide before him had a machete and was whacking away the tall weeds and thick underbrush. The traveler, wearied and hot, asked in frustration, "Where are we? Do you know where you are taking me? Where is the path?!" The seasoned guide stopped and looked back at the man and replied, "I am the path."

We ask the same questions, don't we? We ask God, "Where are you taking me? Where is the path?" And he, like the guide, doesn't tell us. Oh, he may give us a hint or two, but that's all. If he did, would we understand? Would we comprehend our location? No, like the traveler, we are ignorant about this jungle. So rather than give us an answer, Jesus gives us a far greater gift. He gives us himself.

ONE MORE THOUGHT

Have you ever been on a tour with an obnoxious guide, one who makes a dozen bad jokes at every stop? Sometimes it isn't the destination that's makes a trip memorable, but the quality of your company on the journey. You'll never find a better guide than Christ.

Live Forgiven!

Nothing brings on fear like being oblivious to mercy. If you haven't accepted God's forgiveness, you are doomed to fear. Nothing can deliver you from the gnawing realization that you have disregarded your Maker and disobeyed his instruction. No pill, pep talk, or possession can set the sinner's heart at ease. You may deaden the fear, but you can't remove it. Only God's grace can.

Have you accepted the forgiveness of Christ? If not, do so. "If we confess our sins, He is faithful and just to forgive us our sins and to cleanse us from all unrighteousness" (1 John 1:9). Your prayer can be as simple as this: *Dear Father, I need forgiveness. I admit that I have turned away from you. Please forgive me. I place my soul in your hands and my trust in your grace. Through Jesus I pray, amen.*

Having received God's forgiveness, live forgiven! When Jesus sets you free, you are free indeed.

ONE MORE THOUGHT

What does it mean to be set free by Jesus? What does it mean to live forgiven? It's knowing that you've admitted your mistakes to God. It's leaving fear and guilt behind. It's finding peace in his plan. It's trusting him and talking and living truth each day.

His peace will guard your hearts and minds as you live in Christ Jesus.

[Philippians 4:7 NLT]

Perfect Peace

A life lived for God is a life that can be filled with peace. Not a random, wimpy, earthly peace, but *his* peace. Imported from heaven. God offers you the same tranquility that fills his throne room.

Do you think he battles anxiety? You suppose he ever wrings his hands or asks the angels for antacids? Of course not. A problem is no more a challenge to God than a twig is to an elephant. God enjoys perfect peace because God enjoys perfect power.

And he offers his peace to you. A peace that will "guard your hearts and minds as you live in Christ Jesus" (Philippians 4:7 NLT). Paul uses a military metaphor here. The Philippians, living in a garrison town, were accustomed to the Roman sentries maintaining their watch. Before any enemy could get inside, he had to pass through the guards. God gives you the same offer. His supernatural peace overshadows you, guarding your heart.

ONE MORE THOUGHT

Read Philippians 4:4–7. Paul is telling us to tell God about *all* our worries and requests. Only when we give them to him will we be calm in mind and heart. There is peace, and there is *perfect* peace. Choose the kind that comes from the Creator.

Accept teaching from his mouth, and keep his words in your heart.

[Job 22:22 NCV]

God's Language

There is no language God will not speak. Which leads us to a delightful question. What language is he speaking to you? I'm not referring to French or German but to the day-to-day drama of your life.

There are times he speaks the "language of plenty." Is your tummy full? Is your closet well stocked? Got a little jingle in your pocket? Don't be so proud of what you have that you miss what you need to hear. Could it be you have much so you can give much?

Or how about the "language of pain"? Talk about a dialect we try to avoid. But you and I both know how clearly God speaks in hospital hallways and sickbeds. When we're in trouble, his words seem to take on new meaning and urgency. Is God telling you something through your struggles?

God speaks all languages—including yours. What language is God speaking to you?

ONE MORE THOUGHT

We may not hear the audible voice of God, but he finds many other ways to speak to us. How does he speak to you? Do you get a strong sense of his desires when you pray? Do you sense him arranging events in your life? Whatever it is, learn his language so you can know his will.

LORD, remember your mercy and love that you have shown since long ago.

[Psalm 25:6 NCV]

Our Abba

Recently, my daughter Jenna and I spent several days in the old city of Jerusalem. One afternoon, as we were exiting a gate, we found ourselves behind an orthodox Jewish family—a father and his three small girls. One of the daughters, just four or five years old, fell a few steps behind and couldn't see her father. "Abba!" she called to him. He spotted her and immediately took her hand.

When the signal changed, he led her and her sisters through the intersection. In the middle of the street, he reached down and swung her up into his arms as they continued their journey.

Isn't that what we all need? An Abba who will hear when we call? Who will take our hand when we are weak? Who will guide us through the hectic intersections of life? Don't we all need an Abba who will swing us up into his arms and carry us home? We all need a Father.

ONE MORE THOUGHT

Did you have this kind of dad, one who always listened for your cries for help, one who willingly steered you through some of you toughest times? Or was your father too busy or distant to care? No matter. We each have a heavenly Father who takes us into his arms. We can call him Abba.

God has not called us to be dirty-minded and full of lust but to be holy and clean.

[1 Thessalonians 4:7 TLB]

Don't Light the Match

The Internet is a great tool, but it comes with hidden dangers. Pornography is one of them.

For many, many guys, this is a big deal. They figure a few glances won't hurt anybody. They think they can stop when they want. For those who can, unwanted images still imprint on the mind. For those who cannot, an addiction is born.

You can't play with fire and not get burned. So don't light the match. The Bible never says to *battle* sexual sin, *struggle* against sexual sin . . . no, our call is to "run away from sexual sin" (1 Corinthians 6:18 NCV). Just because a girl dresses to get your attention, you don't have to look. Just because pictures appear, you don't have to view them. Cover your eyes and guard your thoughts! You will live tomorrow the thoughts you tolerate today. Use this to your advantage. Want great relationships tomorrow? Think about the strengths of your friendships today. Want to enjoy more faith tomorrow? Meditate on God's Word today. You are what you think.

ONE MORE THOUGHT

Guys are visual. That's how God made us. So gals, help us out here by choosing reserved over racy in your wardrobe. And guys, if you're having a problem with pornography, tell somebody who can help you deal with it. The longer you wait, the harder it is to escape.

AUGUST

───────────

And not only that, but we also glory in tribulations,
knowing that tribulation produces perseverance; and
perseverance, character; and character, hope.

[Romans 5:3–4]

Jesus will keep you strong until the end so that there will be no
wrong in you on the day our Lord Jesus Christ comes again.

[1 Corinthians 1:8 NCV]

God's Not Finished with You

God is not finished with you yet. Oh, you may think he is. You may think you've peaked, that your character and faith won't develop any further, that you'll never amount to more than you are now, that you'll never accomplish much. You may think God's got someone else in mind for the important jobs. If so, think again.

"God began doing a good work in you, and I am sure he will continue it until it is finished when Jesus Christ comes again" (Philippians 1:6 NCV). Did you see what God is doing? A good work in you. Did you see when he will be finished? When Jesus comes again.

You can't yet know what God is doing and will do with you. He's still shaping you on the inside to bring glory to him on the outside. You can't imagine the wonders he has planned. God's not finished with you yet.

ONE MORE THOUGHT

Think of some of the great surprises you've had in your life. Maybe it was the Christmas gift you thought your family couldn't afford or the overseas mission trip you never thought you'd make. God has more happy surprises in store for you, both in who you are and what you'll do. Let him do his wonderful work.

> Don't get angry. Don't be upset; it only leads to trouble.
> [Psalm 37:8 NCV]

Deal with Your Anger

*A*nger. It's easy to define: the noise of the soul. *Anger.* The unseen irritant of the heart. *Anger.* The relentless invader of silence. The louder it gets, the more desperate we become.

You may be thinking, *You don't have any idea how hard my life has been.* And you're right, I don't. Abused? Betrayed? Rejected? Ignored? I don't know your story. But I have a very clear idea how miserable your future will be unless you deal with your anger.

X-ray the world of the enraged, and you'll find a tumor of bitterness: black, menacing, malignant. Cancer of the spirit. Its fatal fibers creep around the edge of the heart and ravage it. Yesterday you can't alter, but your reaction to yesterday you can. The past you cannot change, but your response to your past you can. The Bible has the answer: "Stop being bitter and angry and mad at others. . . . Instead, be kind and merciful, and forgive others, just as God forgave you because of Christ" (Ephesians 4:31–32 CEV).

ONE MORE THOUGHT

When someone hurts you, it's natural to be angry. But if you stay angry, you hurt only yourself. When you forgive, you're not saying what happened to you was okay. You're saying you're not going to let it destroy the rest of your life.

Come, let's worship him and bow down. Let's kneel before the Lord who made us.

[Psalm 95:6 NCV]

Worship: It's Personal

Worship. In two thousand years we haven't worked out how to do it. We still struggle for the right words in prayer. We still fumble over Scripture. We don't know when to kneel. We don't know when to stand. We don't know how to pray. Worship is tough stuff.

For that reason, God gave us the Psalms—a praise book for God's people. This collection of hymns and requests is strung together by one thread—a heart hungry for God. Some psalms are defiant. Others are reverent. Some are to be sung. Others are to be prayed. Some are intensely personal. Others are written as if the whole world would use them.

The very variety should remind us that worship is personal. No secret formula exists. What moves you may be a dead end for another. Some of us like to throw our hands in the air. Others of us close our eyes and silently reflect on God. Each of us worships differently. But each of us should worship.

ONE MORE THOUGHT

Is worship awkward for you? Maybe that's because you're trying to do it the "right" way. Read through the Psalms. Look at all the different ways people praised God. He appreciates all the ways you choose to honor him.

Nothing . . . in the whole world will ever be able
to separate us from the love of God.

[Romans 8:39 NCV]

You're Something Special

Y ou want to know how long God's love will last. Not just on Easter Sunday when your shirt is tucked in and your hair is fixed. Not when you're positive, pumped up, and ready to tackle world hunger. Not then. You know how he feels about you then. Even *you* like you then.

You want to know how he feels about you when you snap at anything that moves, when your thoughts are gutter-level, when your tongue is sharp enough to slice a rock. How does he feel about you then?

Can anything separate us from the love Christ has for us?

God answered our question before we asked it. So we'd see his answer, he lit the sky with a star. So we'd hear it, he filled the night with a choir. So we'd believe it, he did what no man had ever dreamed. He became flesh and came to live among us. He placed his hand on the shoulder of humanity and said, "You're something special."

ONE MORE THOUGHT

Nothing will separate you from the love of God. His grip on you is stronger than the stickiest super glue. No matter what you say, think, or do, you can't escape his love. He sees you and smiles. You will be special to him forever.

For our light and momentary troubles are achieving for us an eternal glory.

[2 Corinthians 4:17 NIV]

For Just a Moment

If grains of sand measured your heavenly and earthly lives, how would they stack up? Heaven would be every grain of sand on every beach on earth, plus more. Earthly life would be one hundredth of one grain of sand. Need a phrase to summarize the length of your life on earth? Try: "Just a moment."

Wasn't this the phrase of choice for Paul? "For our light and *momentary* troubles are achieving for us an eternal glory that far outweighs them all" (2 Corinthians 4:17 NIV). The apostle had been "beaten times without number, often in danger of death." He writes, "Five times I received from the Jews thirty-nine lashes. Three times I was beaten with rods, once I was stoned, three times I was shipwrecked, a night and a day I have spent in the deep" (2 Corinthians 11:23–25 NASB). These, in Paul's words, are light troubles to be endured for just a moment.

What if we took the same attitude toward life? What if we saw our tough times as a grain of sand and saw heaven as endless beaches?

ONE MORE THOUGHT

We *will* have troubles. Jesus told us that. And they *will* hurt. No doubt about it. But in a week, a month, a year—and most certainly from the perspective of heaven—you'll barely remember the stress and pain. Hang on. It gets so much better.

"Whoever compels you to go one mile, go with him two. Give to him who asks you, and from him who wants to borrow from you do not turn away."

[Matthew 5:41–42]

Society of the Second Mile

Jesus created what we might call the Society of the Second Mile. He presented a new option. Serve the ones who hate you; forgive the ones who hurt you. Take the lowest place, not the highest; seek to serve, not to be served. Retaliate, not in kind, but in kindness.

Roman soldiers could legally force Jewish citizens into carrying a soldier's load for one mile.[7] With nothing more than a command, the soldiers could pull a farmer out of his field or a merchant out of his shop.

In such a case, Jesus said, "Give more than requested." At the end of one mile, keep going. Surprise the sandals off the soldier by saying, "I haven't done enough for you. I'm going a second mile." Do more than demanded. And do so with joy and grace!

How can you join the Society of the Second Mile? When your parents ask you to clean the kitchen, pick up your bedroom too. When your sister steals your best T-shirt, offer her two more. You'll shock them. You'll make Jesus smile.

ONE MORE THOUGHT

Going a second mile might sound like a grim assignment. It isn't. The more you do it, the more you'll enjoy the surprised reactions of those you unexpectedly serve. More important, each mile will warm your own heart and move you a little closer to Jesus.

When you believed, you were marked in him with a seal, the promised Holy Spirit.

[Ephesians 1:13 NIV]

Sealed by the Spirit

A soul sealed by God is safe.

For a short time in college, I worked at a vacuum-cleaner plant. We assembled the appliance from plug to hose. The last step on the assembly line was "sealing and shipping." By this point, the company had invested hours and dollars in the machine. So they took extra care to protect their product. They mummified it in bubble wrap, secured it with Styrofoam, wrapped the box with tough-to-tear tape, stamped the destination on the box, and belted it inside the truck. That machine was secure.

But compared to God's care of his children, workers dumped bare machines into the back of a pickup truck. God vacuum-seals us with his strongest force: his Spirit. He slips us into a suit of spiritual armor, surrounds us with angels, and inhabits us himself. Even the president doesn't enjoy that level of security.

Christ paid too high a price to leave us unguarded. "Remember, he has identified you as his own, guaranteeing that you will be saved on the day of redemption" (Ephesians 4:30 NLT). You may slip—indeed you will—but you will not fall from safety.

ONE MORE THOUGHT

What is your most valuable possession? Your laptop? Your iPod? The ring your grandmother gave you? The car you paid for with your own hard-earned money? Whatever it is, no matter how much you treasure it, you mean far more to God. You belong to him.

O God, you are my God; I earnestly search for you. My
soul thirsts for you; my whole body longs for you.

[Psalm 63:1 NLT]

Are You Satisfied?

Satisfied? That is one thing we are not. We are not satisfied.

We buy the latest laptop, the sleekest smart phone, the hottest hair product. Two weeks later, we're already planning our next purchase. We vacation in Hawaii and fill up on sun, fun, and good food. But we're not even on the way home before we dread the end of the trip and begin planning another.

We are not satisfied. As a kid we say, "If only I were a teenager." As a teen we say, "If only I were an adult." As an adult, "If only I were married." As a spouse, "If only I had kids."

We are not satisfied. Why is contentment so difficult? Because there is nothing on earth that can satisfy our deepest longing. We long to see God. And we won't be satisfied until we do.

ONE MORE THOUGHT

Some describe our longing for God as a hole in the heart. Can you feel it? You try to fill the hole with stuff, with friends and good times, with food, with busyness. It can help for a time, but it never lasts. Fill up instead on God. He is the only One who satisfies.

He who heeds the word wisely will find good, and
whoever trusts in the LORD, happy is he.

[Proverbs 16:20]

The Holy Gift of Sex

Run away from sexual sin! No other sin so clearly affects the body as this one does. For sexual immorality is a sin against your own body" (1 Corinthians 6:18 NLT). Paul wrote these words to Corinthians with a sex obsession.

No message swims more upstream than this one. You know the sexual anthem of our day: "I'll do what I want. It's my body." God's firm response? "No, it's not. It's mine."

Be quick to understand, God is not antisex. After all, he developed the whole package. He views sexual intimacy the way I view our family Bible. Passed down from my father's side, it is one hundred years old and twelve inches thick. To me, beyond value. So when I need a step stool, I don't reach for that Bible. If the foot of my bed breaks, I don't use the family Bible as a prop. We reserve it for special times and keep it in a chosen place.

Regard sex the same way—as a holy gift to be opened in a special place at special times. The special place is marriage, and the time is with your spouse.

ONE MORE THOUGHT

The lure of physical attraction is a strong one. Young men and women (older ones too) have been dealing with it since, well, the beginning. Trust God on this one—the short-term pleasure isn't worth the long-term consequences. If you find yourself in a tempting situation, take Paul's advice: run!

In all your ways acknowledge Him, and He shall direct your paths.

[Proverbs 3:6]

Prayer Is This Simple

My father let me climb onto his lap . . . when he drove! Half a century ago, no one cared. Especially on a flat-as-a-skillet West Texas oil field where rabbits outnumber people.

I loved it. Did it matter that I couldn't see over the dash? That my feet stopped two feet shy of the brake and accelerator? Not at all. I helped my dad drive his truck. Did I fear driving into the ditch? Overturning the curve? Running the tire into a rut? Not at all. Dad's hands were next to mine, his eyes keener than mine. I was fearless! Anyone can drive a car from the lap of a father.

And anyone can pray from the same perspective. Prayer is the practice of sitting calmly in God's lap and placing our hands on his steering wheel. He handles the speed and hard curves and ensures safe arrival. And we offer our requests; we ask God to "take this cup away" (Mark 14:36). This cup of disease, betrayal, rejection, conflict, or insecurity. Prayer is this simple.

ONE MORE THOUGHT

God makes it easy for us. We don't need an appointment to talk to him. We don't have to fill out a form or submit questions in advance. Praying is as simple as climbing into a father's lap. Why don't you try it right now?

The heavens declare the glory of God; the skies proclaim the work of his hands.

[Psalm 19:1 NIV]

Our Star Maker

Venture away from the city lights on a clear night, and look up at the sky. That fuzzy band of white light is our galaxy, the Milky Way. One hundred billion stars.[8] Our galaxy is one of billions of others![9] Who can conceive of such a universe, let alone infinite numbers of universes?

No one can. But let's try anyway. Suppose you board a jet and zip through our solar system at a blistering six hundred miles per hour. In 16.5 days you'll reach the moon, in seventeen years you'll pass the sun, and in 690 years you can enjoy dinner on Pluto. After seven centuries you haven't even left our solar system, much less our galaxy.[10]

Our universe is God's finest missionary. "The heavens declare the glory of God" (Psalm 19:1 NIV). A house implies a builder; a painting suggests a painter. Don't stars suggest a star maker? Doesn't creation imply a creator? Look above you.

If God can make a billion galaxies, can't he make good out of our bad and make sense out of our faltering lives? Of course he can. He is God.

ONE MORE THOUGHT

Choose a clear night—maybe tonight. Find a spot where you can really see all those stars. Give them a good look—not just a glance, but a penetrating gaze. Do you think they just "happened" into existence? Or do you think God had something to do with it? Search your heart for your answer.

As all of us reflect the Lord's glory with faces that are not covered with veils, we are being changed into his image with ever-increasing glory.

[2 Corinthians 3:18 GOD'S WORD]

Son Reflectors

What does the moon do? It generates no light. Apart from the sun, the moon is nothing more than a pitch-black, pock-marked rock. But properly positioned, the moon beams. A clod of dirt becomes a source of inspiration and romance. The moon reflects the greater light.

What would happen if we accepted our place as Son reflectors? Such a shift would probably be a big change, however. We've been demanding our way and stamping our feet since God made us. Aren't we all born with a default drive set on selfishness? *I want a girlfriend who makes me happy and friends who always ask my opinion. I want a wardrobe that flatters me and video games that entertain me and a family that serves me.*

How can we be bumped off of self-center? We move from me-focus to God-focus by thinking about him. Talking about him. Following the advice of the apostle Paul: "As all of us reflect the Lord's glory with faces that are not covered with veils, we are being changed into his image with ever-increasing glory" (2 Corinthians 3:18 GOD'S WORD). His light changes us.

ONE MORE THOUGHT

Mirror, mirror, on the wall, who's the worthiest one of all? Believe it or not, it isn't you or me. It's him. The One God. He is the sun to our moon. Our job is simply to put ourselves in position to reflect his brilliance.

He will keep me safe in his dwelling.

[Psalm 27:5 NIV]

God's House

No matter how much we love our home, there are times when we just want to get out of the house for a while, right? Yet David, the man after God's own heart, said, "I'm asking GOD for one thing, only one thing: to live with him in his house my whole life long" (Psalm 27:4 MSG).

What is this house of God that David seeks? Is David describing a physical structure? Does he long for a building with four walls and a door through which he can enter but never exit? No. Our Lord "does not live in temples built by human hands" (Acts 17:24 NIV). When David says, "I will dwell in the house of the LORD forever" (Psalm 23:6 NIV), he's not saying he wants to get away from people. He's saying that he yearns to be in God's presence, wherever he is.

The great thing about being with God? Wherever we are, we're home.

ONE MORE THOUGHT

Home. It's the place where you eat. Sleep. Read. Hang out. Comfortable because it's familiar, because it's where your family is. Yet a big part of your family is with you no matter where you go or live. God is your heavenly Father, and you can live in his house no matter where you are.

God is strong and can help you not to fall.

[Jude v. 24 NCV]

The Climb

Y ou and I are on a great climb. The wall is high, and the stakes are higher. You took your first step the day you accepted Christ as the Son of God. He gave you his harness—the Holy Spirit. In your hands he placed a rope—his Word.

Your first steps were confident and strong, but with the journey came weariness, and with the height came fear. You lost your footing. You lost your focus. You lost your grip, and you fell. For a moment, which seemed like forever, you tumbled wildly. Out of control. Out of self-control. Disoriented. Dislodged. Falling.

But then the rope tightened, and the tumble stopped. You hung in the harness and found it to be strong. You grasped the rope and found it to be reliable. And though you can't see your guide, you know him. You know he is strong. You know he is able to keep you from falling.

And so you climb once more.

ONE MORE THOUGHT

Our faith journey often feels like climbing a mountain. The thrill of starting out. The amazement at the discoveries along the way. The fatigue. The worries. The slips and falls. The excitement as we near our goal. And when we finally reach the mountaintop? There's no joy that compares.

How to Fix a Bad Day

Next time your day goes in the dumpster, here is what you do. Soak yourself in the grace of God. Douse your day in his love. Immerse your mind in his mercy. He has settled your accounts, paid your debt. "Christ carried our sins in his body on the cross" (1 Peter 2:24 NCV).

When you lose your temper with your little sister, Christ intervenes: "I paid for that." When you tell a lie and all of heaven groans, your Savior speaks up: "My death covered that sin." As you desire, boast, crave, or judge, Jesus stands before the tribunal of heaven and points to the blood-streaked cross. "I've already made provision. I've taken away the sins of the world."

What a gift he has given you. You've won the greatest lottery in the history of humanity, and you didn't even pay for the ticket! Your soul is secure, your salvation guaranteed. Your name is written in the only book that matters. You're only a few sand grains in the hourglass from a tearless, graveless, painless existence. What more do you need?

ONE MORE THOUGHT

Do you get how great this news is? You may flunk the quiz, but you've already aced the final. No matter how many problems you face today, you know that they won't matter tomorrow. God's taken care of it. If that's not worthy of singing for joy, I don't know what is.

God is in charge of deciding human destiny.

[James 4:12 MSG]

Down to Your Destiny

Joseph's life went downhill in a hurry. "Put down" by his siblings. "Thrown down" into an empty well. "Let down" by his brothers and "sold down" the river as a slave. "Led down" the road to Egypt. Down, down, down. Stripped of name, status, position. Everything he had, everything he thought he'd ever have, gone. Just like that.

Just like you? Are you down to your final friend, down to your last dime, down on your luck, down on your life . . . down . . . down to Egypt?

Joseph arrived in Egypt with nothing. No big name to stand on. No family to lean on. He lost everything, with one exception. His destiny. He'd had dreams that convinced him God had plans for him. The details were vague, for sure. But Joseph never lost his belief in God's belief in him. While wearing the heavy chains of the slave owners, he remembered, "I've been called to more than this." God had a destiny for Joseph, and the boy believed in it.

Do you believe in God's destiny for you?

ONE MORE THOUGHT

Could Joseph have risen out of slavery to a position of leadership and power if he'd lost his faith in God and his plans? I doubt it. Take a second look at your dreams for your future. Despite your troubles today, your dreams are still possible. Even if you're down to nothing except your destiny.

Rejoice in our confident hope. Be patient in trouble, and keep on praying.

[Romans 12:12 NLT]

Reveal to Heal

Some years ago, a dear friend of mine was called to the funeral home to identify the body of his father, who had been shot in the middle of the night by his ex-wife. The shotgun blast was just another in a long line of angry outbursts and violent family moments. My friend remembers standing near the body and making this resolution: "It stops with me."

Make the same resolve. Your family history may have some sad chapters, but your history doesn't have to be your future. Talk to God and adult Christians you trust about it. Bring it out in the open. Revealing leads to healing. Don't just pray: *Lord, help me forgive.* Give God and others the details: *Every day I come home from school to find Mom drunk, lying on the couch. I have to make dinner, take care of baby brother, do homework on my own. It's not right, God!*

Difficult, for certain. But let God do his work. There is always hope in choosing his future for you.

ONE MORE THOUGHT

When you're in a tough spot, don't try to face it or get through it on your own. One purpose of God's family is to support each other with our problems. Talk to him about what's going on in your life so he can lead you to a pastor, parent, teacher, friend, or other Christian who can help.

Come and See

Philip had just agreed to become a disciple. He found Nathaniel and told him they'd found the One whom Moses wrote about, the One the prophets spoke of. Of all people, it was Jesus, Joseph's son, the man who'd grown up in Nazareth. Nathaniel couldn't believe anyone so important could come from such an out-of-the-way, out-of-touch little town. "'Nazareth! Can anything good come from there?' Nathaniel asked. 'Come and see,' said Philip" (John 1:46 NIV).

Nathaniel's question still lingers, even two thousand years later. Can anything good come out of Nazareth? Come and see the changed lives. The delinquent who is now the do-gooder. The angry, bitter soul who is now full of joy. The depressed and over-whelmed who are now hopeful.

Come and see the pierced hand of God touch the most common heart, wipe the tear from the saddest face, and forgive the ugliest sin. Come and see. He avoids no seeker. He ignores no probe. He fears no search. Come and see what One from Nazareth can do.

ONE MORE THOUGHT

A humble beginning does not mean a useless life. Jesus proved it. Born in a stable. Raised in an obscure village. Savior of the world. Hard to believe? Don't judge a book or a messiah by its cover. Instead, come and see for yourself.

Don't get sidetracked; keep your feet from following evil.

[Proverbs 4:27 NLT]

Danger Zone

When we walk out our front doors each morning, we enter a danger zone. All of us battle a fierce foe called temptation. None of us are immune. The devil has tempted everyone, starting with Adam and including even Jesus. The first with fruit. The second with bread. You and me? It could be with the pretty girl walking by, the wallet lying on the sidewalk, the test answer on the desk next to us.

We can help each other win this fight. A girl chooses a modest outfit, allowing guys to keep their eyes and minds under control. A buddy asks how our God time is going, pointing us toward treasured truth. A friend says, "Are you sure that's a good idea?" providing us with a second chance at a better choice.

When temptation threatens to topple your friends, encourage them to turn to your heavenly Father. He loves to hold the hands of his children. "The LORD directs the steps of the godly" (Psalm 37:23 NLT). He'll lead them—and you—out of the danger zone.

ONE MORE THOUGHT

Read Paul's wise words in 1 Corinthians 10:1–13. You and your friends always have a way out of even the most dangerous situation. It won't come from your willpower. Your escape is provided by God. Watch for it, take it, and don't look back.

I do believe; help me overcome my unbelief!

[Mark 9:24 NIV]

Dealing with Doubt

Someone once said to me, "I'm beginning to doubt whether there really is a God. Can I know he's not just a product of my imagination?"

Belief in God is not blind faith. Doubt is part of the journey to rock-solid conviction. If you're unsure what you believe, it doesn't mean you're a "bad Christian" or that you're doomed. It's okay to ask the hard questions. God can handle it. So how can people get to that place of firm faith? The path varies, but here are a few ideas.

Space: Billions of galaxies and expanding. Where does it end? How did it all begin? *Earth*: So much variety and beauty. How did it come to be? Why does it work in such harmony? *Ethics*: Throughout history, murder is always bad, courage always good. Who programmed us? *Bible*: Examine the wisdom. Experience the stories. *Empty tomb*: So many who claimed to see the risen Lord died with those words on their lips. Would they die for a lie? *Jesus*: No other man in history caused so many questions, stirred so many hearts, gave so many answers. Could he be who he said he was?

ONE MORE THOUGHT

Do you wonder if doubt and faith can coexist? Read the story of the father and his spirit-possessed son in Mark 9:14–27. Despite his doubt, the father was willing to believe that Jesus could heal his son. It was enough. Your faith—even when mixed with doubt—will be enough as well.

Many who have been long dead and buried will wake up,
some to eternal life, others to eternal shame.

[Daniel 12:2 MSG]

Hell Has a Purpose

Does hell serve a purpose? Remove it from the Bible and, at the same time, remove any idea that God is just and that his Word can be trusted.

If there is no hell, God is not fair. If there is no punishment of sin, heaven doesn't care about the rapists and robbers and mass murderers of society. If there is no hell, God is blind toward the victims and has turned his back on those who pray for help. If there is no anger toward evil, then God is not love, for love hates that which is evil.

To say there is no hell is also to say God is a liar and his Scripture untrue. The Bible repeatedly and strongly affirms that each person's history is headed for one of two outcomes. Some will be saved. Some will be lost. God doesn't force us into either destination. He lets us decide. Which do you choose?

ONE MORE THOUGHT

Hell. A place of unimagined misery. How can a loving God allow such a space to exist? Yet how can he not? Does it seem right that those who do evil every day and are never sorry should never face a consequence? God would prefer that hell's hotel remain empty. Let's do all we can to make that idea come true.

> You have not seen Christ, but still you love him. You
> cannot see him now, but you believe in him.
>
> [1 Peter 1:8 NCV]

Look Up

Some years ago a sociologist joined a group of mountain climbers on an expedition. He noticed a connection between cloud cover and contentment. When there were no clouds and the peak was in view, the climbers were energetic and cooperative. When the gray clouds blocked the view of the mountaintop, though, the climbers were sullen and selfish.

The same thing happens to us. As long as our eyes are on God's majesty, there is a bounce in our step. But let our eyes focus on the dirt beneath us and we will grumble about every rock and crevice we have to cross. For this reason Paul urged, "Don't shuffle along, eyes to the ground, absorbed with the things right in front of you. Look up, and be alert to what is going on around Christ—that's where the action is. See things from his perspective" (Colossians 3:1–2 MSG).

You're on your way up. You'll enjoy the climb far more if you keep your eyes on Jesus.

ONE MORE THOUGHT

It's amazing how much difference our view makes. Cold weather and dark clouds can put us in a stormy mood. Sunny days seem to lighten our load. So let your spiritual eyes stay focused on God's majesty. You'll be atop the mountain before you know it.

Jesus is the One whom God raised from the dead.
And we are all witnesses to this.

[Acts 2:32 NCV]

They Couldn't Forget

We don't know where the disciples went when they fled the garden after Jesus was arrested, but we do know what they took: a memory. They took a heart-stopping memory of a man who called himself no less than God in the flesh. And they couldn't get him out of their minds. Try as they might to lose him in the crowd, they couldn't forget him.

If they saw a leper, they thought of his compassion. If they heard a storm, they would remember the day he silenced one. If they saw a child, they would think of the day he held one.

No, they couldn't forget him. As a result, they came back. And, as a result, the church of our Lord began with a group of frightened men in an upper room.

What have you seen Jesus do in your life and in the lives of those around you? Will you remember too?

ONE MORE THOUGHT

For the forgetful among us, a list is a wonderful way to jog a memory. Why don't you make one now of the things Jesus has done for you. Keep it somewhere safe, and add to it as your blessings grow. That way you'll never forget, and your faith will fly.

Love . . . bears all things, believes all things, hopes all things, endures all things.

[1 Corinthians 13:4, 7]

Believe in Others

Everyone else has written off the person you care about. "He's too far gone." "She's too hard . . . too addicted . . . too cold." No one gives a prayer. But you are realizing that God may be at work behind the scenes. Maybe it's too soon to throw in the towel. You begin to believe.

No one believed in people more than Jesus did. He saw something in Peter worth developing, in the adulterous woman worth forgiving, and in John worth harnessing. He saw something in the thief on the cross, and what he saw was worth saving. And in the life of a wild-eyed, bloodthirsty extremist, he saw an apostle of grace. He believed in Saul, who became Paul, one of Christianity's most important voices.

Don't give up on your Saul. When others write him off, give him another chance. Stay strong. Call him brother. Call her sister. Tell your Saul about Jesus, and pray. And remember this: God never sends you where he hasn't already been. By the time you reach your Saul, who knows what you'll find.

ONE MORE THOUGHT

When you're about to take the field or the stage, isn't that encouraging smile worth everything? The one that says, "I believe in you. You can do it!" Someone out there needs that supportive smile or heartwarming word from you.

> "See to it that you are not alarmed."
>
> [Matthew 24:6 NIV]

No Panic

This world stinks sometimes. There's confusion and there's sadness in this world. There's hunger in this world. There are cancer and divorce and death in this world. And sometimes you're going to pray about things, and the prayer isn't going to be answered the way you want.

But Jesus predicted the bad stuff. He said, "In this world you will have trouble" (John 16:33 NIV). It's as if he were telling us, "Don't freak out when things get extreme." If he can predict the problem, he can solve it.

Somewhere between the naïve optimists and the doom-and-gloomers are the sober, honest disciples of Christ who don't panic or lose faith at the presence of problems. They know that all these problems are a natural unfolding of events, part of the plan God laid out long ago.

Our mission is to trust and endure. We're headed for the embrace of heaven, where nothing bad will ever happen again.

ONE MORE THOUGHT

No one likes bad days or bad news. But it's comforting to know that Jesus saw all this coming. He knew we'd find trouble for following him, and he knew the world would get worse before he returned to redeem it. We can be confident in his ultimate victory—and ours.

He will not leave you or forget you.

[Deuteronomy 31:8 NCV]

Welcome Back

When I was seven years old, I ran away from home. I'd had enough of my father's rules and decided I could make it on my own, thank you very much. With my clothes in a paper bag, I stormed out the back gate and marched down the alley. But I didn't go far. I got to the end of the alley and remembered I was hungry, so I went back home. My dad welcomed me back.

Though the rebellion was brief, it was rebellion nonetheless. And had you stopped me, I might have told you how I felt. I might have said, "I don't need a father. I'm too big for the rules of my family."

I didn't hear the rooster crow like Peter did after he lied about knowing Jesus. But I learned from my father on earth what Peter learned from his Father in heaven. Our God is no fair-weather Father. He's not into this love-'em-and-leave-'em stuff. I can count on him to welcome me back no matter how far I go from him. You can too.

ONE MORE THOUGHT

Did you ever run away from home? Are you still doing it today? Maybe not physically, but are you finding small or big ways to rebel against parents, teachers, and God? Maybe it's time to stop running away. God is waiting for you to come home with open arms.

No one is like the LORD our God, who rules from heaven.

[Psalm 113:5 NCV]

God Sees What We Can't

On a trip to the United Kingdom, our family visited a castle. In the center of its garden sat a maze. Row after row of shoulder-high hedges, leading to one dead end after another. Successfully navigate the puzzle, and discover the door to a tall tower in the center of the garden. Were you to look at our family pictures of the trip, you'd see four of our five family members standing on top of the tower. Hmmm, someone is still on the ground. Guess who? I was stuck in the foliage. I just couldn't figure out which way to go.

Ah, but then I heard a voice from above. "Hey, Dad." I looked up to see Sara, peering through the turret at the top. "You're going the wrong way," she explained. "Back up and turn right."

Do you think I trusted her? I didn't have to. But do you know what I did? I listened. Her vantage point was better than mine. She was above the maze. She could see what I couldn't.

Don't you think we should do the same with God?

ONE MORE THOUGHT

Height has its advantages. Teens, unlike toddlers, can see over couches. Lifeguards can survey the beach. An office worker on the thirtieth floor can see the city. A jet pilot's view extends hundreds of miles. But God? He sees it all in a glance—the entire universe and the single next step you need to take.

The Word became flesh and dwelt among us.

[John 1:14]

He Was Reachable

The Word became flesh," John said. In other words . . . he was touchable, approachable, reachable. And, what's more, he was ordinary. If he were here today, you probably wouldn't notice him as he walked through a shopping mall. He wouldn't turn heads by the clothes he wore or the jewelry he flashed.

"Just call me Jesus," you can almost hear him say.

He was the kind of fellow you'd invite to watch the Cubs-Giants game at your house. He'd wrestle on the floor with your little brother, doze on your couch, and cook steaks on your grill. He'd laugh at your jokes and tell a few of his own. And when you spoke, he'd listen to you as if he had all the time in eternity.

And one thing's for sure, you'd invite him back. Because there would be something about him. A peace. A power. A presence. Something you need.

ONE MORE THOUGHT

It happened two thousand years ago, but the concept is still incredible today. God in the flesh. From heaven to human. He loved us so much that he gave up everything to be one of us. When someone does all that, isn't he worth getting to know a little bit better?

He chose us in Him before the foundation of the world.

[Ephesians 1:4]

Headed Home

Search the faces of the Cap Haitian orphanage for Carinette, the girl with the long nose and bushy hair and a handful of photos. The photos bear the images of her future family. She's been adopted.

Her adoptive parents are friends of mine. They brought her pictures, a teddy bear, granola bars, and cookies. Carinette shared the goodies and asked the director to guard her bear, but she keeps the pictures. They remind her of her home-to-be. Within a month, two at the most, she'll be there. She knows the day is coming. Any time now her father will appear. He came once to claim her. He'll come again to carry her home. Till then she lives with a heart headed home.

Shouldn't we all? Our Father paid us a visit too. Have we not been claimed? Adopted? God searched you out. Before you knew you needed adopting, he'd already filed the papers and selected the wallpaper for your room.

ONE MORE THOUGHT

There's something exciting about going home, even if we've never been there before. Like Carinette, we stare at the pictures in our mind of the wonders we'll know there. Today's tough times are far easier to tackle when we know what joys tomorrow will bring.

> Do not try to punish others when they wrong you, but
> wait for God to punish them with his anger.
>
> [Romans 12:19 NCV]

The High Cost of Getting Even

Have you ever noticed in the western movies how the bounty hunter travels alone? It's not hard to see why. Who wants to hang out with a guy who settles scores for a living? Who wants to risk getting on his bad side? More than once I've heard a person spew his anger. He thought I was listening, when really I was thinking, *I hope I never get on his list*. Crabby sorts, these bounty hunters. Best leave them alone. Hang out with the angry and you might catch a stray bullet. Debt-settling is a lonely occupation. It's also an unhealthy one.

If you're out to settle the score, you'll never rest. How can you? For one thing, your enemy may never pay up. As much as you think you deserve an apology, the other person may not agree. You may never get a penny's worth of justice. And if you do, will it be enough?

There is another way. Put away your guns and spurs. Forgive. It's a lot more healthy and a lot more holy.

ONE MORE THOUGHT

Are you a modern bounty hunter, seeking to get even for every insult? If so, you're setting yourself up for a hard and lonely life. It may look cool on screen to wear a gun and track down the bad guys, but in the real world it's a long and miserable ride. Let God do the tracking. You do the forgiving.

> The LORD is my light and my salvation—so why should I be afraid? The LORD
> is my fortress, protecting me from danger, so why should I tremble?
>
> [Psalm 27:1 NLT]

A Life Without Fear

Fear, it seems, has moved into your bedroom and unpacked its things. Oversized and rude, fear is unwilling to share the heart with happiness. Happiness obeys and leaves. Can one be happy and afraid at the same time? Clear thinking and afraid? Confident and afraid? No. Fear is the bully in the school hallway: brash, loud, and unproductive. Fear herds us into detention and slams the doors.

Wouldn't it be great to walk out?

Imagine your life untouched by angst. What if faith, not fear, was your first reaction to threats? If you could hover a fear magnet over your heart and extract every last shaving of dread, insecurity, and doubt, what would be left? Envision a day, just one day, minus the fear of failure, rejection, and disaster. Walking into a class with a genuine, assured smile on your face. Taking the stage with no concerns about messing up. Picturing the future and knowing it's going to be all right.

Jesus asks, "Why are you afraid?" (Matthew 8:26 NCV). He is your light and your salvation. Can you imagine a life with no fear?

ONE MORE THOUGHT

When you become a Christian, it doesn't mean nothing bad will ever happen to you. Sometimes it seems just the opposite! So what is Jesus saying when he asks why you're afraid? That no matter what you're up against, you'll walk through it together. You plus Christ? That's an unbeatable combination.

SEPTEMBER

"Come to Me, all you who labor and are heavy
laden, and I will give you rest. Take My yoke upon
you and learn from Me, for I am gentle and lowly
in heart, and you will find rest for your souls."

[Matthew 11:28–29]

In all the work you are doing, work the best you can. Work
as if you were doing it for the Lord, not for people.

[Colossians 3:23 NCV]

God Is at Work

The State of Texas is rebuilding a highway overpass near my
house. Three lanes have been reduced to one, transforming a
morning commute into a daily stew. Cranes daily hover overhead.
Workers hold signs and shovels, and several million of us grumble.
Well, at least I do. *How long is this going to last?*

My next-door neighbors have a different attitude toward the
project. The husband and his wife are highway engineers. They
endure the same traffic jams and detours as the rest of us, but do
so with a better attitude. Why? They know how these projects
develop. "It will take time," they respond to my grumbles, "but it
will get finished." They've seen the plans.

As you honor workers on Labor Day, also honor God for his
work in your life. His plans for you are grander than any highway
project. "My Father is always at his work to this very day, and I
too am working" (John 5:17 NIV). It will take time. But it will get
finished.

ONE MORE THOUGHT

Think about the traffic jams of your life. What obstacles are keeping you
from going on that mission trip, getting into that class, getting to know that
person? Time? Money? Lack of experience? Lack of confidence? Don't
grumble about it. Give it to God, and let him go to work.

> Come near to God, and God will come near to you.
>
> [James 4:8 NCV]

Secondhand Faith

Some of us have trouble with daily quiet times with God. There are so many distractions. We have a hard time concentrating. And we're *so* busy. So rather than spend time with God, listening for his voice, we let others spend time with him and then rely on their experience. Let them tell us what God is saying. After all, isn't that what preachers get paid to do? And what are spiritual friends for?

If that's your approach, if your spiritual experiences are second-hand and not firsthand, I'd like to challenge you with this thought: Do you do that with other parts of your life? You don't let friends use your concert tickets and tell you about it later. You don't let someone eat on your behalf. You certainly don't send a friend to the dance with *your* date, do you?

There are certain things no one can do for you. One of those is spending time with God.

ONE MORE THOUGHT

How would you feel if your best friend never spent time with you, if she just talked to your other friends to find out what you're doing? Would you feel ignored? Disrespected? Hurt? Now imagine how God feels when you leave him out of your life. Let's make faith a firsthand experience.

Love suffers long and is kind.

[1 Corinthians 13:4]

Kind Hearts

What is your kindness quotient? When was the last time you did something kind for someone in your family—got a blanket, cleaned off the table, made the coffee—without being asked?

Think about your school. Which person is the most overlooked or avoided? A shy student? A grumpy secretary? Maybe he doesn't speak the language. Maybe she doesn't fit in. Are you kind to this person?

Kind hearts are quietly kind. They let the car cut into traffic and the young mom with three kids move up in the checkout line. They pick up the neighbor's trash can that rolled into the street. And they are especially kind at church. They understand that perhaps the neediest person they'll meet all week is the one standing in the foyer or sitting in the row behind them in worship. Paul writes, "When we have the opportunity to help anyone, we should do it. But we should give special attention to those who are in the family of believers" (Galatians 6:10 NCV).

ONE MORE THOUGHT

Becoming kind isn't something we achieve by following a step-by-step plan. It grows out of our understanding of the compassion Jesus felt for us and our need for a Savior. The closer you move to Christ, the more your heart will turn to kindness.

> "If any of you want to be my followers, you must forget about yourself. You must take up your cross each day and follow me."
>
> [Luke 9:23 CEV]

Your God-Designed Task

The phrase "take up your cross" has not fared well through the generations. Ask for a definition, and you'll hear answers like "My cross is my little brother, my geometry class, my allergies, my schedule." The cross, we assume, is any hardship or hassle. God, we think, passes out crosses the way your teacher hands out homework assignments. No one wants one. Each one gets one. Everybody has a cross to bear, and we might as well get used to it.

But really. Is Jesus reducing the cross to hassles and headaches? The cross means so much more. It is God's instrument of salvation—proof of his love for people. To take up the cross, then, is to take up Christ's burden for the people of the world.

Though our crosses are similar, none are identical. We each have our own cross to carry—our individual callings. It's a sweet day when you discover your God-designed task. It fits. It matches your passions and enlists your gifts and talents. Want to blow the cloud cover off your gray day? Accept God's direction. Take up your cross.

ONE MORE THOUGHT

When you're trying to figure out your future, it can be hard to remember that God has a specific path in mind for you—one that is more than boring burden, one that is exciting and fulfilling. One God. One plan. One life. Take up *your* cross. You won't regret it.

He has put a new song in my mouth.

[Psalm 40:3]

A Song of Hope

In the 1760s, a mother and daughter walked up and down a line of recently rescued captives. Their daughter and sister, Regina, had been taken by Indians nearly ten years earlier. Could Regina be among these pale and emaciated souls? None looked familiar. Then someone had an idea: was there a childhood memory or song?

Mother and daughter again walked slowly up and down the rows, singing a song from the girls' childhood. Suddenly a tall, slender girl rushed out of the crowd toward her mother, embraced her, and began to sing the verse. Regina had not recognized her family, but she remembered the song placed in her heart as a young girl.[11]

God places a song in the hearts of his children too. A song of hope and life. Sometimes this song falls silent. Life's hurts and happenings mute the music within. Yet God's never-ending grace calls us home. Even when we mess up. Even if we are lost, cut off from his family for years. Eventually we hear his voice, and something within us awakens. And when it does, we begin to sing again.

ONE MORE THOUGHT

Music is powerful. It can inspire us, move us, even bring us to tears. Write down a few of your favorite songs and reasons why they are meaningful to you. Then consider the song of hope that God offers to each of us. His music is the most moving of all.

Let us run with endurance the race God has set before
us. We do this by keeping our eyes on Jesus.

[Hebrews 12:1–2 NLT]

Look at the Son

More mornings than not I drag myself out of bed and onto the
street. I run because I don't like heart doctors.

Since heart disease runs in our family, I run in our neighborhood. As the sun is rising, I am running. And as I am running, my
body is groaning. It doesn't want to cooperate. My knee hurts. My
hip is stiff. My ankles complain.

Things hurt. And as things hurt, I've learned that I have three
options. Go home. (Denalyn would laugh at me.) Meditate on my
hurts until I start imagining I'm having chest pains. (Pleasant
thought.) Or I can keep running and watch the sun come up. If I
watch God's world go from dark to golden, guess what? The same
happens to my attitude. The pain passes and the joints loosen.
Everything improves as I fix my eyes on the sun.

Wasn't that the same advice the author of Hebrews gave us—
keep our eyes on the Son?

ONE MORE THOUGHT

Read Hebrews 12:1–12. The author makes it clear that we will sometimes
struggle against our own misguided desires and will be disciplined for it.
The solution is to focus on our perfect example, Jesus, the Son who shines
his light for all.

If we walk in the light, as he is in the light, we have fellowship with one another.

[1 John 1:7 NIV]

Confess to One Another

Your stayed when you should have gone, looked when you should have turned, flirted when you should have walked away, hurt when you should have helped, denied when you should have confessed. So talk to God about it. Go to him as you would go to a trusted family member. Explain the pain, and revisit your mistake together.

When you mess up and fess up, God may send you to talk to another Christian. "Confess your sins to *one another*, and pray for one another so that you may be healed" (James 5:16 NASB). James calls us not only to confess *up* to God but also to confess *out* to each other.

People are attracted to honesty. You should be too. Find a Bible study or youth group with guys and gals that believe in fessing up. Avoid gatherings where everyone claims to be perfect—you won't fit in there anyway. Instead, hang out where people admit their sins and show humility. Healing happens in places like this.

Confessors find a freedom that deniers don't.

ONE MORE THOUGHT

We need each other. I'm not talking about fake friends who vanish the moment you have a crisis. I mean fellow God-believers who have your back. Be real with these people. They are God's gift of encouragement to you.

> "Be strong and of good courage; do not be afraid, nor be dismayed,
> for the Lord your God is with you wherever you go."
>
> [Joshua 1:9]

Live with Jesus

Now when [the accusers] saw the boldness of Peter and John, and perceived that they were uneducated and untrained men, they marveled. And they realized that they had been with Jesus" (Acts 4:13).

Peter and John had lingered long and delightfully in the presence of the resurrected King. Awakening with him, walking with him. And because they had, silence was no longer an option. "We cannot but speak the things which we have seen and heard" (v. 20).

Could you use some high-octane boldness? As long as you are stationary, no one will complain. Dogs don't bark at parked cars. But as soon as you accelerate—once you step out of dishonesty into integrity or laziness into compassion—expect the yapping to begin. Expect to be criticized. Expect to be mocked.

So how can we prepare ourselves? Simple. Imitate the disciples. Linger long and often in the presence of Christ. Meditate on his grace. Ponder his love. Memorize his words. Gaze into his face. Talk to him. Courage comes as we live with Jesus. As we meditate on Christ's life, we find strength for our own.

ONE MORE THOUGHT

Feeling fearful about tomorrow? Do like the disciples—spend time with Jesus. Talk to him. Read his words. Reflect on his life and love for you. He has power and strength like none other, and he's more than willing to share some with you.

> He made the storm be still, and the waves of the sea were hushed.
>
> [Psalm 107:29 ESV]

A Cut Above

The word *holy* means "to separate." The term can be traced back to an ancient word that means "to cut." To be holy, then, is to be a cut above the norm, superior, excellent. The Holy One dwells on a different level from the rest of us. What frightens us does not frighten him. What troubles us does not trouble him.

I'm a pastor, not a sailor, but I've puttered around in a bass boat enough to know the secret for finding land in a storm. You don't aim at another boat. You certainly don't stare at the waves. You set your sights on an object unaffected by the wind—a light on the shore—and go straight toward it.

When you set your sights on our God, you focus on One "a cut above" any storm life may bring. Finals? Broken friendships? A family that constantly fights? He's the One who can make the storm be still. In him, you find peace.

ONE MORE THOUGHT

Isn't it good to know there's a level above all the junk we live with? A place that's holy instead of horrible? A place of peace instead of storms? This is where God lives, and he wants you to enjoy it with him. So aim toward him, and paddle with all your might.

> "I am the Lᴏʀᴅ, the God of every person on the
> earth. Nothing is impossible for me."
> [Jeremiah 32:27 ɴᴄᴠ]

Read the Story

We need to hear that God is still in control. We need to hear that it's not over until he says so. We need to hear that life's mistakes, mishaps, and tragedies are not reasons to bail out. They are simply reasons to sit tight. Corrie ten Boom used to say, "When the train goes through a tunnel and the world gets dark, do you jump out? Of course not. You sit still and trust the engineer to get you through."

Yes, you will say the wrong thing, write down the wrong answer, and pick the wrong friend. You will have days—and weeks—that feel like the end of the world, and you will be discouraged.

The way to deal with discouragement? The cure for disappointment? Go back and read the story of God. Read it again and again. Be reminded that you aren't the first person to cry. And you aren't the first person to be helped. Read the story, and remember—the story is yours!

ONE MORE THOUGHT

You get up late. Miss the bus. Mess up a midterm. Forget about meeting a friend for lunch. Drop your homework in the mud. Yes, it's discouraging! So pick up your Bible. It's full of stories about people just like you and the victories that God raised from the ruins.

> I pray that you, being rooted and established in love, may . . . grasp
> how wide and long and high and deep is the love of Christ.
>
> [Ephesians 3:17–18 NIV]

He Didn't Quit

Lee Ielpi is a retired firefighter, a New York City firefighter. He gave twenty-six years to the city. But on September 11, 2001, he gave much more. He gave his son. Jonathan Ielpi was a fireman as well. When the Twin Towers fell, he was there.

Firefighters are a loyal clan. When one perishes in the line of duty, the body is left where it is until a firefighter who knows the person can come and literally pick it up. Lee made the discovery of his son's body his personal mission. He dug daily with dozens of others at the sixteen-acre graveyard. On Tuesday, December 11, three months after the disaster, his son was found. And Lee was there to carry him out.

The father didn't quit. Why? Because his love for his son was greater than the pain of the search. Can't the same be said about Christ? Why didn't he quit? Because the love for his children was greater than the pain of the journey.

ONE MORE THOUGHT

Love isn't there just for the fun times or when it's convenient. It believes when no one else does and sticks around when no one else does. It is wide and long and high and deep. It doesn't quit. And like the love of Christ, it always stands ready to carry us home.

"Weren't we excited when he talked with us on the road?"

[Luke 24:32 GOD'S WORD]

The Fire Within

When [the disciples] saw who he was, he disappeared. They said to each other, 'It felt like a fire burning in us when Jesus talked to us on the road and explained the Scriptures to us'" (Luke 24:31–32 NCV).

Don't you love that verse? They knew they had been with Jesus because of the fire within them. God reveals his will by setting a torch to your soul. He gave Jeremiah a fire for hard hearts. He gave Nehemiah a fire for a forgotten city. He set Abraham on fire for a land he'd never seen. He set Isaiah on fire with a vision he couldn't resist. Forty years of unproductive preaching didn't put out the fire of Noah.

Mark it down: Jesus comes to set you on fire! He walks as a torch from heart to heart, warming the cold and thawing the chilled and stirring the ashes. Following Christ is not some dull, endless journey. It is an exciting quest for your destiny. Feel the heat—he's already on his way!

ONE MORE THOUGHT

Some people think that being a Christian is boring, that it's sitting in church and memorizing ancient ideas. They just don't get it. God's love and power and passion will spread within you like a wildfire. There's no thrill like marching with Jesus! It is life itself.

> "I will make you my promised bride forever. I will be good
> and fair; I will show you my love and mercy."
>
> [Hosea 2:19 NCV]

The Choice Is Ours

For all its strange twists and unique characters, the Bible has a simple story. God made man. Man rejected God. God won't give up until he wins him back.

God will whisper. He will shout. He will touch and tug. He will take away our problems; he'll even take away our blessings. If there are a thousand steps between us and him, he will take all but one. But he will leave the final one for us. The choice is ours. "If you declare with your mouth, 'Jesus is Lord,' and believe in your heart that God raised him from the dead, you will be saved" (Romans 10:9 NIV).

Please understand. His goal is not to make you happy. His goal is to make you his. His goal is not to get you what you want; it is to get you what you need.

ONE MORE THOUGHT

How often does God whisper, shout, or tug at you without you noticing? That time you sensed you should go to church but ended up sleeping in? That morning you meant to pray? He pursues you every day, inviting you to make the choice to be with and follow him.

> We worked hard all night and caught nothing.
>
> [Luke 5:5 NASB]

Try Again

Peter had fished all night with no luck when Jesus told him to try again. Do *you* have any worn, wet, empty nets? Do you know the feeling of a sleepless, fishless night? Of course you do. For what have you been casting?

Faith? "I want to believe, but . . ." Healing? "I've been sick so long . . ." Hope? "Nothing seems to make a difference . . ."

You've worked hard all night and caught nothing. You've felt what Peter felt. You've sat where Peter sat. And now Jesus is asking you to go fishing. He knows your nets are empty. He knows your heart is weary. He knows you'd like nothing more than to turn your back on the mess and call it a life. But he urges, "It's not too late to try again."

See if Peter's reply won't help you decide on your own. "I will do as You say and let down the nets" (Luke 5:5 NASB).

ONE MORE THOUGHT

Peter obeyed Jesus and caught so many fish his nets began to break. What will your obedience and perseverance lead to? What is more blessing than you can imagine? Jesus enjoys going beyond what we expect, but it takes our faith and obedience to see the surprise.

"Shouldn't you have mercy on your fellow servant, just as I had mercy on you?"

[Matthew 18:33 NLT]

The Grace-Given

A servant owed more money to his king than he could ever repay. He'd sooner find an iPod in his cereal than cash for the debt. So the king ordered that he, his family, and everything he had be sold to pay the debt. But the man begged, "'Please, be patient with me, and I will pay it all.' Then his master was filled with pity for him, and he released him and forgave his debt" (Matthew 18:25–27 NLT).

The man hurried to the house of a person who owed him a few dollars. You would expect the just-blessed man to be quick-to-bless, right? Not in this case. He demanded payment. He turned a deaf ear to the fellow's pleas for mercy and locked him in debtors' prison. When the king found out, he threw *his* servant in prison.

How could the servant be so coldhearted? We're left to speculate, and I speculate this much: grace never happened to him. The self-centered servant didn't get it. The grace-given give grace.

ONE MORE THOUGHT

We're blessed every day, but sometimes we forget to notice. There's the bed your parents gave you to sleep on. The teacher who granted extra time for homework. The friend who listened to your problems. The grace-given, giving grace. Make sure grace happens to you—then give it to someone else.

"Rescue the weak and the needy; deliver them from the hand of the wicked."

[Psalm 82:4 ESV]

Stand Up to Bullies

Jesus had business to do with bullies. So do we.

When a group of finger-pointing Pharisees pushed a woman accused of adultery in front of Jesus, he lifted himself until his shoulders were straight and his head was high. He stood, not to preach, for his words would be few. Not to instruct his followers; he didn't address them. He stood on behalf of the woman. He placed himself between her and the lynch mob and said, "Let the one who has never sinned throw the first stone!" (John 8:7 NLT).

We also should stand up for those who can't defend themselves, should "encourage the disheartened, help the weak" (1 Thessalonians 5:14 NIV). Does someone in your school or neighborhood need your help? Turn the other cheek doesn't mean turn away when a bully threatens—with words or fists—a smaller, younger, or weaker victim. Jesus showed us the way. So step forward. Love stands up to bullies.

ONE MORE THOUGHT

You don't want to be bullied. Who does? Certainly not the guy or gal pinned in a corner by a gang of "tough" guys. Or the classmate who isn't quick enough to defend against words that hurt. Who will stand up to the bullies? You will—because that's what Jesus did.

> "Look at the birds in the air. They don't plant or harvest or store food in barns, but your heavenly Father feeds them."
>
> [Matthew 6:26 NCV]

God's Workshop

Our globe's weight has been estimated at six sextillion (that's a six with twenty-one zeroes!) tons. Yet it is precisely tilted at twenty-three degrees; any more or any less and our seasons would be lost in a melted polar flood. Although our globe revolves at the rate of one thousand miles per hour or twenty-five thousand miles per day or nine million miles per year, none of us tumbles into orbit.

As you stand observing God's workshop, let me pose a few questions. If he is able to place the stars in their sockets and suspend the sky like a curtain, do you think it is remotely possible that God is able to guide your life? If your God is mighty enough to ignite the sun, could it be that he is mighty enough to light your path? If he cares enough about the planet Saturn to give it rings or Venus to make it sparkle, is there an outside chance that he cares enough about you to meet your needs?

Ever wonder about God's ability to influence your life? The answer is in his workshop.

ONE MORE THOUGHT

It's amazing how our universe fits together to allow us to live on this planet we call Earth. Only God has the power and plan to make it happen. Do you think he would do all this yet neglect his children? Me either.

> Don't copy the behavior and customs of this world, but let God transform you into a new person by changing the way you think.
>
> [Romans 12:2 NLT]

Fitting In

A minister invited me to his house for high tea. I had never heard of it. In the spirit of adventure, I gladly accepted the invitation. I even acted enthused at the sight of the tea and cookie tray. But then came the moment of truth: the hostess asked what I would like in my tea. She offered two options. "Lemon? Milk?" I had no clue, but I didn't want to be rude, and I sure didn't want to miss out on anything so I said, "Both."

The look on her face left no question: I'd goofed. "You don't mix lemon and milk in the same cup," she softly explained, "unless you want a cup of curdle."

Some of us try so hard to fit in this world, but we end up simply looking foolish. Jesus says that if we're believers, we shouldn't try. "They are not of the world any more than I am of the world" (John 17:14 NIV). If our goal is to fit in with God, we won't miss a thing.

ONE MORE THOUGHT

We worry so much about what others will think. We dress, talk, and walk so we'll fit in. Maybe it's time to start worrying less about what people in this world think and start caring more about what God thinks.

The Simple Life

The most powerful life is the simplest life. The most powerful life is the life that knows where it's going, that knows where its strength comes from, and that stays free of clutter and hurry.

Being busy is not a sin. Jesus was busy. Paul was busy. Peter was busy. Nothing of significance is achieved without effort and hard work and weariness. Being busy, in and of itself, is not a sin. But being busy in an endless pursuit of things that leave us empty and hollow and broken inside—that cannot be pleasing to God.

One source of man's weariness is the pursuit of things that can never satisfy; but which one of us has not been caught up in that? Our pleasures, possessions, and pride—these are all dead things. When we try to get life out of dead things, we end up tired and unsatisfied. Keep it simple. Love and follow God.

ONE MORE THOUGHT

Doesn't life sometimes seem too complicated? So much to do, so many new gadgets to try, so many people to please. And all of it so unsatisfying. It doesn't have to be this way. Choose a simple life. Focus on the only One who will satisfy in the end.

> Since God has shown us great mercy, I beg you to
> offer your lives as a living sacrifice to him.
>
> [Romans 12:1 NCV]

A Raging Fire

Resentment is the cocaine of the emotions. It causes our blood to pump and our energy level to rise. But, also like cocaine, it demands increasingly larger and more frequent dosages. There is a dangerous point at which anger ceases to be an emotion and becomes a driving force. A person bent on revenge moves unknowingly further and further away from being able to forgive, for to be without the anger is to be without a source of energy.

Do you know someone caught in this trap, always angry, always plotting how to get back at someone? Are you there yourself? This is why the Bible tells us, "Don't get so angry that you sin. Don't go to bed angry" (Ephesians 4:26 CEV).

Hatred is the rabid dog that turns on its owner. Revenge is the raging fire that consumes the arsonist. Bitterness is the trap that snares the hunter.

And mercy is the choice that can set them all free.

ONE MORE THOUGHT

Has this ever happened to you? Have you used anger or hate like a drug to give you energy, to allow you to stay mad? It's a story with an unhappy ending. Choose God's way and forgive. Put out the fire of anger before it burns you up.

> "Before I made you in your mother's womb, I chose you."
>
> [Jeremiah 1:5 NCV]

God's Signature

With God in your world, you aren't an accident or an incident; you are a gift to the world, a divine work of art, signed by God.

One of the finest gifts I ever received is a football signed by thirty former professional quarterbacks. There is nothing unique about this ball. For all I know it was bought at a discount sports store. What makes it unique is the signatures.

The same is true with us. When you just look at all of nature, humans are not entirely unique. We aren't the only creatures with flesh and hair and blood and hearts. What makes us special is not only our body but the signature of God on our lives. We are his works of art. We are created in his image to do good deeds. We are significant, not because of what we do, but because of whose we are.

God has put his autograph on you. That makes you valuable beyond measure.

ONE MORE THOUGHT

A signature means everything to collectors. A baseball signed by Babe Ruth? A painting signed by Rembrandt? People pay thousands or even millions for such items. But who can put a price on the signature of God?

Be careful what you think, because your thoughts run your life.

[Proverbs 4:23 NCV]

Your Thoughts Run Your Life

Two types of voices command your attention today. Negative ones fill your mind with doubt, bitterness, and fear. Positive ones provide hope and strength. Which ones will you choose to listen to? You have a choice, you know. "We take every thought captive so that it is obedient to Christ" (2 Corinthians 10:5 GOD'S WORD).

Do you let anyone who knocks on your door enter your house? Don't let every thought that surfaces make a home in your mind. Take it captive . . . make it obey Jesus. If it refuses, don't think it.

Negative thoughts never strengthen you. How many times have you changed a test score with your grumbles? Does groaning about zits make them disappear? Why moan about your aches and pains, problems and challenges?

"Be careful what you think, because your thoughts run your life" (Proverbs 4:23 NCV).

ONE MORE THOUGHT

Minds race. Minds wander. Minds can turn mindless. The ideas and thoughts that hike through your head are like sheep—they need to be corralled. Let's put them in the pen with the "positive" sign on the gate. They'll be much happier there, and so will you.

Before a downfall the heart is haughty, but humility comes before honor.

[Proverbs 18:12 NIV]

Blind Ambition

Blind ambition. Success at all cost. Becoming a legend in one's own time. Climbing the ladder to the top. King of the mountain. Top of the heap. "I did it my way."

We make heroes out of people who are ambitious. We hold them up as models and put their pictures on the covers of our magazines. And rightly so. This world would be in sad shape without people who dream of touching the heavens. Ambition is that grit in the soul that creates disenchantment with the ordinary and puts the dare into dreams.

But without God's guiding hand it becomes an addiction to power and fame; a roaring hunger for achievement that devours people as a lion devours an animal, leaving behind only the skeletal remains of relationships.

God won't tolerate it. Blind ambition is a giant step away from God and one step closer to catastrophe.

ONE MORE THOUGHT

What does blind ambition look like in your life? Classmates who copy an essay off the Internet? Guys who take steroids to muscle up? People who put down others to make themselves look better? Whatever the case, it's a road to ruin. Walk God's way instead.

> "The water I give will become a spring of water
> gushing up inside . . . giving eternal life."
>
> [John 4:14 NCV]

Spiritual Water

Any athlete will agree that a water bottle is a must. Deprive your body of necessary fluid, and your body will tell you. Dry mouth. Swollen tongue. Dizziness and fatigue.

Spiritual water is also a must. Deprive your soul of it, and your soul will tell you. Dehydrated hearts send desperate messages. Snarling tempers. Waves of worry. Growling mastodons of guilt and fear. You think God wants you to live with these? Hopelessness. Sleeplessness. Loneliness. Resentment. Irritability. Insecurity. These are warnings. Symptoms of a dryness deep within.

Treat your soul as you treat your thirst. Take a gulp. Guzzle moisture. Flood your heart with a good swallow of water.

Where do you find water for the soul? In Christ. "Let anyone who is thirsty come to me and drink. If anyone believes in me, rivers of living water will flow out from that person's heart, as the Scripture says" (John 7:37–38 NCV).

ONE MORE THOUGHT

You've been there. After a hard run or game, you're dying of thirst. You can't wait to gulp down waves of water. We should feel the same about Jesus. When life leaves us feeling dry and deserted, he is the One who floods our soul with hope.

Worship the LORD with gladness. Come before him, singing with joy.

[Psalm 100:1–2 NLT]

Reasons for Joy

How's life?" someone asks. And even though we've been saved by Jesus, we say, "Well, things could be better." Or "Couldn't get into the class I wanted." Or "My parents won't let me go to the party." Or "People won't leave me alone so I can finish my report on selfishness."

Are you so focused on what you don't have that you can't see what you do?

> *You have a ticket to heaven no thief can take,*
> *an eternal home no divorce can break.*
> *Every sin of your life has been cast to the sea.*
> *Every mistake you've made is nailed to the tree.*
> *You're blood-bought and heaven-made.*
> *A child of God—forever saved.*
> *So be grateful, joyful—for isn't it true?*
> *What you don't have is much less*
> *than what you do.*

ONE MORE THOUGHT

It's one of the simplest lessons of life. You can spend your time thinking about what you don't have. Or you can spend your time thinking about what you do. One is far greater than the other. Can you guess which one?

> If we say we have no sin, we are fooling ourselves, and the truth is not in us.
>
> [1 John 1:8 NCV]

A Band-Aid Isn't Enough

Some time ago my daughter Andrea got a splinter in her finger. I took her to the restroom and set out tweezers, ointment, and a Band-Aid. She didn't like what she saw. "I just want the Band-Aid, Daddy."

Sometimes we are just like Andrea. Maybe we've lied to a friend, stayed out past a curfew, or smoked something we shouldn't have. We come to Christ with our mistake, but all we want is a covering. We want to skip the treatment. We want to hide our sin. And one wonders if God, even in his great mercy, will heal what we conceal.

How can God heal what we deny? How can God touch what we cover up? A Band-Aid does no good if the splinter is still there underneath. Don't deny. Confess everything to him. Give God the chance to remove the splinters of sin in your life. It's the only way to be truly healed.

ONE MORE THOUGHT

Think back over the last week. Have you offended God with any of your actions or attitudes? Have you talked to him about it and asked for his forgiveness? The guilt and shame won't go away until you do. Let God do

Praise the LORD! . . . For His merciful kindness is great toward us.

[Psalm 117:1–2]

Soak in God's Grace

You messed up yesterday. You spoke when you should have listened, walked when you should have waited, judged when you should have trusted, gave in when you should have resisted. You messed up, but you'll mess up more if you let yesterday's mistakes sabotage today's attitude.

God's mercies are new every morning. Receive them. Learn a lesson from the Cascade forests of Washington State. Some of its trees are hundreds of years old, far surpassing the typical life span of fifty to sixty years. One leaf-laden fellow dates back seven centuries! What makes the difference? Daily drenching rains. Downpours keep the ground moist, the trees wet, and the lightning ineffective.[12]

Lightning strikes you as well. Thunderbolts of regret can ignite and consume you. Counteract them with torrents of God's grace, daily washings of forgiveness. Once a year won't do. Once a month is insufficient. Weekly showers leave you dry. Sporadic mistings leave you combustible. You need a solid soaking every day. "The LORD's love never ends; his mercies never stop. They are new every morning" (Lamentations 3:22–23 NCV).

ONE MORE THOUGHT

God's grace is like that—a cleansing shower that washes away every last trace of sorrow, guilt, and regret. We need it because we do find ways to keep messing up. How did you mess up yesterday? Or today? It's time, right now, to talk to God about it. I already hear a shower headed your way.

He has created us anew in Christ Jesus, so we can do
the good things he planned for us long ago.

[Ephesians 2:10 NLT]

A Life That Matters

By the time you knew what to call it, you were neck deep in it. It's called life. No one else has your version. You'll never bump into yourself on the sidewalk. You'll never meet anyone who has your exact blend of loves and longings.

This life of yours is racing, and if you aren't careful, you'll look up and see it passing you by. Some people don't bother with such thoughts. They grind through their days without lifting their eyes to look. They live and die and never ask why. But you aren't numbered among them. It's not enough for you to do well. You want to do good. You want your life to matter. You want to live in such a way that the world will be glad you did.

We are each given an opportunity to make a big difference during a difficult time. What if we did? What if we rocked the world with hope? Filled all corners with God's love and life?

We are created by a great God to do great works.

ONE MORE THOUGHT

God has a plan for you. A big one. A great one. Can't see it yet? Don't worry, it's out there waiting for you to discover it. So keep watching for it. Preparing for it. Praying for it. God doesn't waste his creations. He won't waste the one called "you."

The strength of those who wait with hope in the Lord will be renewed.

[Isaiah 40:31 God's Word]

A Slow Boil

Do you struggle with patience? You want to be taller, thinner, stronger—now. You want to understand algebra—now. You want a boyfriend or girlfriend—now!

You've heard the saying "A watched pot never boils." Patience is a slow boil. It doesn't turn up the flame. It waits for the burner to heat the pan, which heats the water to 212 degrees. You must sit back and allow it to happen.

Life is often this way. It's our nature to decide on what we want then dive in and make it happen. But if we jump ahead of God and the perfect timing of his plan for us, we only set ourselves up for a hard landing. When we patiently wait on him, he meets our needs at just the right moment.

If you have the Holy Spirit, then you have the potential of making patience a part of your life. Thankfully, God is patient while you find that patience.

ONE MORE THOUGHT

Do you pray when you're feeling impatient? When the pace of life leaves you stamping your feet, talking to God is always a good idea. He's the One who can tell you if it's time to plunge ahead or pull back. You just have to take

He is not far from each one of us.

[Acts 17:27]

God at the Bottom

J. J. Jasper and his little boy, Cooper, were having a blast riding in a dune buggy. Then the buggy flipped. And before he knew it, J. J. found himself doing the unthinkable: selecting a casket, planning a funeral, and imagining life without his only son. J. J. told me, "There is no class or book on this planet that can prepare you to have your five-year-old son die in your arms. . . . We know what the bottom looks like."

The bottom. The place where rejection, humiliation, and tragedy live. Where hope takes the highway. Friends too. Who's left? God is.

David asked, "Where can I go from Your Spirit? Or where can I flee from Your presence?" (Psalm 139:7). He then listed the places he found God: in "heaven . . . hell . . . [in] the morning . . . in the uttermost parts of the sea" (vv. 8–9). God, everywhere.

You will never go where God is not. Standing in front of a class? Crying alone in your room? Stuck at the bottom? God will be there. And he brings the comfort and strength that only a Father can.

ONE MORE THOUGHT

Up one moment, down the next. Life can flip faster than a dune buggy, leaving us on the bottom, wondering what happened and feeling very alone. But we're not alone. God will find you even here, and he offers his unlimited power to lift you back up.

OCTOBER

Yes, the LORD will give what is good.

[Psalm 85:12]

There is no longer Jew or Gentile, slave or free, male and
female. For you are all one in Christ Jesus.

[Galatians 3:28 NLT]

The New Kid

I've tried to be a friend to a new kid in our school. He's from another culture, and most of the kids in school treat him like dirt. Now they're making fun of me for being friends with him. This really hurts, but I feel sorry for him. I'm his only friend right now. What should I do?"

Here's how I answered this question from a student: "I would remain a friend to the new kid no matter what is said. The new kid is an unknown, but you are making him known. The first few jokes always sting, but over time the prejudice fades, the jokes get old, and people see that their mockery won't make a difference. Others look only at the surface and see differences. You obviously look deeper into this friend and see similarities."

Heaven is not divided into neighborhoods. Iranians over here. Peruvians here. Popular crowd in the middle. Rejects in the corner. In fact, when the colors of heaven are mentioned, they are always expressed as a rainbow (Revelation 4:3; 10:1). In heaven, no one eats alone.

ONE MORE THOUGHT

When people don't understand, they attack and divide. Deep down, we're really all the same. We want to love and be loved. We want to live with meaning. We want what God offers each of us—membership in his forever

> "Whoever hears my word and believes him who sent me has eternal life."
>
> [John 5:24 NIV]

The Bottom Line

Many Christians live with anxiety. Why? They're worried about eternity. They *think* they are saved, *hope* they are saved, but still they doubt, wondering, *Am I* really *saved?*

It's a universal question. Kids who accept Christ ask it. Rebels ask it. It surfaces in the heart of the struggler. It seeps into the thoughts of the dying. When we forget our vow to God, does God forget us? Is our ticket still good, or are heaven's doors closed?

Jesus' language couldn't be stronger. "And I give them eternal life, and they shall never lose it or perish throughout the ages. . . . And no one is able to snatch them out of My hand" (John 10:28 AMP).

Jesus promised a new life that could not be lost or terminated. Bridges are burned, and the transfer is accomplished. Ups and downs may mark our days, but they will never ban us from his kingdom. Jesus bottom-lines our lives with grace.

ONE MORE THOUGHT

Do you ever doubt your future with God? Don't. Reread Jesus' promises in John 3:16, 5:24, 10:28, and 11:25–26. Of all we don't know in life, we know this: we hold a ticket to heaven that will be honored. We have a

"You will always have the poor with you, but you will not always have me."

[John 12:8 NCV]

What Is Important?

Jesus visits two sisters. One, Mary, drops everything to sit at his feet. The other, Martha, scurries about, trying to tidy the house and prepare a meal for their distinguished guest. And she's not happy about it. "Lord, don't you care that my sister has left me alone to do all the work?" (Luke 10:40 NCV).

Martha's life was cluttered. She needed a break. "Martha, Martha, you are worried and upset about many things," the Master explained to her. "Only one thing is important. Mary has chosen [it]" (Luke 10:41–42 NCV).

Do you need a break? Are you hurrying through life, trying to impress others or even God? There's nothing wrong with trying to earn top grades, with doing your best in band, baseball, and the science club. But if the only reason you do it is to impress the world, let it go. Choose instead to sit at the feet of Christ. God is more pleased with the quiet attention of a sincere servant than the noisy service of a sour one.

ONE MORE THOUGHT

Sometimes the expectations pile up from parents, peers, and teachers. Life seems to be all about grades, clubs, volunteering, and college scholarships. Just remember that none of that comes from God. He just wants you to sit at his feet. He's the One thing that's important.

Trust the LORD with all your heart, and don't depend on your own understanding.

[Proverbs 3:5 NCV]

God Knows Best

The problem with this world is that it doesn't fit. It's like a T-shirt that's two sizes too small. Oh, it will do for now, but it isn't tailor-made. We were made to live with God, but on earth we live by faith. We were made to live forever, but on this earth we live but for a moment.

We must trust God. We must trust not only that he does what is best but that he knows what's ahead. Think about the words of Isaiah 57:1–2: "The good men perish; the godly die before their time, and no one seems to care or wonder why. No one seems to realize that God is taking them away from evil days ahead. For the godly who die shall rest in peace" (TLB).

What a thought. God is taking them away from the evil days ahead. Could death be God's grace? As bad as the grave seems now, could it be God's protection from the future?

Only God knows what's around the corner. Maybe we should let him do the driving.

ONE MORE THOUGHT

Are you a backseat driver, always telling the person at the wheel what to do? I bet that's how we often seem to God. We're always telling him what he needs to do and what needs to happen. Except he's the only One who knows where we're all going. Have we got it all backward?

He put a new song in my mouth, a song of praise to our God.

[Psalm 40:3 NCV]

Changed by Praise

God invites us to see his face so he can change ours. He uses our uncovered faces to display his glory. The makeover isn't easy. The sculptor of Mount Rushmore faced a lesser challenge than does God. But our Lord is up to the task. He loves to change the faces of his children. By his fingers, wrinkles of worry are rubbed away. Shadows of shame and doubt become portraits of grace and trust. He relaxes clenched jaws and smooths furrowed brows. His touch can remove bags of exhaustion from beneath the eyes and turn tears of despair into tears of peace.

How? Through worship.

We'd expect something more complicated, more demanding. A forty-day fast or the memorization of the Gospels, perhaps. No. God's plan is simpler. Our singing, praising, and shouting about his goodness does something good to us. What happens inside is reflected on the outside. God changes our faces through worship.

ONE MORE THOUGHT

It's tough to be a grouch when you're giving a compliment. It's hard to worry when you're singing in celebration. For us, worship is a physical reminder of God's spiritual glory. It has the wonderful side effect of turning

Devote yourselves to prayer, being watchful and thankful.

[Colossians 4:2 NIV]

Redefining Prayer

Early Christians were urged to "pray without ceasing" (1 Thessalonians 5:17 NASB); "keep on praying" (Romans 12:12 NLT); and "pray . . . at all times and on every occasion" (Ephesians 6:18 NLT).

Sound like an impossible assignment? Are you wondering, *My homework needs to get done, my parents expect me to do chores, my coach needs me to practice. How can I sit around praying all day?*

Do this: change your definition of prayer. Think of prayers less as an activity for God and more as an awareness of God. Seek to live in uninterrupted awareness. Acknowledge his presence everywhere you go. As you stand in line to get on the bus, think, *Thanks, God, for being with me through my day.* In the mall as you shop, *Lord, you love each and every one of these people, including me. Thank you.* As you put away the dishes, worship your Maker. Prayer isn't a task to check off your list. Prayer is an ongoing conversation with God.

ONE MORE THOUGHT

How often do you talk or text with your best friends each day? Your relationship with God can be like that and more. He'll never tell you to turn off your phone or your prayers. He's always available and always listening. He wants to hear from you.

The LORD is near to all who call upon Him, to all who call upon Him in truth.

[Psalm 145:18]

Never Alone

Is God distant? How can the touching, helping, healing presence of God come to us? Should we light a candle, sing chants, build an altar, give a backpack full of money? What invites the presence of God?

God's present is his presence. God's greatest gift is himself. Sunsets steal our breath. Caribbean blue stills our hearts. Newborn babies stir our tears. But take all these away—strip away the sunsets, oceans, and cooing babies—and leave us in the Sahara, and we still have reason to dance in the sand. Why? Because God is with us.

God wants us to know. We are never alone. Ever. God loves you too much to leave you alone, so he hasn't. He hasn't left you alone with your fears, your worries, your disease, or your death. So kick up your heels for joy.

He is a personal God who loves and heals and helps. He doesn't respond to magic potions or clever slogans. He looks for more. He looks for reverence, obedience, and God-hungry hearts. And when he sees them, he comes!

ONE MORE THOUGHT

Feeling abandoned and alone? It might not seem like it, but your loneliness may be an opportunity. God longs to be your friend, the One you always turn to. He is there for you. So reach out to him with praise and prayer. He is closer than you think.

> "Anyone who becomes as humble as this little child
> is the greatest in the Kingdom of Heaven."
>
> [Matthew 18:4 NLT]

Bend Low

One morning on the side of a Swiss mountain, a man watched two goats headed down a narrow path from opposite directions, one going up, the other down. At one point the narrow trail prevented them from passing each other. When they saw each other, they backed up and lowered their heads, as though ready to lunge. But then a wonderful thing happened. The ascending goat lay down on the path. The other stepped over his back. The first animal then arose and continued his climb to the top. The man observed that the first goat made it higher because he was willing to bend lower.

What works for goats also works for people. When we're willing to bend low and allow others to get their way, it's usually true that both sides get what they want. It's a form of humility. "Do nothing out of selfish ambition or vain conceit. Rather, in humility value others above yourselves" (Philippians 2:3 NIV).

Our model, as always, is Jesus, who "humbled himself by becoming obedient to death—even death on a cross!" (v. 8 NIV).

ONE MORE THOUGHT

You can show humility in the simplest of ways, such as when you and another person reach the cafeteria line at the same time, and you say, "You go ahead." You know it's taking root in your life when you pray, *Please, God, you lead the way, and I'll follow you.*

Give all your worries to him, because he cares about you.

[1 Peter 5:7 NCV]

Don't Worry About It

Worry makes you forget who's in charge.

And when the focus is on yourself, you worry. You become anxious about many things. You worry that:

Your classmates won't appreciate you.
Your teachers will overwork you.
Your parents won't understand you.
Your friends will outshine you.

With time, your agenda becomes more important than God's. You're more concerned with making yourself look good than with making him happy. You may even find yourself doubting God's judgment.

God has gifted you with talents. He has done the same to your friends. If you concern yourself with your friends' talents, you will neglect yours. But if you concern yourself with simply doing the best you can with yours, you could inspire both you and your friends to let God be in control. He is anyway, you know.

Try it—and don't worry about it.

ONE MORE THOUGHT

Someone once said that a day of worry is more exhausting than a week of work. I believe it. Worry is a waste of time and energy. Worse, it distracts you from the business of pleasing God. So give up worrying already—I'm worried about you!

> "You must change and become like little children. Otherwise,
> you will never enter the kingdom of heaven."
>
> [Matthew 18:3 NCV]

Heart of a Child

Bedtime is a bad time for young kids. No child understands the logic of going to bed while there is energy left in the body or hours left in the day.

My children were no exception. Years ago, after many objections and countless groans, the girls were finally in their gowns, in their beds, and on their pillows. I slipped into the room to give them a final kiss. Andrea, the five-year-old, was still awake, just barely, but awake. After I kissed her, she lifted her eyelids one final time and said, "I can't wait until I wake up."

Oh, for the attitude of a five-year-old! That simple passion for living that can't wait for tomorrow. A philosophy of life that reads, "Play hard, laugh hard, and leave the worries to your father." A bottomless well of optimism flooded by a perpetual spring of faith. Is it any wonder Jesus said we must have the heart of a child before we can enter the kingdom of heaven?

ONE MORE THOUGHT

Do you remember how bedtime felt when you were little? The excitement of anticipating another day of play? You can recapture that feeling. Make this your motto too: "Play hard. Laugh hard. Leave the worries to your Father."

> "Are you doing anything remarkable if you welcome
> only your friends? Everyone does that!"
>
> [Matthew 5:47 GOD'S WORD]

Open Arms

You know, probably all too well, about cliques. They're tight groups of people who are always talking and hanging out together. And the people in them tend to treat everyone else like they have a disease.

Maybe you're in a clique now. Or maybe there's a group you're dying to join. But are cliques all they're cracked up to be? What good is a group that makes others feel left out?

God shows us another approach. He has a white-hot passion to save the children of every jungle, neighborhood, village, and slum. His vision for the end of history includes "people for God from every tribe, language, people, and nation" (Revelation 5:9 NCV). He loves the gypsies of Turkey, the hippies of California, the cowboys and rednecks of West Texas. He has a heart for science club presidents and football team captains.

Christ has little use for cliques. He opens his arms to all.

ONE MORE THOUGHT

You know how awful it feels to be the outsider. That's what cliques do—they send the unspoken message that "You don't belong." Contrast that with the message of Christ, who invites the whole world into his family. Which group would you rather join?

Peace of mind means a healthy body, but jealousy will rot your bones.

[Proverbs 14:30 NCV]

Put an End to Envy

Joseph had a jealousy problem. Not his, but the jealousy of his ten older brothers. Their father pampered Joseph like a prized calf. The brothers worked all day. Joseph played all day. They wore clothes from a secondhand store. Jacob gave Joseph a hand-stitched, multicolored cloak with embroidered sleeves. Jacob treated the eleventh-born like a firstborn. The brothers spat at the sight of Joseph.

The brothers dealt with their jealousy by selling Joseph into slavery. Not the best solution. Joseph rose to power in Egypt and threw his brothers into prison for a time.

Acting out on your envy isn't the best solution for you either. Do your parents treat little sister Cindy Lou better than you? Does a friend own a better car? Does another friend get all the guys? Getting mad at your parents or your friends won't help. Giving in to jealousy ruins relationships and robs you of joy. It's better when you focus on what you have instead of what you want. God's already given you what you need.

ONE MORE THOUGHT

If we're feeling jealous, that's an air-raid warning. Our mind is saying, "I want more for *me*." Can't we be happy for whatever blessings God has given someone else? Don't be a slave to envy. Live with a thankful heart. That's freedom.

Since we have been united with him in his death,
we will also be raised to life as he was.

[Romans 6:5 NLT]

Safe to Believe

This world teaches us that everything has an ending. Songs. Movies. School days. Lives. But Jesus taught a different lesson. "When Jesus was raised from the dead it was a signal of the end of death-as-the-end" (Romans 6:5–6 MSG). Don't you love that sentence? The resurrection is an exploding flare announcing to all sincere seekers that it is safe to believe. Safe to believe in ultimate justice. Safe to believe in eternal bodies. Safe to believe in heaven as our mansion and the earth as its porch. Safe to believe in a time when questions won't keep us awake and pain won't keep us down. Safe to believe in open graves and endless days and genuine praise.

Jesus died, but it wasn't the end. Because Jesus walked out of his tomb, your death won't be the end either. Because we can accept the resurrection story, it is safe to accept the rest of the story.

ONE MORE THOUGHT

It's the answer to every question about Christ and Christianity. Jesus died on a cross, his body was sealed in a tomb, and on the third day he threw the stone aside and walked into the sun. Who else comes back to life? We do, when we give up this life on earth and join Jesus in heaven.

"You will be judged in the same way that you judge others."

[Matthew 7:2 NCV]

No Judging

Don't you hate it when people judge you? When they make fun of you for flunking a test, not knowing you were too sick to study? When they insult your shoes, not understanding that your family is short on funds? We need to be careful that we don't do the same to others.

Are they too loud? Perhaps they fear being neglected again. Are they too quiet? Perhaps they fear failing again. Too slow? Perhaps they fell the last time they hurried. You don't know. Only someone who has followed yesterday's steps can be their judge.

Not only are we ignorant about yesterday, we are ignorant about tomorrow. Dare we judge a book while chapters are yet unwritten? Should we comment on a painting while the artist still holds the brush? How can you dismiss a soul until God's work is complete? "God began doing a good work in you, and I am sure he will continue it until it is finished when Jesus Christ comes again" (Philippians 1:6 NCV).

ONE MORE THOUGHT

Few people truly understand you. Your friends, sometimes. Your parents, maybe only once in a while. So it's not such a good idea to assume you understand everyone else. They're probably dealing with things you can't even imagine. Let your goal be, instead of judging them, to understand them.

> God, with undeserved kindness, declares that we are righteous.
>
> [Romans 3:24 NLT]

Free to Go

Barabbas sat in a jail cell waiting for his execution, anger in his heart and blood on his hands. Defiant. Violent. A trouble-maker. A life taker. Guilty and proud of it.

We're like Barabbas. Sinners. Murderers. It doesn't matter if we've literally killed someone. The point is that we are rebels against God. We roar, "I want to run my own life, thank you very much!" We tell God to get out, get lost, and not come back. Like Barabbas, we deserve to die. Four prison walls, thickened with fear, hurt, and hate, surround us. We have been found guilty. And we have nothing to offer in trade for our lives.

Our executioner's footsteps echo against stone walls. We don't look up as he opens the door. We know what he's going to say. "Time to pay up." But we hear something else. "You're free to go. They took Jesus instead of you."

What just happened? Grace happened.

ONE MORE THOUGHT

Aren't we all world-class rebels? Selfish instead of selfless? More interested in Gabby's new wardrobe than God's Word? How do we live with ourselves? Jesus is how. He crosses out the *guilty* on our name tag and writes in *grace*. That's freedom. That's living.

> Why spill the water of your springs in the streets, having sex with just anyone?
>
> [Proverbs 5:16 NLT]

What Will It Hurt?

He *really* likes you. You *really* like him. What's the big deal if you end up having sex? What will it hurt?

Glad you asked. It's important to think about how you'll react when this situation comes up. *Before* it comes up. Think about what you will say, and what your decision will be. Make your decision now.

Sex outside of marriage pretends we can give the body and not affect the soul. We can't. All that we are as humans is so connected that whatever touches the body deeply impacts mind and heart as well. Get too close too soon and guilt and shame are the natural result. On top of that, there are the fears about pregnancy and disease. The me-centered phrase "as long as no one gets hurt" sounds noble, but the truth is, a lot of hurt can come from losing self-control with sexual temptation.

God created this wonderful gift, and he wants you to enjoy it—on his terms—within the covenant of marriage. Sex is a celebration of permanence, a tender moment in which the body continues what the mind and the soul have already begun. It's a time when no one gets hurt. A time that brings joy to man and wife and honor to God.

ONE MORE THOUGHT

There's nothing wrong with sexual feelings—God gave them to you. It's what you do with them (and when) that matters. A smart strategy is to decide what you believe, and what will please God, before you get into a steamy situation. Then hold your ground no matter what.

Remember God's Goodness

A great storm arose on the lake so that waves covered the boat, but Jesus was sleeping" (Matthew 8:24 NCV).

Now there's a scene. The disciples scream; Jesus dreams. Thunder roars; Jesus snores. His snooze troubles the disciples. "Teacher, don't you care that we're going to drown?" (Mark 4:38 NLT). They do not ask about Jesus' strength, his knowledge, or his know-how. They raise doubts about Jesus' character: "Do you not care . . ."

Fear does this. Fear wears down our confidence in God's goodness. It also muffles our memory. The disciples had reason to trust Jesus. By now they'd seen him "healing all kinds of sickness and all kinds of disease among the people" (Matthew 4:23). They had witnessed him heal a leper with a touch and a servant with a command (8:3, 13).

Did they remember the accomplishments of Christ? Maybe they didn't. Fear creates a form of spiritual amnesia. It makes us forget what Jesus has done and how good God is.

ONE MORE THOUGHT

You've rehearsed for the choir solo for a month and nailed it every time—only when you step on stage, fear can make you forget all those perfect practices. Kind of like us with God. It's one reason we worship. It's spiritual rehearsal—a way to remind ourselves of his amazing power and love

> We all have different gifts, each of which came because of the grace God gave us.
>
> [Romans 12:6 NCV]

What Are Your Strengths?

There are some things we want to do but simply aren't able. I, for example, have the desire to sing. Singing for others would give me wonderful satisfaction. The problem is, it wouldn't give the same satisfaction to my listeners as they held their ears.

Paul gives good advice in Romans 12:3: "Have a sane estimate of your capabilities" (PHILLIPS).

In other words, be aware of your strengths. When you explain, do people understand? When you lead, do people follow? When you organize, do things improve? Where are you most productive? A big part of the teen years is trying different things to find out where you excel and what you most enjoy. Identify your strengths, and then major in them. Failing to focus on your strengths may prevent you from accomplishing the unique tasks God has called you to do. Preaching? Writing? Singing? Pray about your future, and let God lead you to the gifts he wants you to use.

ONE MORE THOUGHT

Figuring out your future can feel like a heavy burden. You may feel that God forgot about you, that you don't have any gifts. Not true! Some do take longer to discover than others, so be patient. God will show you your strengths and your future when the time is right.

Pressing the Pause Button

Jesus understands the frenzy of life. People back-to-backed his calendar with demands. They brought Jesus more than sick bodies and seeking souls. They brought him agendas. Itineraries. Unsolicited advice.

They do the same with you. Look over your shoulder, my friend. The crowd is one step back. Moreover, they seem to know more about your life than you do. Who you should hang out with. What you should study. Where you should spend your Saturday. Your mental hard drive is full already!

Follow the example of Jesus. "Now when it was day, He departed and went into a deserted place" (Luke 4:42). *Deserted* doesn't necessarily mean desolate, just quiet. Jesus was after peace. "I need to get away. To think. To ponder. To rechart my course." He determined the time, selected a place. With resolve, he pressed the pause button on his life.

God rested after six days of work, and the world didn't collapse. What makes us think it will if we do?

ONE MORE THOUGHT

You're not a superhero, you know. You need time to rest and recharge, to chill and change your stress level. To pray and praise God. If even Jesus needed a break, maybe we should give ourselves one too.

> Don't insist on getting even; that's not for you to do. "I'll
> do the judging," says God. "I'll take care of it."
>
> [Romans 12:19 MSG]

No Room for Revenge

Your enemies still figure into God's plan. Their pulses are proof: God hasn't given up on them. They may be out of God's will, but not out of his reach. You honor God when you see them not as his failures, but as his projects.

Besides, who assigned us the task of vengeance? God occupies the only seat on the supreme court of heaven. He wears the robe and refuses to share the gavel. Revenge removes God from the equation. We seek to displace and replace him. "Did you see what she did to me, Lord? I'm not sure you can handle this one. You may punish too little or too slowly. I'll take this matter into my hands, thank you."

Is this what you want to say? Jesus didn't. No one had a clearer sense of right and wrong than the perfect Son of God. Yet, "when he suffered, he didn't make any threats but left everything to the one who judges fairly" (1 Peter 2:23 GOD'S WORD).

Only God assesses accurate judgments. Vengeance is his job. Leave your enemies in the hands of the perfect Judge.

ONE MORE THOUGHT

The desire to get back at those who wrong you is so strong. He stole your sweatshirt. She stole your boyfriend. They deserve the worst you can dish out, and then some! Except that's a call we're not allowed to make. God is umpire, linesman, judge, and jury. Let him rule, or you may be next in line

The prayer of a person living right with God is something powerful.

[James 5:16 MSG]

Flip the Switch

One of our Brazilian church leaders met Christ during a stay in a drug-rehab center. His therapy included three one-hour sessions of prayer a day. Patients didn't have to pray, but they had to attend the prayer meeting. Dozens of recovering drug addicts spent sixty uninterrupted minutes on their knees.

I was amazed. I admitted that my prayers were short and formal. He invited (dared?) me to meet him for prayer. We knelt on the concrete floor of our small church auditorium and began to talk to God. Change that. I talked; he cried, wailed, and pleaded. He pounded his fists on the floor, shook a fist toward heaven, confessed and reconfessed every sin. He recited every promise in the Bible as if God needed a reminder.

Our passionate prayers move the heart of God. "The prayer of a person living right with God is something powerful to be reckoned with" (James 5:16 MSG). Prayer does not change God's nature. Prayer does, however, impact the flow of history. God has wired his world for power, but he calls on us to flip the switch.

ONE MORE THOUGHT

Crying. Shouting. Begging. Not your style of prayer? God isn't asking you to put on a show for him. He does, however, want you to show your true feelings. No holding back. So find a time and place—like right now—to give it all to him, then watch him go to work.

God alone, who gave the law, is the Judge.

[James 4:12 NLT]

Let Jesus Be Judge

Even though you knew better, you drank beer with your girl-friends after the dance. Or maybe your parents were gone and you spent an hour looking at Internet pictures you knew you shouldn't see. You blew it and confessed to God. You realize he's forgiven you, but you're finding it hard to forgive yourself.

Welcome to the Court of Shame. Look around. See anyone you know? Recognize that judge in the long black robe? It's you. In fact the prosecutor looks pretty familiar. You again. Glance over to the jury. Yep. Twelve of you, all giving you the evil eye and saying, "Guilty." When it comes to shame, we are our harshest judges.

After hearing the heart of the woman having an affair, Jesus declared, "I also don't judge you guilty. You may go now, but don't sin anymore" (John 8:11 NCV). If Jesus judged her and found her not guilty, what do you think he says about you?

At times like this, you must ask yourself a question: who makes a better judge—you or Jesus?

ONE MORE THOUGHT

To see what kind of judge Jesus is, find your Bible and read the full story of the woman caught in adultery in John 8:1–11. Does he desire to condemn her—or you? No. He just wants us to stop doing wrong and start doing right. Compassion and wisdom. My kind of judge.

I will praise You, for I am fearfully and wonderfully made; marvelous
are Your works, and that my soul knows very well.

[Psalm 139:14]

You Are God's Idea

Fashion designers tell us, "You'll be somebody if you wear our jeans. Stick our name on your rear end, and insignificance will vanish." For a while, fashion redeems us from the world of littleness and nothingness, and we are something else. But then, horror of horrors, the styles change, the fad passes, and we're left wearing yesterday's jeans, feeling like yesterday's news.

Fear of insignificance creates the result it dreads. If a basketball player stands at the foul line repeating, "I'll never make the shot," guess what? He'll never make the shot. If you pass your days mumbling, "I'll never make a difference; I'm not worth anything," guess what? You will be sentencing yourself to a life of gloom.

Even more, you are disagreeing with God. According to him you were "skillfully wrought" (Psalm 139:15). You were "fearfully and wonderfully made" (v. 14). If you could count his thoughts of you, "they would be more in number than the sand" (v. 18).

Why does he love you so much? The same reason the artist loves his paintings or the boat builder loves his vessels. You are his idea.

ONE MORE THOUGHT

When was the last time you worked really hard to create something special? Was it a model? A drawing? A book report? A batch of chocolate chip cookies? When you put your heart into something, it matters to you. A lot. That's how God feels about you.

You shall walk in all the way that the LORD your God has commanded you, that you may live, and that it may go well with you.

[Deuteronomy 5:33 ESV]

Walk Through with God

God gets us through stuff. *Through* the Red Sea onto dry ground (Exodus 14:22), *through* the wilderness (Deuteronomy 29:5), *through* the valley of the shadow of death (Psalm 23:4), and *through* the deep sea (Psalm 77:19).

In fact, *through* is one of God's favorite words: "When you pass *through* the waters, I will be with you; and *through* the rivers, they shall not overflow you. When you walk *through* the fire, you shall not be burned, nor shall the flame scorch you" (Isaiah 43:2).

What are you trying to get through today? Trouble with your parents? A friendship that's fading? A class you're failing? Whatever you're up against, God has already been through it, and he'll walk through it with you. The journey may not be easy. It may not be quick. But God promises to be at your side, lighting the way for each step. "Your word is a lamp to guide my feet and a light for my path" (Psalm 119:105 NLT).

ONE MORE THOUGHT

Ever taken a long walk alone at night—without a light? It can be a little creepy and scary—and sometimes a lot creepy and scary! Kind of like walking through life without the light of God to show you the way. So read the Bible and talk to him daily. You'll find it a much better way to travel.

There is surely a future hope for you, and your hope will not be cut off.

[Proverbs 23:18 NIV]

Impossible Dreams

Do your parents doubt your dreams? I'm not talking about the ones when you're asleep, but the ones when your eyes are open. Dreams like wanting to be a dancer, diver, or diplomat, a doctor serving the poor or a missionary serving in Malaysia. Without their support, it feels impossible.

We forget that *impossible* is one of God's favorite words. He dreams impossible dreams. Why? If you accomplish a possible dream, then you get all the glory. But if you accomplish an impossible dream, then God gets the glory. It shows the world that an incredible, unbelievable God still exists and works in the lives of people. It begins with dreams like yours.

Although it may seem your parents are dousing your passion, they could just be injecting some much-needed wisdom into your plans. Practicality and logic aren't all bad. Doubt may be caution in disguise.

In the end you must ask yourself, whose dream am I going to follow: mine, my parents', or God's? God's dreams are always bigger, better, and more unbelievable.

ONE MORE THOUGHT

Yes, parents can be a drag on dreams. But they usually mean well! Keep talking to them, and to God, about your goals. Mix in a heavy dose of patience and perseverance. If God is behind your dream, it will happen in his timing. If not, he has something even better in mind.

> Where God's love is, there is no fear, because God's perfect love drives out fear.
>
> [1 John 4:18 NCV]

Soaked in Love

We fear rejection, so we follow the crowd. We fear not fitting in, so we take the drugs. For fear of standing out, we wear what everyone else wears. For fear of blending in, we wear what no one else wears. For fear of being alone, we sleep with anyone. For fear of not being loved, we search for love in all the wrong places.

But God flushes those fears. Those soaked in God's love don't sell out to win the love of others. They don't even sell out to win the love of God.

Do you think you need to? Do you think, *If I cuss less, pray more, drink less, study more . . . if I try harder, God will love me more?* Sniff and smell Satan's stench behind those words. We all need improvement, but we don't need to pursue God's love. We change because we already have God's love. God's perfect love.

ONE MORE THOUGHT

Read 1 John 4:16–21, some of the most important words about love ever written. Do you ever find yourself trying to win God's love through your performance? What do these verses say to you about perfect love and God's love for us?

He had compassion on them.

[Matthew 14:14 NIV]

He Feels and Heals Our Hurts

The Greek word for compassion is *splanchnizomai*, which won't mean much to you unless you're taking Introduction to "Splanchnology" at school. If so, you know that "splanchnology" is a study of . . . the gut.

When Matthew writes that Jesus had compassion on the people, he is not saying that Jesus felt casual pity or a little bit sorry for them. No, the term is far more graphic and intense. Matthew is saying that Jesus felt their hurt in his gut. He felt the limp of the crippled. He felt the hurt of the diseased. He felt the loneliness of the leper. He felt the embarrassment of the sinful.

Jesus has felt everything you've felt and then some. Rejection. Humiliation. Torture. Execution with nails on a cross. When you allow him into your heart, he feels your pain too. And once he feels your hurts, he can't help but heal them.

ONE MORE THOUGHT

When you're having the absolute worst day of your life, you figure no one can understand, not even Jesus. Except he's God, remember? He's inside of you. He *does* understand. Share your pain with him. No one can make it better like he can.

> No one who is dishonest will live in my house; no liars will stay around me.
>
> [Psalm 101:7 NCV]

Lying Leads to Death

Do you know the story of Ananias and Sapphira (Acts 5:1–11)? Both tried to deceive the church and God, and both apparently died because of it. More than once I've heard people refer to that story with a nervous chuckle and say, "I'm glad God doesn't still strike people dead for lying." I'm not so sure he doesn't.

It seems to me that the result of deceit is still death. Not death of the body, perhaps, but death all the same. Relationships (falsehoods are termites in the walls of any marriage or friendship). A conscience (the tragedy of the second lie is that it's always easier to tell than the first). A career (just ask the grad student who got booted out for cheating if the lie wasn't fatal).

We could also list the deaths of intimacy, trust, peace, credibility, and self-respect. But perhaps the most tragic death caused by our lying is when it happens to our statements about Jesus. The court won't listen to the testimony of a lying witness. Neither will the world.

ONE MORE THOUGHT

Read about Ananias and Sapphira in your Bible. Do *you* think that God overlooks lying today? That there's no consequence for fibs, whether big or little? When we disobey God, we harm not only ourselves but also those around us, sometimes in ways we can't imagine. Make it easy on everyone—just tell the truth.

When I was helpless, he saved me.

[Psalm 116:6 NCV]

God Is on Our Team

When I was young, the minute we neighborhood kids got home from school we'd drop the books and hit the pavement. The kid across the street had a dad with a strong addiction to football. As soon as he was home from work we'd start yelling for him to come and play. Out of fairness he'd always ask, "Which team is losing?" Then he would join that team, which often seemed to be mine.

His appearance in the huddle changed the whole ballgame. He was confident, strong, and most of all, he had a plan. We'd circle around him, and he'd say, "Okay, boys, here is what we're going to do." The other side was groaning before we left the huddle. You see, we not only had a new plan, we had a new leader.

He brought new life to our team. God does precisely the same for us. We didn't need a new play; we needed a new plan. We didn't need to trade positions; we needed a new player. That player is Jesus Christ, God's firstborn Son.

ONE MORE THOUGHT

Do you ever feel that way—that you're on a losing team with little hope for a comeback? That no matter how hard you try to move the ball, you end up losing yardage? There is One with a playbook designed specifically for your situation. One God. One plan. One life. Trust him with yours.

I want to know Christ and the power that raised him from the dead. . . .
Then I have hope that I myself will be raised from the dead.

[Philippians 3:10–11 NCV]

The Other Side of the River

Jesus saw people enslaved by their fear of death. He explained that the river of death was nothing to fear. The people wouldn't believe him. He touched a boy and called him back to life. The followers were still unconvinced. He whispered life into the dead body of a girl. The people were still cynical. He let a dead man spend four days in a grave and then called him out. Is that enough?

Apparently not. It was necessary for him to enter the river and submerge himself in the water of death before people would believe that death had been conquered.

But after he did, after he came out on the other side of death's river, it was time to sing . . . it was time to celebrate!

Are you afraid of death's river? Don't be. Jesus shows us that there is a bank on the other side, and that he has the power to take us there.

ONE MORE THOUGHT

People usually fear the unknown, and most of us have little experience with death. Jesus, however, knows all about it. He's been there, done that. He says, "Those who give up their lives for me will have true life" (Matthew 16:25 NCV). I'm trusting the One with power over death.

> But the Lord is faithful; he will strengthen you and guard you from the evil one.
>
> [2 Thessalonians 3:3 NLT]

Ultimate Good

Have you read Genesis 3? That's the chapter about the entry of evil into the world. Disaster came in the form of Lucifer, the fallen angel. And as long as Satan "prowls around like a roaring lion" (1 Peter 5:8 NIV), he will wreak havoc among God's people. He will lock preachers, like Paul, in prisons. He will afflict the friends of Jesus, like Lazarus, with diseases. He will assault you with the lie that no one loves you.

Yet Satan's strategies will backfire. The imprisoned Paul will write books of the Bible. The cemetery of Lazarus will become a stage for one of Christ's greatest miracles. And you will learn that God loves you more than you can imagine. Intended evil becomes ultimate good.

We can be thankful that the tricks of the devil will always be trumped by the "treat" of a God who "will rescue me from every evil deed and bring me safely into his heavenly kingdom" (2 Timothy 4:18 ESV).

ONE MORE THOUGHT

This night may be marked by candy, kids in masks, and made-up monsters, but the real creatures of the dark are not to be trifled with. Let's rely on a loving and rescuing God to put down evil whenever and wherever it strikes.

NOVEMBER

"And you shall know the truth, and
the truth shall make you free."

[John 8:32]

Losing your temper causes a lot of trouble, but staying calm settles arguments.

[Proverbs 15:18 cev]

Deal with Your Drips

You get ticked off these days over the smallest things. Now even your friends avoid you. What are you supposed to do about all this anger?

I wonder what formed the Grand Canyon. Maybe a few drips here and there. A leaky underground faucet or a gentle rain on a peaceful night. Slowly more and more water built up. Thunderstorms. Lightning. Angry expressions from the sky spilling out in the raging river called the Colorado, carving a crevasse.

Our anger builds like the Colorado. Slowly, small things drip down, annoying, irritating, finally enraging. *Get out of my way!* Drip. *You do this all the time!* Drip. *Don't tell me what to do!* Drip. The pressure and the buildup explodes, unleashing a frenzy of anger, pouring out in words, sweeping away our friends, our family, our peace.

Don't wait until you have a roaring river. Go after the small drips. Address every little irritant with forgiveness and prayer. Do it before anger digs a canyon in your life . . . with you on one side and everyone you know on the other.

ONE MORE THOUGHT

Got anger management issues? Go to God with them. He knows how to help you and what's really bugging you. He can speak to you through a godly friend, teacher, or family member too. Talk to them now—before the next temper tornado.

> "The work God wants you to do is this: Believe the One he sent."
>
> [John 6:29 NCV]

"I Am the Way"

Some historians clump Christ with Moses, Muhammad, Confucius, and other spiritual leaders. But Jesus refuses to share the page. He declares, "I am the way, and the truth, and the life; no one comes to the Father, but by me" (John 14:6 RSV). He could have been politically correct and said, "I know the way," or, "I show the way." Yet he speaks of who he is: *I am the way.*

Many flinch at this absolute. It sounds primitive in our era of broadbands and broad minds. The world is shrinking, cultures are blending, borders are bending; this is the day of inclusion. All roads lead to heaven, right?

But how can all religions lead to God when they are so different? We don't tolerate such illogic in other matters. We don't pretend that all roads lead to London or all ships sail to Australia.

Jesus cleared a one-of-a-kind passageway uncluttered by human effort. Christ came, not for the strong, but for the weak; not for the righteous, but for the sinner. We enter his way with the confession of our need, not the completion of our deeds. He dies and we live. He invites and we believe.

ONE MORE THOUGHT

Do you have friends who struggle with this idea? Do you wrestle with it yourself? Jesus does not intend to exclude. He's just being clear. He is God. No one else. The road goes through him. No shortcuts and no detours. One God. One way. Make your choice.

The LORD created the heavens. He is the God who formed the earth and made it.

[Isaiah 45:18 NCV]

The God You Need

You don't need what Dorothy found. Remember her discovery in *The Wizard of Oz* movie? She and her trio of friends followed the yellow-brick road only to discover that the wizard was a wimp! Nothing but smoke and mirrors and tin-drum thunder. Is that the kind of god you need?

You don't need to carry the burden of a lesser god . . . a god on a shelf, a god in a box, or a god in a bottle. No, you need a God who can place 100 billion stars in our galaxy and 100 billion galaxies in the universe. You need a God who can shape two fists of flesh into 75 to 100 billion nerve cells, each with as many as 10,000 connections to other nerve cells, place it in a skull, and call it a brain.

And you need a God who, while so mind-numbingly mighty, can also make the gentlest of snowflakes and care about the smallest of creatures. A God of power and of love.

ONE MORE THOUGHT

We all lean on lesser gods at times. Status. Popularity. Money. Grades. A cool car. The "right" friends. Whatever we think will carry us through. But none of these gods satisfies for long. We don't need an "Over the Rainbow" god. We need the One who created rainbows!

Come back to the LORD your God, because he is kind and shows mercy.

[Joel 2:13 NCV]

Whatever It Takes

How far do you want God to go in getting your attention? If God has to choose between your eternal safety and your earthly comfort, which do you hope he chooses?

What if he moved you to another land? (As he did Abraham.) What if he called you to confront an ornery ruler? (Remember Moses?) How about a ride in the bowel of a fish? (You've heard of Jonah.) A promotion like Daniel's? A demotion like Samson's?

God does whatever it takes to get our attention. Isn't that the message of the Bible? The relentless pursuit of God. God on the hunt. God in the search. Peeking under the bed for hiding kids, stirring the bushes for lost sheep. Have you thought about this? Your illness, your heavy homework load, your long list of rejections—all could be God waving his hand, letting you know it's time to come back and spend time with him.

Aren't you glad he's still there?

ONE MORE THOUGHT

God won't *make* you walk with him. He's too much of a gentleman for that. But he has a thousand ways to get you to notice what's missing in your life. You're facing one crisis after another? It could be the devil. It could just be life. But it also could be the holy hand of heaven, pointing the way home.

Whatever you say or do should be done in the name of the Lord Jesus.

[Colossians 3:17 CEV]

Our Work Honors God

Work, work, work. Chores in the morning. Classes all day. Dishwashing after dinner. Homework at night. Part-time job on the weekend. Does it ever end? Does any of it matter to God?

God has ordained your work as something good. Before he gave Adam a wife or a child, even before he gave Adam britches, God gave Adam a job. "Then the LORD God took the man and put him into the garden of Eden to cultivate it and keep it" (Genesis 2:15 NASB). God calls all the physically able to till the gardens he gives. He honors work. So honor God in your work. "And whatever you do, whether in word or deed, do it all in the name of the Lord Jesus, giving thanks to God the Father through him" (Colossians 3:17 NIV).

Whatever you do! Do it as if Jesus is grading your report or autographing your project. Then give thanks to God for the tasks he gives you and the opportunity to make a difference in the world. Even if it's by washing dishes.

ONE MORE THOUGHT

There's no glamour in scrubbing out the toilet or rewriting an English essay. Much of our work is like that. But you know what? We honor and worship God with the quality of our labor. Mundane becomes meaningful. Work becomes wondrous. God becomes glad.

> "There will be no more death or mourning or crying or pain,
> for the old order of things has passed away."
>
> [Revelation 21:4 NIV]

Looking Ahead to Heaven

Do you ever find life a little . . . boring? That will change one day. You won't be bored in heaven because you won't be the same you in heaven. Boredom emerges from weeds that heaven doesn't allow. The weed of weariness: our eyes tire. The weed of mental limitations: information overload dulls us. The weed of self-centeredness: we grow disinterested when the spotlight shifts to others. The weed of tedium: meaningless activity steals our energy. But there are no weeds in heaven. You're left with a keen mind, endless focus, and God-honoring assignments.

Yes, you will have assignments in heaven. "[God's] servants shall serve Him" (Revelation 22:3). What is service if not responsible activity? Those who are faithful over a few things will rule over many (Matthew 25:21).

You might oversee the orbit of a distant planetary system . . . design a mural in the new city . . . monitor the expansion of a new species of plants or animals. What does a Creator do but create? What do his happy children do but serve him?

ONE MORE THOUGHT

Dull days. We all have them. Not much we can do about it either. Part of life is persevering through the predictable. But maybe we'll find the journey a little easier when we remember what's ahead. The best is yet to come. Heaven awaits.

Plant the good seeds of righteousness, and you will harvest a crop of love.

[Hosea 10:12 NLT]

Planting Peace

Want to see a miracle? Plant a word of love deep in a person's heart and life. Nurture it with a smile and a prayer, and watch what happens.

Compliment your friend on the way her hair looks today. Thank a buddy for his positive example. Give your teacher a note of appreciation at the end of the term. Bake cookies and take them to the single mom and her kids down the street. Help your brother with his homework. Hug your mom before you leave for school. Honor your dad by asking him about his day.

Sowing seeds of peace is like sowing beans. You don't know why it works; you just know it does. Seeds are planted, and top-soils of hurt are shoved away. Anger fades. Conflicts decline. Peace sprouts and spreads.

Don't forget the principle. Never underestimate the power of a seed.

ONE MORE THOUGHT

A single seed, when properly cared for, will eventually grow into towering timber. You can create a forest of peace and love around you with the simplest methods. Plant encouraging words. Water them daily with friendship and prayer. Stand back as they stretch to the sky.

> He faced all of the same testings we do, yet he did not sin. So
> let us come boldly to the throne of our gracious God.
>
> [Hebrews 4:15–16 NLT]

He's Been There

Do you avoid talking to God because you don't think he'll understand your troubles? According to the Bible he can: "Jesus understands every weakness of ours, because he was tempted in every way that we are. But he did not sin!" (Hebrews 4:15 CEV).

It's as if the writer of Hebrews knows we will say, "God, it's easy for you up there. You don't know how hard it is down here." So he boldly proclaims Jesus' ability to understand. Look at the wording again. *Jesus*. Not an angel. Not an ambassador. Jesus himself. *Understands every weakness*. Not some of them. Not most. Every one. *Was tempted in every way that we are*. He's been through every hurt and ache, every stress and strain, and knows how they weaken us.

Every page of the Gospels hammers home this key point: God knows how you feel. When you say you've reached your limit, he gets what you mean. When you shake your head at impossible deadlines, he shakes his too. When your plans are interrupted by people with other plans, he nods because he knows.

He's been there.

ONE MORE THOUGHT

Does it bug you when parents or friends say, "I know what you mean," but they really don't? That never happens with Jesus. He *does* know what you mean. He's been through it all, and when living inside you, he's going through it all again with you.

The Spirit of God has made me; the breath of the Almighty gives me life.

[Job 33:4 NIV]

Commanded to Love

Observant guy, Paul. He noticed something about the way we treat people. He said it about marriage, but the principle applies in any relationship. "The man who loves his wife loves himself" (Ephesians 5:28 NCV). There's a connection between the way you feel about yourself and the way you feel about others. If you are at peace with yourself—if you like yourself—you will get along with others.

The opposite is also true. If you don't like yourself, if you are ashamed, embarrassed, or angry, other people are going to know it.

Why is this important? Because Jesus told us the two greatest commandments are "Love the Lord your God with all your heart and with all your soul and with all your mind" (Matthew 22:37 ESV) and "Love your neighbor as yourself" (v. 39 ESV). So give yourself a break! You are incredibly valuable, a creation of God, *commanded* to love. Our assignment is to love fully, with heart, soul, and mind—and that includes loving ourselves.

ONE MORE THOUGHT

You've made mistakes. You keep falling short. No one seems to value you. I get all that. But God forgives you, loves you, believes in you, has a wonderful plan for you. Who are you to reject the one opinion that counts? Love him. Love others. Love yourself. Because he commands it.

The LORD is close to everyone who prays to him, to all who truly pray to him.

[Psalm 145:18 NCV]

Help Is Near

Healing begins when we do something. Healing begins when we reach out. Healing starts when we take a step.

God's help is near and always available, but it is only given to those who seek it. Nothing results from sitting around, waiting for God to notice us. Sometimes the whole purpose of our problems is to get us to move closer to him. To pray to him. To praise him. To shout, "God, do something!" We must request his help and have faith that he will act.

God honors radical, risk-taking faith. When arks are built, lives are saved. When staffs are raised, seas still open. When a lunch is shared, thousands are fed. And when in faith you call on him to provide courage to confront a friend or healing to cure a sick sibling, you can expect an amazing response. He is always near, ready to step in. The first move is up to us.

ONE MORE THOUGHT

Have you ever thought of that? Maybe you've been ignoring God lately. Maybe the point of your problems is to get you talking to God again. He may not solve your problems exactly how and when you want. That's okay. You're still moving in the right direction.

> "When two of you get together on anything at all on earth and make a prayer of it, my Father in heaven goes into action."
>
> [Matthew 18:19 MSG]

Praying to Win

Moses and the Israelites once battled the Amelekites. The military strategy of Moses was a strange one. He sent Joshua to lead the fight in the valley below. Moses ascended the mountain to pray. But he did not go alone. He took his two lieutenants, Aaron and Hur.

While Joshua led physical combat, Moses engaged in a spiritual one. Aaron and Hur stood on either side of their leader to hold up his arms in the battle of prayer. The Israelites prevailed because Moses prayed. Moses prevailed because he had a community to pray with him.

What battle are you facing today? Depression? Worry? A fight with a brother or sister? On this day when we honor those who fought for our country and freedom, don't go to war alone. Tell Christian family and friends about it so they can "hold up your arms," praying for you and with you. And tell God. When he's fighting on your side, you're sure to prevail.

ONE MORE THOUGHT

Whether the battle is physical, emotional, or spiritual, what's your first response when you face a challenge? Head into the fray? Run and hide? Moses had it right. To win at war or anything else, the first thing to do is gather your forces and pray.

We all live off his generous bounty, gift after gift after gift.

[John 1:16 MSG]

Never-Ending Grace

Can God run out of grace?

Plunge a sponge into Lake Erie. Did you absorb every drop? Take a deep breath. Did you suck the oxygen out of the atmosphere? Pluck a pine needle from a tree in Yosemite. Did you wipe out the forest's foliage? Watch an ocean wave crash against the beach. Will there never be another?

Of course there will. No sooner will one wave crash into the sand than another appears. Then another, then another. This is a picture of God's never-ending grace. *Grace* is simply another word for his tumbling, rumbling reservoir of strength and protection. It comes at us not in occasional drips but in titanic torrents, wave upon wave. We've barely regained our balance from one breaker, and then, *bam*, here comes another.

"Grace upon grace" (John 1:16 NASB). We dare to stake our hope on the gladdest news of all: if God permits the challenge, he will provide the grace to meet it.

ONE MORE THOUGHT

Dating. Drugs. Disease. Your parents' divorce. Sometimes the problems pile so high, it feels like even God can't handle them. Don't believe it! His grace reservoir *never* runs dry. He has more than enough to solve every dilemma, wipe every tear, and answer every question.

I praise you because you made me in an amazing and wonderful way.

[Psalm 139:14 NCV]

Play Your Best

Antonio Stradivari was a seventeenth-century violin maker whose name in its Latin form, *Stradivarius,* is now linked with excellence. He once said that to make a violin less than his best would be to rob God, who could not make Antonio Stradivari's violins without Antonio.

He was right. God could not make Stradivarius violins without Antonio Stradivari. Certain gifts were given to that craftsman that no other violin maker possessed.

There are also certain things you can do that no one else can. Maybe you're a computer whiz. Maybe you paint. Perhaps you work well with animals or small children or you're really good at encouraging the discouraged. It's very possible you haven't yet discovered your greatest gifts. But there are things that *only* you can do, and you are alive to do them. In the great orchestra we call life, you have an instrument and a song, and you owe it to God to play them both with your very best.

ONE MORE THOUGHT

Do you know your God-designed gifts? Pull out a piece of paper and write down a few of the things you seem to be good at. Now make another list of the things you enjoy doing. Are any the same? This may be a step toward discovering what you can do best to bring glory to God.

So now, those who are in Christ Jesus are not judged guilty.

[Romans 8:1 NCV]

Not Guilty

If you have ever wondered how God reacts when you fail, frame these words and hang them on your wall: "I also don't judge you guilty. You may go now, but don't sin anymore." They are the words of Jesus to the woman caught in bed with a man not her husband (John 8:1–11 NCV). Read them. Ponder them. Memorize them.

Or better still, take Jesus with you to your canyon of shame. Invite Christ to journey with you, to stand beside you as you retell the events of the darkest nights of your soul. The night you lied to your parents. The night you stole at the store. The night you gave up your virginity.

And then listen. Listen carefully. He's speaking . . . "I don't judge you guilty."

And watch. Watch carefully. He's writing. He's leaving a message. Not in the sand, but on a cross. Not with his hand, but with his blood. His message has two words: not guilty.

ONE MORE THOUGHT

Maybe you've blown it. Big-time. Don't let guilt drag you into the dirt. Take your crime to Jesus. Confess the whole thing to him. Ask him to forgive you. Then hear the words that give so much hope: "I don't judge you guilty. Go. Don't sin anymore."

> We don't look at the troubles we can see now; rather,
> we fix our gaze on things that cannot be seen.
>
> [2 Corinthians 4:18 NLT]

The Weaver

Over a hundred years ago in England, a mine collapsed, killing many of the workers inside. A bishop was asked to comfort the mourners. Standing in front of the mine, he said, "It is very difficult for us to understand why God should let such an awful disaster happen, but we know him and we trust him, and all will be right. I have at home, an old bookmark given to me by my mother. It is worked in silk, and, when I examine the wrong side of it, I see nothing but a tangle of threads, crossed and re-crossed. It looks like a big mistake. One would think that someone had done it who did not know what she was doing. But, when I turn it over and look at the right side, I see there, beautifully embroidered, the letters GOD IS LOVE.

"We are looking at this today," he counseled, "from the wrong side. Someday we shall see it from another standpoint and shall understand."[13]

Indeed we will. Until then, focus less on the tangled threads and more on the hand of the weaver.

ONE MORE THOUGHT

Tangled threads. Isn't that a good description of how life often feels? Relationship misunderstandings. Homework hassles. Strands that don't fit together—today. But just maybe, later, we'll see how all this was necessary, directed by an expert weaver's hand.

Now that you've found you don't have to listen to sin tell you what to do, and have discovered the delight of listening to God telling you, what a surprise!

[Romans 6:22 MSG]

No More Slobs

Before Jesus, our lives were out of control, sloppy, and self-focused. Remember that? We didn't even know we were slobs until we met him.

Then he moved in. Things began to change. What we threw around before, we began putting away. What we neglected we cleaned up. What had been clutter became order. Oh, there were and still are moments when we blow it, but by and large he got our house in order.

Suddenly we find ourselves wanting to do good. Helping family. Encouraging friends. Go back to the old mess? Are you kidding? "In the past you were slaves to sin—sin controlled you. But thank God, you fully obeyed the things that you were taught. You were made free from sin, and now you are slaves to goodness" (Romans 6:17–18 NCV).

Who wants to be a self-centered slob? Following God and doing good feels so much better.

ONE MORE THOUGHT

Do you ever stop to look at your life? What's it like when you are close to Jesus and follow his teaching? What's it like when you don't? I don't know about you, but without Jesus, my life is a mess. I prefer letting him clean up. How about you?

Jesus went to them, walking on the sea. . . . And they cried out for fear.

[Matthew 14:25–26]

Don't Miss the Light

Every so often a storm will come, and I'll look up into the blackening sky and say, "God, a little light please?"

The light came for the disciples. They were at sea on a stormy night when a figure came to them, walking on the water. It wasn't what they expected. Perhaps they were looking for angels to descend or heaven to open. We don't know what they were looking for. But one thing is for sure, they weren't looking for Jesus to come walking on the water. And since Jesus came in a way they didn't expect, they almost missed seeing the answer to their prayers.

Unless we look and listen closely, we risk making the same mistake. Are tidal waves of trouble threatening to overturn the boat of your life? God is on his way. His lights in our dark nights are as numerous as the stars, if only we'll look for them.

ONE MORE THOUGHT

Has someone you love moved away or died? Has someone you trusted turned his back on you? Our lives sure do feel like dark storms at times. When you're in one, don't miss God's light. He may surprise you with his approach, but he is surely coming for you.

I have learned in whatever state I am, to be content.

[Philippians 4:11]

Choosing to Be Content

In his book *Money: A User's Manual*, Bob Russell describes a farmer who once grew discontent with his farm. He griped about the lake on his property always needing to be stocked and managed. And those fat cows lumbering through his pasture. And all the fencing and feeding—what a headache!

He called a realtor and made plans to list the farm. A few days later the agent phoned, wanting approval for the advertisement she intended to place in the local paper. She read the ad to the farmer. It described a lovely farm in an ideal location—quiet and peaceful, contoured with rolling hills, carpeted with soft meadows, nourished by a fresh lake, and blessed with well-bred livestock. The farmer said, "Read that ad to me again."

After hearing it a second time, he decided, "I've changed my mind. I'm not going to sell. I've been looking for a place like that all my life."

ONE MORE THOUGHT

Aren't we a lot like the farmer? We complain about our family, our friends, our school, our clothes. In our minds, we even complain about God. But when we look at it from another person's perspective, we might realize that we already have just what we're looking for.

Tremendous power is made available through a good man's earnest prayer.

[James 5:16 PHILLIPS]

Desperate Faith

Great acts of faith are seldom born out of calm and ordered thinking.

It wasn't logic that caused Moses to raise his staff on the bank of the Red Sea and expect the water to withdraw. It wasn't common sense that caused Paul to abandon his life as a Pharisee and embrace grace. And it wasn't a confident committee that prayed in a small room in Jerusalem for Peter's release from jail. It was a fearful, frantic band of backed-into-a-corner believers. It was a church with no options. A congregation of have-nots pleading for help. "The church was earnestly praying to God for him" (Acts 12:5 NIV). And never were they stronger. They prayed Peter right out of prison.

Last-chance prayers often have the most power. The impact of impulsive acts can spread like wildfire. *If*, that is, they depend on God's fuel to ignite the spark. At the beginning of every great deed of faith, there is often more than a flicker of desperation.

ONE MORE THOUGHT

Would you describe your faith as desperate? Do your prayers possess the intensity of a last chance? God hears your every word, but he is most moved when your prayers are sincere pleas and when your faith comes from the heart as well as the head.

> "If anyone desires to be first, he shall be last of all and servant of all."
>
> [Mark 9:35]

Be Last, Not First

We regularly face subtle yet significant decisions, all of which fall under the category of who comes first: do they or do I? When you eat lunch with the neglected kids rather than the cool ones. When you spend your Saturday with your grandmother at the dementia unit. When you turn away from personal dreams for the sake of others, you are denying yourself. "If any of you wants to be my follower, you must turn from your selfish ways, take up your cross, and follow me" (Matthew 16:24 NLT).

Behold the most surprising ingredient of a great day: self-denial.

Don't we assume just the opposite? Great days emerge from the soil of self-interest, self-expression, and self-celebration. But deny yourself? When was the last time you read this ad copy: "Go ahead. Deny yourself and have the time of your life!"?

Jesus could have written the words. In his world the least are the greatest (Luke 9:48); the last will be first (Mark 9:35); the chosen seats are the forgotten seats (Luke 14:8–9). Does he have it backward? What do you think?

ONE MORE THOUGHT

Not so easy to serve others when so much of our interest centers on self. Practice helps. What can you do in the next five minutes to put someone else first? What are you waiting for?

God Is for You

Paul's question echoes through the centuries: "If God is for us, who can be against us?" The question is not simply, "Who can be against us?" You could answer that one. Who is against you? Disease, disasters, people, pimples. Homework hassles and worries that wear on you. A crisis around every corner. Were Paul's question, "Who can be against us?" we could list our enemies much easier than we could fight them. But that is not the question. The question is, *If God is for us, who can be against us?*

God is for you. Your parents may have forgotten you, your teachers may have neglected you, your siblings may be ashamed of you; but within reach of your prayers is the maker of the oceans—God!

No matter how bad your life gets, you have someone on your side who can take out your toughest opponent. Even on the most horrible day, that's a reason for hope.

ONE MORE THOUGHT

Mickey and Minnie. Lewis and Clark. Batman and Robin. When you're facing trouble, it helps to have a partner who's fully committed to you, who will stand with you in battle. And when that someone is God, you can be totally confident that ultimate victory is yours.

> If we live, we are living for the Lord, and if we die, we are dying
> for the Lord. So living or dying, we belong to the Lord.
>
> [Romans 14:8 NCV]

Eye to Eye

My dad was in the hospital, bedridden. The end was near. A little girl named Ginger made a get-well card in her Sunday school class. She and her mom delivered it in person.

Somehow, Ginger had a moment alone with my dad and asked as only a six-year-old can, "Are you going to die?" He touched her hand and told her to come near. "Yes, I am going to die. When? I don't know."

She asked if he was afraid to go away. "Away is heaven," he told her. "I will be with my Father. I am ready to see him eye-to-eye." About this point in the visit, Ginger's mother and mine returned. Ginger gave my dad a big, beautiful smile. He did the same—and winked.

A man near death, winking at the thought of it. Years later, Ginger wrote me a note about that day. My dad had taught her something about facing trouble, about facing even death. "The worst thing that could happen," she wrote, "is getting to see 'my Father eye-to-eye.'"

ONE MORE THOUGHT

When you take on a big challenge, do you ever ask yourself, *What's the worst thing that could happen?* We often think of dying as the ultimate "worst." But that's the funny thing about God. He turns our thinking upside down. And when you really think about it, "worst" is actually best.

We are God's masterpiece.

[Ephesians 2:10 NLT]

God's Work of Art

Over a hundred years ago, a group of fishermen were relaxing in a Scottish seaside inn. One of the men gestured widely, and his arm struck the serving maid's tea tray, sending the teapot flying into the whitewashed wall. The innkeeper looked at the damage and sighed, "The whole wall will have to be repainted."

"Perhaps not," offered a stranger. "Let me work with it."

Having nothing to lose, the innkeeper agreed. The man pulled pencils, brushes, and pigment out of an art box and went to work. In time, an image began to emerge: a stag with a great rack of antlers. The man inscribed his signature at the bottom, paid for his meal, and left. His name: Sir Edwin Landseer, famous painter of wildlife.

In Sir Edwin's hands, a mistake became a masterpiece. God's hands do the same, over and over. To show his love, he draws together the disjointed blotches in our life and turns them into a beautiful work of art.

ONE MORE THOUGHT

When you look at all the mistakes you've made, you see a mess. Like the innkeeper, you just want to repaint it and start over. But God sees what you can't. He sees a canvas with unique possibilities. When he goes to work on you, the result is breathtaking.

"I am Yahweh."

[Exodus 6:2 NLT]

In Awe of the Almighty

The Israelites considered the name *Yahweh* too holy to be spoken by human lips. Whenever they needed to say *Yahweh*, they substituted the word *Adonai*, which means "Lord." If the name needed to be written, the scribes would take a bath before they wrote it and destroy the pen afterward.

Do we treat God with the same respect today? Are we still in awe of the Almighty? I wonder if we've lost our wonder. Our society practically worships the modern celebrity. Whether it's a movie star, a rock icon, or a top athlete, we roar with appreciation when they appear on the screen, stage, or field. Do we worship in church with the same intensity?

Moses sang, "Who among the gods is like you, LORD? Who is like you—majestic in holiness, awesome in glory, working wonders?" (Exodus 15:11 NIV). The Israelites did not dare even to say his name. Surely we can dare to show him our love, appreciation, and respect.

ONE MORE THOUGHT

Awesome is a word that gets thrown around a lot these days. The new dress Ally is wearing? *Awesome*. That double burger you had for lunch? *Awesome*. No homework tonight? *Awesome!* Maybe, though, we should think about what's *truly* awesome. That would be God. Nothing else comes close.

A Positive Power

Nathaniel Hawthorne came home heartbroken. He'd just been fired from his job in the custom house. His wife, rather than responding with anxiety, surprised him with joy. "Now you can write your book!"

He wasn't so positive. "And what shall we live on while I'm writing it?" To his amazement she opened a drawer and revealed a wad of money she'd saved out of her housekeeping budget. "I always knew you were a man of genius," she told him. "I always knew you'd write a masterpiece."

She believed in her husband. And because she did, he wrote. And because he wrote, every library in America has a copy of *The Scarlet Letter* by Nathaniel Hawthorne.

You have the power to change someone's life simply by the words you speak. "Death and life are in the power of the tongue." Use your power wisely, and you may soon witness a masterpiece.

ONE MORE THOUGHT

The Bible says we should "encourage one another daily" (Hebrews 3:13 NIV). Mark Twain once said, "I can live for two months on a good compliment." Do you doubt the power of words? Build up others with your words, and change the world.

"Spiritual life comes from the Spirit."

[John 3:6 NCV]

Freedom from Suffering

Maybe your parents and siblings are the definition of a dysfunctional family: disagreements and divorce. Maybe you've seen raw evil: anger and abuse. And now you have to make a choice. Do you rise above the past and make a difference? Or do you remain controlled by the past and make excuses?

"If only I'd been born somewhere else." "If only I'd been treated fairly." Maybe you've used those words. Maybe you have every right to use them. If so, go to John's gospel and read Jesus' words: "Human life comes from human parents, but spiritual life comes from the Spirit" (John 3:6 NCV).

Jesus understands your pain because he's been there. He offers you an alternative to the humiliation and hurt. Love him. Live for him. Reach for him so you can hear the words he once spoke to a woman in misery: "Daughter, your faith has healed you. Go in peace and be freed from your suffering" (Mark 5:34 NIV).

ONE MORE THOUGHT

When we put our faith in Christ, we have a reason to get up in the morning no matter how terrible the day before. Faith is the weapon that can outlast any enemy. It's what gives our life meaning. Leave the past behind. Put your faith in Jesus and the spiritual life to come.

> Be cheerful no matter what; pray all the time; thank God no matter what happens. This is the way God wants you who belong to Christ Jesus to live.
>
> [1 Thessalonians 5:16–18 MSG]

An Attitude of Gratitude

If you look long enough and hard enough, you'll find something to gripe about. So quit looking! Lift your eyes off the weeds. Major in the grace of God. And . . .

Measure the gifts of God. Collect your blessings. Catalog his kindnesses. Assemble your reasons for gratitude and recite them. "Always be joyful. Pray continually, and give thanks whatever happens. That is what God wants for you in Christ Jesus" (1 Thessalonians 5:16–18 NCV).

Look at the totality of those terms. *Always* be joyful. Pray *continually.* Give thanks *whatever* happens. Learn a lesson from Sidney Connell. When her brand-new bicycle was stolen, she called her dad with the bad news. He expected his daughter to be upset. But Sidney wasn't crying. She was honored. "Dad," she boasted, "out of all the bikes they could have taken, they took mine."

Make gratitude your default emotion, and you'll find yourself giving thanks for even the problems of life.

ONE MORE THOUGHT

Let's practice what we've just learned. Pull out a pen and paper and write down ten things you're thankful for. Go ahead, I'll wait. Not a bad list, right? You might be surprised how much life changes when you linger on this list instead of your problems. Try it. You might like it.

> "This happened so that the works of God might be displayed in him."
>
> [John 9:3 NIV]

The Greatest of Good

When you slurp a chocolate milkshake and say, "This is good," what are you saying? The machine with the ice cream is good? The ice cream itself is good? The chocolate syrup is good? The milk? The cup? The straw? No, none of these. *Good* happens when the ingredients are worked together: the machine churns out the ice cream, chocolate and milk are added, the whole concoction is stirred in a cup, and you get to enjoy it through a straw. It is the collective cooperation of the elements that creates good.

Nothing in the Bible would cause us to call a famine *good* or a heart attack *good* or a terrorist attack *good*. These are catastrophes. Yet every message in the Bible compels us to believe that God will mix them with other ingredients and bring good out of them.

But we must let God define *good*. Our definition includes health, success, and popularity. His definition? In the case of his Son, the good life consisted of struggle, storms, and death. But God worked it all together for the greatest of good: his glory and our salvation.

ONE MORE THOUGHT

Our lives are a little like a milkshake. Ingredients get mixed together. Some of the ingredients are unimpressive by themselves. Some—rejections, disappointments, failures—are awful at the time. Yet God shakes them up and pours them out into a concoction that is delicious and good.

Don't destroy yourself by getting drunk, but let the Spirit fill your life.

[Ephesians 5:18 CEV]

Just One Drink

A friend slides a beer bottle in your direction. A classmate offers a marijuana joint. Your mind seeks ways to explain and excuse, the reasons popping up like weeds after a summer rain. *It won't hurt anyone. I won't get caught. I'm only human.*

You've heard so many messages about the evils of drinking and drugs that your head is ready to explode. But could there be some truth behind the endless words of warning? You better believe it. I've seen it in my own family. "Just one drink" makes it easier to say yes again the next night. Two hits become a habit. A habit turns into addiction and a life you can't control.

Of course, that happens to other people, not you. But what if the example of your one drink helps lead a friend into a life of alcoholism? How might that one joint hurt the heart of the Father watching over you?

Do everyone a favor. Trade the one drink for the wisdom of the One.

ONE MORE THOUGHT

Not everyone is bound for a life of substance abuse and addiction—but the moment you think you're untouchable is the moment you're most likely headed for trouble. If you're going to be obsessed with something, make God your choice. That's a habit worth keeping.

"People judge by outward appearance, but the LORD looks at the heart."

[1 Samuel 16:7 NLT]

God Sees Hearts

The LORD does not see as man sees; for man looks at the outward appearance, but the LORD looks at the heart" (1 Samuel 16:7).

Those words were written for the misfits and outcasts of society. God uses them all. Moses ran from justice. Jonah ran from God. Rahab ran a brothel. God used them.

And David? God saw a teenage boy serving him in the backwoods of Bethlehem, at the intersection of boredom and anonymity, and through the voice of a brother, God called, "David! Come in. Someone wants to see you." Human eyes saw a gangly teenager enter the house. Yet, "the LORD said, 'Arise, anoint him; for this is the one!'" (1 Samuel 16:12).

God saw what no one else saw: a God-seeking heart. David, for all his faults, sought God like a lark seeks sunrise. In the end, that's all God wanted or needed, all he wants or needs. Others measure your waist size or wallet. Not God. He examines hearts. When he finds one set on him, he calls it and claims it.

ONE MORE THOUGHT

You're overweight? Covered with acne? Hair won't comb? Too tall or short? Clumsy? Mathematically challenged? Think too slow to create witty comebacks? None of that matters to God. He sees what's in your heart. Allow him to make use of yours.

DECEMBER

For unto us a Child is born,
Unto us a Son is given;
And the government will be upon His shoulder.
And His name will be called
Wonderful, Counselor, Mighty God,
Everlasting Father, Prince of Peace.

[Isaiah 9:6]

"Those who see the Son and believe in him have eternal
life. . . . This is what my Father wants."

[John 6:40 NCV]

Knowing God's Heart

We learn God's plan for our lives by spending time in his presence. The key to knowing God's heart is having a relationship with him. A *personal* relationship. God will speak to you differently than he will speak to others. Just because God spoke to Moses through a burning bush, that doesn't mean we should all sit next to a bush waiting for God to speak. God used a fish to convict Jonah. Does that mean we should have worship services at Sea World? No. God reveals his heart personally to each person.

For that reason, regular time with God is essential. We won't understand his desires for us after an occasional chat or weekly visit. We learn his will as we walk and talk with him throughout every single day. At breakfast. On the bus. In class. At basketball practice. Before playing that video game. At bedtime.

Walk with him long enough and you come to know his heart.

ONE MORE THOUGHT

Breathing is automatic for us. We need air to live, but we don't think about the process of getting it as we go about our day. We just breathe. That's how our relationship with God should be. Automatic. We don't think about needing to talk to God. It just happens, all day long.

> We know that in everything God works for the good of those who love him.
>
> [Romans 8:28 NCV]

Helpful Hassles

We don't usually think so at the time, but our hassles can help us. They allow us to grow into the people God intended. He uses our struggles to build character.

James makes the point in the Bible. "When troubles come your way, consider it an opportunity for great joy. For you know that when your faith is tested, your endurance has a chance to grow. So let it grow, for when your endurance is fully developed, you will be perfect and complete, needing nothing" (James 1:2–4 NLT).

Today's trial makes you better and stronger tomorrow. Hasn't the oyster taught us this principle? The grain of sand invades the shell, and how does the oyster respond? Does he shell out a bunch of money on a shopping binge to get over the pain? No. He emits the substance that transforms the irritation into a pearl. Every pearl is simply a victory over irritations.

How do we handle our hassles in the meantime? We trust, remembering that "in everything God works for the good of those who love him" (Romans 8:28 NCV).

ONE MORE THOUGHT

The words of Romans 8:28 should encourage you a ton. God uses *everything* for your good. He may not always cause it, but he knows what to do with it. Your woe is not wasted. One day, it will lead you to joy.

We put no confidence in human effort.

[Philippians 3:3 NLT]

God's Perfect Plan

Is pressure getting to you? There's so much of it. Pressure from parents to get top grades to get scholarships to get into the best college. Pressure at your part-time job at the Snow Cone to show up earlier, serve faster, smile bigger. Pressure from the band teacher to keep those rowdy sophomore sax players in line. Pressure from one group of friends to say and wear the right thing. Pressure from another group to work less and hang out more.

And then there's the pressure you put on yourself. You *want* to be the best. Sure, it's tough keeping everyone happy. But it's all part of the plan. You just need to be perfect. That's what God expects, right?

Actually, God has a better idea: "For by grace you have been saved through faith, and that not of yourselves; it is the gift of God" (Ephesians 2:8). We contribute nothing. Nada. As opposed to the merit badge of the Scout, salvation of the soul is unearned. A gift. Our merits merit nothing. God's work merits everything.

ONE MORE THOUGHT

There's a problem with pushing for perfection—we'll never get there. Good? Maybe. Stressed? For sure. But perfect? That's God's turf. Salvation is one thing we don't *do*. Just confess your sins and believe. It's God's perfect plan.

Possession Obsession

In 1900 the average person living in the United States wanted seventy-two different things and considered eighteen of them essential. Today the average person wants five hundred things and considers one hundred of them essential.

Our obsession with stuff carries a hefty price tag. Eighty percent of people battle the pressure of overdue bills. We spend 110 percent of our available money trying to manage debt. And you know that some of your friends—maybe you too—can't wait to get their hands on the latest album release, iPhone upgrade, and brand-name shoes.

Who can keep up? We no longer measure ourselves against the Joneses next door but against the star on the screen or the hunk on the magazine cover. Hollywood's diamond-studded earrings make yours look like gumball-machine toys. If we always think we need more, will we ever have enough? No. For that reason Jesus warns, "Be on your guard against every form of greed" (Luke 12:15 NASB).

ONE MORE THOUGHT

Take a moment right now to think about the stuff in your life. How much of it do you really need? Is paying for it, playing it, caring for it, storing it, or fixing it taking time away from God, family, and friends? We think we own our stuff. Too often, it owns us.

"Let your good deeds shine out for all to see, so that
everyone will praise your heavenly Father."

[Matthew 5:16 NLT]

Daily Kindness

In the final days of Jesus' life, he shared a meal with his friends Lazarus, Martha, and Mary. For Mary, however, giving the dinner was not enough. "Mary came in with a jar of very expensive aromatic oils, anointed and massaged Jesus' feet, and then wiped them with her hair. The fragrance of the oils filled the house" (John 12:3 MSG). Jesus received this as a generous demonstration of love, a friend surrendering her most treasured gift.

Follow Mary's example.

There is an elderly man in your community who just lost his wife. An hour of your time would mean the world to him. Some kids in your school have no dad. No father takes them to movies or baseball games. Maybe you and yours can.

Or how about this one? Down the hall from your bedroom is a person who shares your last name. Shock that person with kindness. Something radical. Your homework done with no complaints. Coffee served before he awakens. A love letter written to her for no special reason. Daily do a deed for which you cannot be repaid.

ONE MORE THOUGHT

We never know how much a "Mary moment" will mean to someone. Comforting? Probably. Encouraging? For sure. Maybe even more. Sometimes your God-inspired gesture is exactly what a hurting soul needs to survive another day.

Don't become partners with those who reject God. How can
you make a partnership out of right and wrong?

[2 Corinthians 6:14 MSG]

The Right Partner

You've daydreamed about getting married someday. But how will you choose a lifelong partner?

A person makes two big decisions in life. The first has to do with faith. The second has to do with family. The first defines the second. Your God defines your family. If your God is yourself, then you call your own shots because your marriage is for your pleasure and nothing more. But if your God is Christ, then he calls the shots because your marriage is for his honor. And he has an opinion about your choice in a mate. "Don't become partners with those who reject God. How can you make a partnership out of right and wrong?" (2 Corinthians 6:14 MSG).

Marry someone who loves God more than you do. The longer you date a nonbeliever, the longer you postpone the opportunity for God to bring the right person your way. If you are a child of God and you marry a child of the Devil, you're going to have trouble with your father-in-law.

ONE MORE THOUGHT

Your friend comes by to take you for a drive. You want to go to the store. He wants to go to Mexico. You have a problem! It's like that when you get married. If your partner's goal is to get rich and yours is to get to heaven, it's going to be a long, hard journey.

Jesus Christ always does the right thing, and he will speak to the Father for us.

[1 John 2:1 CEV]

God Gets Your Groans

Did you know that if you are involved in a legal trial, you don't always have to be present in court? Sometimes your lawyer can speak for you. He understands court cases when you don't, and he speaks legalese while you stumble over the words.

You may have never gone to court, but you can still be living in crisis. The kind that has you so wiped out and stressed out that you can't talk even to God. The good news is you also have an advocate standing before the Father. When you are timid, Jesus speaks. He stands in for us when we just can't speak for ourselves. And we have support from the Holy Spirit, who "intercedes for us through wordless groans" (Romans 8:26–27 NIV). Those gross sounds coming from your tired soul? It's okay. The Holy Spirit speaks Groan-ese. "Uuuggghhh"—Help me, Lord. Get me out of this misery. "Uhhhhhh"—I don't know what to do. The pain is too much. "Ooohhhhhh"—Where is everyone?

God understands when you're so overwhelmed that you can't pray. With Jesus as your advocate and the Holy Spirit as your prayer partner, I bet you've been praying more than you think.

ONE MORE THOUGHT

God gets it. When you reach out to him, he's not looking for fancy words that would impress your English teacher. He sees your heart. A groan, a look, a sigh—he speaks every language. He understands.

He gives strength to those who are tired and more power to those who are weak.

[Isaiah 40:29 NCV]

Seeing the Unseen

An example of faith was found on the wall of a concentration camp. On it a prisoner had carved the words:

"I believe in the sun, even though it doesn't shine. I believe in love, even when it isn't shown. I believe in God, even when he doesn't speak."

I try to imagine the person who etched those words. I try to picture his skeleton-like hand gripping the broken glass or stone that cut into the wall. I try to imagine his eyes squinting through the darkness as he carved each letter. What hand could have cut such a conviction? What eyes could have seen good in such horror?

There is only one answer: Eyes that understand the words of Paul. "So we fix our eyes not on what is seen, but on what is unseen, since what is seen is temporary, but what is unseen is eternal" (2 Corinthians 4:18 NIV). Do you see the unseen?

ONE MORE THOUGHT

How is your eyesight? Are you able to see beyond your problems to the goodness and love beyond? This is where God lives—behind the scenes, at work, arranging your troubles of today into a brighter tomorrow.

I said, "I will confess my sins to the LORD," and you forgave my guilt.

[Psalm 32:5 NCV]

The Bridge of Confession

Once there were a couple of farmers who couldn't get along with each other. A wide ravine separated their two farms, but as a sign of their mutual distaste for each other, each constructed a fence on his side of the gulch to keep the other out.

In time, however, the daughter of one met the son of the other, and the couple fell in love. Determined not to be kept apart by their foolish fathers, they tore down the fences and used the wood to build a bridge across the ravine.

Confession does that. Confessed sin becomes the bridge that allows us to walk back into the presence of God. Is there a ravine in your relationship with God? Are you keeping anything from him? Bad behavior? Bad attitude? Dishonesty? Doubt?

Tell God about it right now. Tear down the fences. Build a bridge back to him.

ONE MORE THOUGHT

Read Psalm 32. What happened to David when he kept silent about his wrongs? What changed when he confessed? Don't you feel closer to friends who trust you enough to tell you everything? That's just what God wants from you.

After you have suffered a little while, he will restore, support, and strengthen you.

[1 Peter 5:10 NLT]

Grace Is All You Need

Paul wrote, "I was given a thorn in my flesh, a messenger from Satan to torment me and keep me from becoming proud. Three different times I begged the Lord to take it away. Each time he said, 'My grace is all you need'" (2 Corinthians 12:7–9 NLT).

Such vivid imagery. The sharp end of a thorn pierces the soft skin of life and lodges beneath the surface. Every step is a reminder of the thorn in the flesh. The disease in the body. The sadness in the heart. The sister in the rehab center. The dad moving out. The D on the report card. The craving to be one of the cool crowd.

"Take it away," you've pleaded. This wound oozes pain, and you see no sign of tweezers coming from heaven. But what you hear is this: "My grace is all you need."

God's grace is not a gentle shower washing away the problem. It is a raging, roaring river whose current knocks you off your feet and carries you into the presence of God.

ONE MORE THOUGHT

God's great grace wipes out everything else on the landscape. It is not puny but plentiful. Not teeny but torrential. Not mini but majestic. It meets us right now and equips us with courage, wisdom, and strength. So hang on— the next wave is coming!

Long before [God] laid down earth's foundations, he had us
in mind, had settled on us as the focus of his love.

[Ephesians 1:4 MSG]

Chosen

Don't we all yearn to be loved and accepted? To belong? So many messages tell us we don't. We get cut from the basketball team. Dropped from the honor roll. Left off the sleepover list. Everything from acne to anorexia leaves us feeling like the kid with no date to the prom.

We react. We validate our existence with a flurry of activity. We do more, buy more, achieve more. We try to say the right things, get the right look, hang with the right people. We try to fit in. All of it is a way of asking the burning question in our hearts: "Do I belong?"

God has an answer. His grace—outrageous, overflowing, stretching beyond the stars and back again—is the definitive reply. "Be blessed, my child. I love you. I accept you. I have adopted you into my family."

Adopted children are chosen children.

ONE MORE THOUGHT

Take a moment to consider this. Make sure you understand it. Accept it. Enjoy it! There is something in you that God loves. *You* cause his eyes to widen, his heart to beat faster. He *chose* you to be in his family. Never doubt it. Never forget it.

We capture every thought and make it give up and obey Christ.

[2 Corinthians 10:5 NCV]

Captured Thoughts

Capturing thoughts is serious business. It was for Jesus. Remember the thoughts that came his way courtesy of the mouth of Peter? Jesus had just predicted his death, burial, and resurrection, but Peter couldn't bear the thought of it. "Peter took Jesus aside and told him not to talk like that. . . . Jesus said to Peter, 'Go away from me, Satan! You are not helping me! You don't care about the things of God, but only about the things people think are important'" (Matthew 16:22–23 NCV).

See the decisiveness of Jesus? A trashy thought comes his way. He is tempted to entertain it. Skipping death on the cross would be nice. But what does he do? He stands at the gangplank of the dock and says, "Get away from me." As if to say, "You are not allowed to enter my mind."

What if you did that? What if you took every thought captive?

ONE MORE THOUGHT

I'm guessing you've had a trashy thought or two come your way. Especially after someone leaves cash on the cafeteria table. Especially after someone insults you. Can you be as decisive as Jesus? The moment you spot the invader, try saying, "Get away from me!"

He will cover you with his feathers, and under his wings you can hide.

[Psalm 91:4 NCV]

God, Your Guardian

My college friends and I barely escaped a West Texas storm before it pummeled the park where we were spending a Saturday afternoon. As we were leaving, my buddy brought the car to a sudden stop and pointed to a tender sight on the ground. A mother bird sat exposed to the rain, her wing extended over her baby who had fallen out of the nest. The fierce storm kept her from returning to the tree, so she covered her child until the wind passed.

From how many winds is God protecting you? His wing, at this moment, shields you. A bully heading down the hall in your direction is interrupted by a teacher's question. A burglar on the way to your house has a flat tire. A drunk driver runs out of gas before your car passes his. "For he will order his angels to protect you wherever you go" (Psalm 91:11 NLT). God, your guardian, protects you.

ONE MORE THOUGHT

Are you feeling exposed to the storms of life? Read Psalm 91, a wonderful promise from God. When we love him and tell others about that love, he moves to protect us. "I will be with them in trouble. I will rescue and honor them" (v. 15 NLT).

Thanks be to God for his gift that is too wonderful for words.

[2 Corinthians 9:15 NCV]

God's Great Gifts

Why did he do it? A shack would have sufficed, but he gave us a mansion. Did he have to give the birds a song and the mountains a peak? Was he required to put stripes on the zebra and the hump on the camel? Why wrap creation in such splendor? Why go to such trouble to give such gifts?

Why do you? I've seen you searching for a gift. I've seen you stalking the malls and walking the aisles. I'm not talking about the have-to gifts. I'm talking about that extra-special person and that extra-special gift. Why do you do it? You do it so the heart will stop. You do it so the jaw will drop. You do it to hear those words of disbelief, "You did this for me?"

That's why you do it. And that is why God did it. Next time a sunrise steals your breath or a meadow of flowers leaves you speechless, be still. Say nothing and listen as heaven whispers, "Do you like it? I did it just for you."

ONE MORE THOUGHT

Do you get excited when you find just the right gift for friends or family members? Do you look forward to watching their faces when they open your present? As you exchange gifts this Christmas season, remember the pleasure God takes in our joy at his gifts.

Those who believe in the Son have eternal life.

[John 3:36 NCV]

Computer Christians

Computerized Christianity. Push the right buttons, enter the right code, insert the correct data, and bingo, print out your own salvation.

You do your part and the Divine Computer does his. No need to pray (after all, you control the keyboard). No emotional attachment necessary (who wants to hug circuits?). And worship? Well, worship is a lab exercise—insert the rituals and see the results.

Religion by computer. That's what happens when you replace the living God with a cold system. When you replace inestimable love with a by-the-numbers budget. When you replace the ultimate sacrifice of Christ with the puny achievements of man.

And what about the personal, you ask? What about relationship with a rescuer? What about joining God's family? "I will walk among you and be your God, and you will be my people" (Leviticus 26:12 NIV). That's something else entirely. That's real faith.

ONE MORE THOUGHT

Faith in God is about so much more than applying logic and following rules. It's not an abstract concept that's just for study. It's connecting with Christ on an intimate, personal level. It's emotional and spiritual as well as intellectual. It's alive. It's love.

> "Rejoice with those who rejoice, and weep with those who weep."
>
> [Romans 12:15 NASB]

When Love Is Real

The summer before my eighth-grade year I made friends with a guy named Larry. He was new to town, so I encouraged him to go out for our school football team. The result was a good news–bad news scenario. The good news? He made the cut. The bad news? He won my position. I tried to be happy for him, but it was tough.

A few weeks into the season Larry fell off a motorcycle and broke a finger. I remember the day he stood at my front door holding up his bandaged hand. "Looks like you're going to have to play." I tried to feel sorry for him, but it was hard. The Bible passage was a lot easier for Paul to write than it was for me to practice. "Rejoice with those who rejoice, and weep with those who weep" (Romans 12:15 NASB).

You want to find out if your love for someone is real? See how you feel when that person succeeds. God will rejoice. I hope you will too.

ONE MORE THOUGHT

Are you happy when your friends do well, or do your comments actually bring them down? Are you sympathetic when your friends go through trials, or do you "encourage" them with clichés? Love meets people where they are. Kind of like how Christ meets us.

Our light and momentary troubles are achieving for us
an eternal glory that far outweighs them all.

[2 Corinthians 4:17 NIV]

The Master Composer

Every Christmas, musicians around the world gather to perform George Frederic Handel's famous oratorio *The Messiah*. The entire work is over a hundred pages long. But suppose at the time George was writing it, his wife came upon one page on their kitchen table. On it, her husband had written only one measure, in a minor key, one that didn't work on its own. Suppose she, armed with this fragment of discord, marched into his studio and said, "This music makes no sense. You are a lousy composer." What would he think?

Perhaps something similar to what God thinks when we do the same. We point to our minor key, our broken leg, our divorced parents, our sick brother. "This makes no sense!" Yet, of all of his creation, how much have we seen? Only a doorway peephole. And, of all his work, how much do we understand? Only a sliver. What if God's answer to the question of suffering requires more megabytes than our puny minds have been given?

Think about it.

ONE MORE THOUGHT

Imagine the genius of someone like Beethoven, composing beautiful symphonies even after he was deaf, hearing the blend of each complex part only in his mind. Now multiply that genius by a billion and more and you begin to get a vague idea of what God does as he composes the symphony of our lives.

> Today in the town of David a Savior has been born to you.
>
> [Luke 2:11 NIV]

The Perfect Gift

I know we shouldn't complain. But, honestly, when someone hands you Christmas candy from two years ago and says, "This is for you," don't you detect a lack of creativity? But when a person gives a genuine gift, don't you cherish the presence of affection? The home-baked cookies, the tickets to see your favorite obscure band, the personalized poem, the Lucado book. Such gifts convince you that someone planned, prepared, saved, searched. Last-minute decision? No, this gift was just for you.

Have you ever received such a gift? Yes, you have. Sorry to speak on your behalf, but I know the answer as I ask the question. You have been given a perfect personal gift. One just for you. "There has been born *for you* a Savior, who is Christ the Lord" (Luke 2:11 NASB).

An angel spoke these words. Shepherds heard them first. But what the angel said to them, God says to anyone who will listen. "There has been born *for you* . . ." Jesus is the gift.

ONE MORE THOUGHT

So you've made your Christmas list? Checked it twice? Before we get too carried away dreaming about the CD or Xbox game we've just *got* to have, let's be thankful for the One gift we already have—the best gift of all.

And we are confident that he hears us whenever
we ask for anything that pleases him.

[1 John 5:14 NLT]

Ask and Believe

If you believe, you will get anything you ask for in prayer" (Matthew 21:22 NCV).

Don't reduce this grand statement to the category of a new Xbox or new guitar, a bigger room or better clothes, more pizza or more popularity. Don't limit the promise of this passage to the selfish pool of perks and favors. The fruit God assures is far greater than earthly wealth. His dreams are much more ambitious than temporary pleasures and possessions.

God wants you to fly. He wants you to fly free of yesterday's guilt. He wants you to fly free of today's fears. He wants you to fly free of tomorrow's grave. Sin, fear, and death. These are the mountains he has moved. These are the prayers he will answer. That is the fruit he will grant when you ask for what pleases him. This is what he longs to do.

ONE MORE THOUGHT

Read the words of 1 John 5:14–15 near the end of your Bible. It seems that when we are close enough to God to understand what he desires and we ask for it in prayer, we can be sure it's ours. That's exciting! It should make us want to pray every chance we get.

"When you go to the people of Israel, tell them, 'I AM sent me to you.'"

[Exodus 3:14 NCV]

The One Who Is

D o you know anyone who goes around saying, "I am"? Neither do I. When we say "I am," we always add another word. "I am *happy*." "I am *sad*." "I am *strong*." "I am *Max*." God, however, starkly states, "I AM" and adds nothing else.

"You are what?" we want to ask. "I AM," he replies. God needs no descriptive word because he never changes. God is what he is. He is what he has always been. His unalterable nature motivated the psalmist to declare, "But thou art the same" (Psalm 102:27 KJV). The writer is saying, "You are the One who is. You never change."

There's so much you have to adjust to in life. It seems that everything changes. New classes each term. New friends when old ones ignore you. New feelings as your body develops. New rules as you grow older. Isn't it good to know you can count on something permanent? Yahweh is an unchanging God.

ONE MORE THOUGHT

Everything starts somewhere, right? All things must have a beginning. All, that is, except God. He was, is, and always will be. His unchanging nature and love is one of the great mysteries of the universe and great gifts of our lives.

"We had to celebrate and be happy because your
brother . . . was lost, but now he is found."

[Luke 15:32 NCV]

No Price Is Too High

When our oldest daughter, Jenna, was two, I lost her in a department store. One minute she was at my side, and the next she was gone. I panicked. All of a sudden only one thing mattered—I had to find my daughter. Shopping was forgotten. The list of things I came to get was unimportant. I yelled her name. What people thought didn't matter. For a few minutes, every ounce of energy had one goal—to find my lost child. (I did, by the way. She was hiding behind some jackets!)

No price is too high for a parent to pay to redeem his child. No energy is too great. No effort too demanding. A parent will go to any length to find his or her own.

So will God.

Mark it down. God's greatest creation is not the flung stars or the gorged canyons; it's his eternal plan to reach his children.

ONE MORE THOUGHT

Imagine suddenly losing track of your little brother or sister or favorite pet. In an instant, you have to face the idea that you might never again see this person or pet you love. You would do almost anything to get him or her back, right? That's a glimpse of how God feels about you.

Always be full of joy in the Lord. I say it again—rejoice!

[Philippians 4:4 NLT]

A Letter of Joy

Go with me back in history a couple of thousand years. Let's go to Rome, to a rather drab little room. Inside we see a man seated on the floor. He's an older fellow, shoulders stooped and balding. Chains are on his hands and feet. It is the apostle Paul. The apostle who was bound only by the will of God is now in chains—stuck in a dingy house—attached to a Roman officer.

Paul the prisoner has a message to communicate. No e-mail here, however. No Facebook either. So Paul writes a letter. No doubt it is a complaint letter to God. No doubt it is a list of grievances. He has every reason to be bitter and complain. But he doesn't. Instead, he writes a letter that two thousand years later is still known as the treatise on joy—Philippians.

How can a man in chains write about being "full of joy in the Lord" (Philippians 4:4 NLT)? The answer for him—and for you—is in Jesus, who brings joy to the world.

ONE MORE THOUGHT

Paul had been through it all: threats, torture, health issues, imprisonment. Yet as he sat under Roman guard writing his letter to the Philippians, the emotion that came through was joy. Read it for yourself and discover his secret.

> God has given a son to us. . . . His name will be Wonderful
> Counselor, Powerful God, . . . Prince of Peace.
>
> [Isaiah 9:6 NCV]

What We Need

Every Christmas I read this reminder from Roy Lessin that came in the mail several years ago:

"If our greatest need had been information, God would have sent an educator. If our greatest need had been technology, God would have sent us a scientist. If our greatest need had been money, God would have sent us an economist. But since our greatest need was forgiveness, God sent us a Savior."

Do Christmas card messages strike you as corny? Maybe they are. Yet their simple phrases can cut through the chaos and capture the reason for the season. God knew what we needed. He became like us so that we could become like him. Angels still sing and the star still signals us to come closer.

And he still loves each one of us like there was only one of us to love.

ONE MORE THOUGHT

The Christmas season can be crazy. Too much shopping. Too many parties with your parents where you don't know anybody. None of that is important. But God becoming a baby so we could find new life with him? That's important.

> "Here I am! I stand at the door and knock."
>
> [Revelation 3:20 NCV]

Room for God?

Some of the saddest words on earth are: "We don't have room for you." Whether it's about a ride to the game or a place on the team, the words hurt.

Jesus knew the sound of those words. He was still in Mary's womb when the innkeeper said, "We don't have room for you." And when he was hung on the cross, wasn't the message one of utter rejection? "We don't have room for you in this world."

Even today Jesus is given the same treatment. He goes from heart to heart, asking if he might enter. Every so often, he is welcomed. Someone throws open the door of his or her heart and invites him to stay. And to that person Jesus gives this great promise: "In My Father's house are many rooms" (ESV).

What a delightful promise he makes us! We make room for him in our hearts, and he makes room for us in his house.

ONE MORE THOUGHT

Mary was a pregnant teenager, Joseph not so much older, when the innkeeper turned them away. Jesus was born into an earthly family that knew rejection well. Maybe that's one reason he is so determined to invite

A Humble Birth

She looks into the face of the baby. Her son. Her Lord. His Majesty. At this point in history, the human being who best understands who God is and what he is doing is a teenage girl in a smelly stable. She can't take her eyes off him. Somehow Mary knows she is holding God. So this is he. She remembers the words of the angel. "His kingdom will never end."

He looks like anything but a king. His face is prunish and red. His cry, though strong and healthy, is still the helpless and piercing cry of a baby. And he is absolutely dependent upon Mary for his well-being.

Majesty in the midst of the mundane. Holiness in the filth of sheep manure and sweat. God entering the world on the floor of a stable, through the womb of a teenager, and in the presence of a carpenter.

A birth that couldn't be more humble. A birth that changed the world—including mine and yours. Can we ever thank him enough?

ONE MORE THOUGHT

As we open gifts, gather around the dinner table, and enjoy time with family, let's remember the real reason we celebrate this day. A birth in a stable. A king in the form of a baby. God among us. Joy to the world!

An angel of the Lord appeared to them, and the
glory of the Lord shone around them.

[Luke 2:9 NIV]

No Ordinary Night

An ordinary night with ordinary sheep and ordinary shepherds. You might have called it boring. If not for a God who loves to hook an "extra" on the front of the ordinary, the night would have gone unnoticed. The sheep would have been forgotten, and the shepherds would have slept the night away.

But God dances amid the common. And that night he showed some of his best moves.

The black sky exploded with brightness. Trees that had been shadows jumped into clarity. Sheep that had been silent became a chorus of curiosity. One minute the shepherd was dead asleep, the next he was rubbing his eyes and staring into the face of an alien. The night was ordinary no more.

The angel came in the night because that is when lights are best seen and that is when they are most needed. God comes into the common for the same reason. His most powerful tools are the simplest.

ONE MORE THOUGHT

Life can be downright dull sometimes. Yet when you least expect it, God will light up the sky and announce something incredible. He already sent his Son to be born in a manger. Need I say more?

He and Mary were soon married, just as the Lord's angel had told him to do.

[Matthew 1:24 CEV]

A Home for Christ

Joseph had to make the biggest decision of his life. Mary was pregnant, but the baby was not his. His first thought was to quietly release Mary from their engagement and save her from public judgment and stoning. But then an angel in a dream told him not to be afraid to take Mary as his wife.

Joseph made his choice. He tanked his reputation for a pregnant fiancée and an illegitimate son. He placed God's plan ahead of his own. Rather than make a name for himself, Joseph made a home for Christ. And because he did, a great reward came his way. "He called His name JESUS" (Matthew 1:25).

By now, millions have spoken the name of Jesus. Look at the person selected to stand at the front of the line. Joseph. Of all the saints, sinners, prodigals, and preachers who have spoken the name, Joseph, a blue-collar, small-town construction worker said it first. He cradled the wrinkle-faced prince of heaven and with an audience of angels and pigs, whispered, "Jesus . . . You'll be called Jesus."

ONE MORE THOUGHT

Joseph made his choice. What will you choose? Will you make a home for Christ in your heart, even though it might look foolish to others? I hope so. If you do, God will reward you in ways you can't even imagine.

God will help you overflow with hope in him through
the Holy Spirit's power within you.

[Romans 15:13 TLB]

God Gives Hope

Heaven's hope does for your world what the sunlight did for my grandmother's cellar. I owe my love of peach preserves to her. She canned her own and stored them in an underground cellar near her West Texas house. It was a deep hole with wooden steps, plywood walls, and a musty smell. As a youngster I used to climb in, close the door, and see how long I could last in the darkness. I would sit silently, listening to my breath and heartbeats, until I couldn't take it anymore and then would race up the stairs and throw open the door. Light would avalanche into the cellar. What a change! Moments before I couldn't see anything—all of a sudden I could see everything.

Just as light poured into the cellar, God's hope pours into your world. Upon the sick, he shines the ray of healing. To the lonely, he gives the promise of relationship. To the confused, he offers the light of Scripture.

When you have God, you always have hope.

ONE MORE THOUGHT

"I hope we win the game tonight." "I hope I pass my final tomorrow." We often use the word *hope* as a wish for something to happen. But *hope* in God is something far deeper. It's knowing that he's in control, that he loves us, and that our future is secure in him.

Love patiently accepts all things. It always trusts,
always hopes, and always endures.

[1 Corinthians 13:7 NCV]

Love Accepts All Things

Wouldn't it be nice if love were like a cafeteria lunch line? What if you could look at the people you live with and select what you want and pass on what you don't? What if your parents could've done this with you? "I'll take a plate of good grades and cute smiles, and I'm passing on the teenage identity crisis and tuition bills." What if you could've done the same with your parents? "Please give me a helping of allowances and free lodging but no rules or curfews, thank you."

And your future spouse? "Hmm, how about a bowl of good health and good moods. But job transfers, in-laws, and laundry are not on my diet."

Wouldn't it be great if love were like a cafeteria line? It would be easier. It would be neater. It would be painless and peaceful. But you know what? It wouldn't be love. Love doesn't accept just a few things. Love is willing to accept all things.

ONE MORE THOUGHT

What are the little (or not so little) things that your family and friends do that annoy you? It isn't easy to accept *all* things about the people in your life. Yet that's what God calls us to do. After all, he does it with us. That's love.

To everything there is a season, a time for every purpose under heaven.

[Ecclesiastes 3:1]

Face the Future with God

What person passes through life with no surprises? Remember the summary of Solomon? "To everything there is a season, a time for every purpose under heaven" (Ecclesiastes 3:1).

God administers life the way he manages the universe: through seasons. When it comes to the earth, we understand God's management strategy. Nature needs winter to rest and spring to awaken. We don't dash into underground shelters at the sight of spring's tree buds. Earthly seasons don't upset us. But unexpected personal ones certainly do. The move to a new city. The breakup you never saw coming.

Are you on the eve of change? Do you find yourself looking into a new chapter? Are the leaves of your world showing signs of a new season? Heaven's message for you is clear: when everything else changes, God's presence never does. He may surprise you. But he wants you to know: you'll never face the future without his help.

ONE MORE THOUGHT

Think back to the big changes in your life. You lived through them, right? And when you remembered to lean on God, wasn't it easier to manage? He was there then, and he'll be there for the next one. Now is a good time to thank him for guiding you through every season.

I work . . . using Christ's great strength that works so powerfully in me.

[Colossians 1:29 NCV]

Deliver Christ to the World

The birth of Jesus in the manger is more, much more, than a Christmas story; it is a picture of how close Christ will come to you. The first stop on his journey was a womb. Where will God go to touch the world? Look deep within Mary for an answer.

Better still, look deep within yourself. What he did with Mary, he offers to us! He issues a Mary-level invitation to all his children. "If you'll let me, I'll move in!" What is the mystery of the gospel? "Christ in you, the hope of glory" (Colossians 1:27 NIV).

Christ grew in Mary until he had to come out. Christ will grow in you until the same thing happens. He will come out in your speech, in your actions, in your decisions. Every place you live will be a Bethlehem, and every day you live will be a Christmas. You, like Mary, will deliver Christ into the world.

ONE MORE THOUGHT

A whole new year is waiting for you. I pray that you'll pray for Jesus to grow in you, for everything you say and think and do to reflect more and more of him. For you and me, every day *can* be Christmas. Let's present the world with the greatest gift of all: Jesus.

Sources

Devotional material has been excerpted and revised from the following books written by Max Lucado and published by Thomas Nelson. All copyrights to the original books are held by the author, Max Lucado.

You'll Get Through This (2013)
Wild Grace (2012)
Live Loved (2011)
Max on Life (2010)
Grace for the Moment, Volume 2 (2006)
Grace for the Moment, Volume 1 (2000)

Notes

1. Rubel Shelly, *The ABCs of the Christian Faith* (Nashville, TN: Wineskins, 1998), 21–22.
2. *1041 Sermon Illustrations, Ideas, and Expositions: Treasury of the Christian World*, ed. A. Gordon Nasby (1953; repr., Harper & Brothers, Ann Arbor, Michigan), 109.
3. Eugene H. Peterson, *Run with the Horses: The Quest for Life at Its Best* (Madison, WI: InterVarsity Press, 1983), 115.
4. Rick Reilly, "Matt Steven Can't See the Hoop. But He'll Still Take the Last Shot," Life of Reilly, ESPN.com, March 11, 2009, http://sportsespn.go.com/espnmag/story?id=39678087. See also Gil Spencer, "Blind Player Helps Team See the Value of Sportsmanship," *Delaware County Daily Times*, February 25, 2009, www.delcotimes.com/articles/2009/02/25/sports/doc49a4c50632d09134430615.
5. C. J. Mahaney, "Loving the Church," audiotape of message at Covenant Life Church, Gaithersburg, MD, n.d., quoted in *Heaven* by Randy Alcorn (Wheaton, IL: Tyndale House, 2004), xxii.
6. Christine Caine, *Undaunted: Daring to Do What God Calls You to Do* (Grand Rapids: Zondervan, 2012), 48.
7. Frederick Dale Bruner, *The Christbook: Matthew—A Commentary*, rev. and exp. Ed. (Dallas: Word Publishing, 1987), 210.
8. Andy Christofides, *The Life Sentence: John 3:16* (Waynesboro, GA: Paternoster Publishing, 2002), 11.
9. Guillermo Gonzalez and Jay W. Richards, *The Privileged Planet: How Our Place in the Cosmos Is Designed for Discovery* (Washington, DC: Regenery Publishing, 2004), 143.
10. "Liftoff to Space Exploration," NASA, http://liftoff.msfc.nasa.gov/academy/universe_travel.html.
11. Tracy Leininger Craven, *Alone, Yet Not Alone* (San Antonio, TX: His Seasons, 2001), 19, 29–31, 42, 153–54, 176, 190–97.
12. Gary L. Thomas, *Sacred Marriage: What If God Designed Marriage to Make Us Holy More Than to Make Us Happy?* (Grand Rapids: Zondervan, 2000), 46–47.
13. F. W. Boreham, *Life Verses: The Bible's Impact on Famous Lives, Vol. Two* (Grand Rapids: Kregel Publications, 1994), 114–155.

Reading the Bible

Your teachers may pile on the reading assignments, but the Bible is *the* most important book you will ever read. It's God's plan for your life, telling you what is right, what is wrong, and how to get to heaven. When life comes at you fast and hard, the Bible can be your answer book, so it's a good idea to read something from it every day.

Try one of these reading plans to help you get started. Put a check next to each one as you read it. *30 Days with Jesus* walks you through the life of Jesus while he was here on earth. *90 Days Through the Bible* gives you all the major happenings of the Old and New Testaments, beginning with the Creation in Genesis and going all the way through to Revelation.

30 Days with Jesus

1. John 1:1–51 ____
2. Luke 2:1–52 ____
3. Mark 1:1–11 ____
4. Luke 4:1–44 ____
5. John 3:1–36 ____
6. Luke 5:1–39 ____
7. John 4:1–54 ____
8. Luke 6:1–49 ____
9. Luke 7:1–50 ____
10. Luke 8:1–56 ____
11. Mark 8:1–38 ____
12. Luke 10:1–42 ____
13. Matthew 5:1–48 ____
14. Matthew 6:1–34 ____
15. Matthew 7:1–29 ____
16. Luke 14:1–35 ____

17. Luke 15:1–32 _____
18. Luke 16:1–31 _____
19. John 8:1–59 _____
20. Luke 17:1–37 _____
21. Luke 18:1–43 _____
22. John 9:1–41 _____
23. Luke 19:1–48 _____
24. Luke 20:1–47 _____
25. John 10:1–42 _____
26. John 11:1–57 _____
27. Mark 13:1–37 _____
28. Luke 22:1–71 _____
29. Matthew 27:1–66 _____
30. Luke 24:1–53 _____

90 Days Through the Bible

1. Genesis 1:1–2:3 _____
2. Genesis 3:1–24 _____
3. Genesis 6:9–7:24 _____
4. Genesis 8:1–9:17 _____
5. Genesis 17:1–22 _____
6. Genesis 22:1–19 _____
7. Genesis 25:19–34 _____
8. Genesis 27:1–28:9 _____
9. Genesis 37:1–36 _____
10. Genesis 41:1–57 _____
11. Genesis 45:1–28 _____
12. Exodus 1:8–2:15 _____
13. Exodus 3:1–4:17 _____
14. Exodus 5:1–6:13 _____
15. Exodus 12:1–42 _____
16. Exodus 13:17–14:31 _____
17. Exodus 20:1–21 _____
18. Numbers 13:1–33 _____
19. Joshua 2:1–24 _____

Wild Grace
978-1-4003-2084-4 | $14.99

Make Every Day Count
978-1-4003-1822-3 | $14.99

**Available at bookstores everywhere or online at
www.thomasnelson.com**

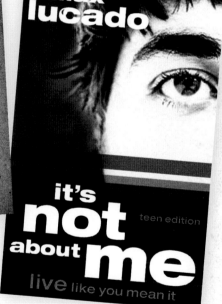